RENOVATING THE BILLIONAIRE

(Pine Grove Novel, book 3)

Jean C. Joachim

Moonlight Books

Dedication

To my Book Buddies, love you all.

Acknowledgment

Thank you to my editor, Sherri Good, and my proofreader, Renee Waring. A special "thank you" to Vicki Locey, whose daily encouragement keeps me on track. Thank you to the Joachim men, Larry, David & Steve for keeping me grounded and believing in me.

ABOUT THE E-BOOK YOU HAVE PURCHASED: Your non-refundable purchase of this e-book allows you to only ONE LEGAL copy for your own personal reading on your own personal computer or device. **You do not have resell or distribution rights without the prior written permission of both the publisher and the copyright owner of this book.** This book cannot be copied in any format, sold, or otherwise transferred from your computer to another through upload to a file sharing peer to peer program, for free or for a fee, or as a prize in any contest. Such action is illegal and in violation of the U.S. Copyright Law. Distribution of this e-book, in whole or in part, online, offline, in print or in any way or any other method currently known or yet to be invented, is forbidden. If you do not want this book anymore, you must delete it from your computer.

WARNING: The unauthorized reproduction or distribution of this copyrighted work is illegal. Criminal copyright infringement, including infringement without monetary gain, is investigated by the FBI and is punishable by up to 5 years in federal prison and a fine of $250,000.

Chapter One

THE BUS RIDE TO THE prison in Fishkill and back provided reading time for Jess Lennox. She settled into a window seat and opened her book. A man slid in next to her. Jess pulled the paperback closer. Feeling his stare, she squeezed up against the glass.

"You visiting a relative?" he asked, eying her up and down.

She nodded. The last thing she needed was some chatty, middle-aged man hitting on her.

"My wife. Shoplifting. Minimum security."

Jess ignored him and kept reading.

"It gets lonely with her gone," he continued.

Anger bubbled up in her chest. Damn it! She worked hard, and this trip once a month was her only time off.

"Your boyfriend in the slammer?" he asked.

Her patience evaporated like water boiling on the stove. Jess slammed the book shut and faced the insensitive clod.

"My mother. She's in for murder. She killed my father. They say murderous tendencies run in families," she said, shooting him the meanest glare she could muster.

The man paled, nodded once and pushed to his feet.

"I can see you don't want to be disturbed," he muttered and headed for another seat. Jess smiled and opened her novel, *If I Loved You.* Totally absorbed by the story, tears formed in her eyes as she identified with the trials the characters endured.

Jess ate up love stories borrowed from the library. Romance books kept her believing that things could work out, that life could get better—and happiness did exist. When the bus pulled up to the Pine Grove stop, she scooted past the annoying man, down the steps, and ran for her car.

She stowed the book in the glove compartment until her next visit and put the vehicle in gear.

The story stuck with her. What would she do if she ever met a man like Chaz Duncan? Would she even recognize his good heart under his arrogant attitude? With a short laugh, she figured she wouldn't. Jess hated egotistical men, men so in love with themselves they couldn't see anyone else.

She'd only met one man who had cracked her hard veneer. Chip Matthews won her heart in high school. He'd taken her virginity then, too. But she didn't care. He had provided respite from the anger, fighting, and hostile atmosphere in her home. He'd been her refuge.

Pulling into the parking lot of Java the Hut, she turned off the car and plucked a dollar bill from her purse. Inside, an iced coffee-to-go waited on the counter. Marge, the waitress, looked up. Jess picked up the paper cup and slid her buck across the shiny Formica. She shot a small smile at the older woman and headed back to her vehicle.

Next stop, the old mansion on Route 113. She turned on the radio and cranked up the volume to banish the reality of how many more trips she'd make to Fishkill over the next thirty years. Taking the winding road that hugged Cedar Lake refreshed her spirits.

There it was, in all its glory. Way below ramshackle, the 1825 four-story mansion stood with whatever pride it could muster. All the windows were broken and there were bare spots on the roof, including one large hole—providing entry for a variety of wildlife.

When she was only eighteen, Jess had stumbled on the house and fallen in love. Minnie West, the old woman who owned it, had invited her in for tea and cookies. Jess gained entry to every room by volunteering to sweep and dust. Including bathrooms, there were forty rooms in the mansion.

The third floor resembled a rabbit warren of tiny rooms only big enough for a single bed and small dresser. Jess guessed those were the servants' quarters. At the end of the floor was the longest staircase she'd ever seen. It went straight down from the top floor to the kitchen.

Minnie chatted about the history of the house and how, years ago, she'd raised her nephew there. The older lady didn't go on much about him, and he never visited—at least not when Jess was around. As time went on, Jess noticed the place sink further and further into disrepair. When she asked Minnie about it, the woman had explained.

"Oh, I have money, but I spend it on saving animals. A house is just a thing. Animals are alive. So many need help, you know. I do what I can. I give to several shelters."

While Jess agreed with the worthiness of the cause, she doubted the wisdom of putting it ahead of upkeep for Minnie's home. Years passed, and Jess had less and less time for visits. Providing for her brother and herself had turned out to be more than a full-time job. She and Minnie lost touch.

After studying cooking in high school, Jess had become a pretty fair baker. She eked out a meager living baking and selling her pies to restaurants, shops, and hotels. She conjured up a dream of buying the fixer-upper from Minnie for a song, repairing it, and running a bed and breakfast.

One day, while spying on his big sister, Will had discovered her secret. He promised not to tell anyone and vowed that he'd fix it. He told her that new paint, hammer, nails, and a ton of elbow grease could restore the splendor of the mansion. Jess believed every word.

From that day on, they had shared the secret. Jess sold her cakes and pies while Will did odd jobs and a bit of carpentry when he could get it. They worked toward making the dream come true.

When Minnie got too old to live alone, she moved to an assisted living facility several counties away. Year after year, Jess spied the weather-beaten for sale sign staked in the front lawn.

From time to time, a real estate agent brought someone by, but they left quickly. The only one with a vision for the decrepit house, Jess smiled every time a car carried away someone shaking their head and wrinkling their nose.

A few pangs for the dotty old woman who had lived in the mansion tweaked Jess's heart. She'd waited patiently for the old woman to put the building up for sale at a rock-bottom price.

Now thirty, with Will a sturdy twenty-five, she figured they were ready to take on the world's biggest renovation and make her dream come true. Even after such a long wait, Jess had never given up. She simply baked her pies, did odd jobs for folks in town and kept house for her and her brother. They put away a few bucks when they could and waited.

Today she circled around back, eying the snarled weeds, wiry brambles, and tree stumps in the backyard. Jess planned where she'd plant her garden. Fresh veggies and herbs would make her food better than anyone's for miles.

She found a patch of grass and lay down, staring at the pitched roof and the top floor that, in its day, had cooks, butlers, and maids filling its rooms. As she picked at a weed, she made a mental list of the seeds and plants she'd buy when the place was hers.

The clouds cleared, and the sun shone down. Jess believed in guardian angels. How else had she and Will survived without parents these past twelve years?

She glanced around. Something wasn't right. Jess sat up. What was missing? The "for sale" sign had disappeared. She picked up her phone and called her brother.

"Haven't you heard? Old Minnie West finally kicked the bucket," he said.

Jess put down her phone. Did this mean that her time to buy the place had come? If that was true, where was the sign?

STRYKER ALEXANDER WEST hated funerals. He didn't see the point. The person being honored was dead. They couldn't see or hear, so why go through all the rigamarole for someone who wouldn't appreciate it? He'd rather be in his study, going over the financials for his newest private airport. A young man approached.

"Here's your eulogy for your aunt, Mr. West."

"Thank you, Chris," the dark-eyed mogul replied. As he thumbed through the document, he frowned. "Bit long, isn't it?"

"You were her favorite nephew."

"I was her only nephew. Is there a place where I can edit this down?"

"Of course. Right this way," Chris led the tall, attractive man to a small, private study in the funeral home. As he passed the sanctuary, he took note of the large number of people milling about and remarked to his aunt who was no longer there.

"Well done, Minnie. You've attracted quite a crowd to see you off. Even I'm impressed. For a woman who didn't go out much, you found a way to make friends," he said with a chuckle.

Stryker sat at the wooden desk and pulled out a fountain pen from his breast pocket. He scratched out about half of the speech, changed a few words, then read it over.

Aunt Minnie had been his father's big sister. She was lively, happy, and inquisitive, always poking into his personal business and giving him unwanted advice. She'd been a one-woman matchmaker, trying to marry him off until two years ago, when he turned forty. Then even Minnie West threw in the towel, declaring that he was not marriage material. So what? He doubted he was missing anything other than a messy, expensive divorce.

Stryker West enjoyed playing the field, taking his pleasure whenever and wherever he could. He'd never been at a loss for female companionship. His billions, his most attractive quality, he assumed, made marriage a risk he preferred not to take.

Quite content with his life, Stryker created plenty of challenges for his nimble brain. Finding just the right spot to build a private airport, where executives could fly the old-fashioned way—with no security lines and perfect service, occupied his days.

Stryker's luxurious airlines flew short hops from Los Angeles, New York, Boston, Chicago, Washington, Atlanta, and Toronto. He also owned and leased private jets and limousines. He had everything the busy CEO could want to make travel fast and painless.

Although he was licensed for flights only within the United States, he had a team of lawyers working on making expansion to Europe possible. In the meantime, movie stars, athletes, businessmen, and simply wealthy folks lined up to pay top dollar and enjoy luxury treatment as they jetted from Boston to Washington, From Los Angeles to San Francisco. .

His current project was an airport outside of Dallas. After he said goodbye to Minnie a final time, he'd take one of his planes to Texas.

As he read over the eulogy, memories returned. Aunt Minnie had taken an interest in precocious Stryker early on. His father, a letter carrier, barely made enough money to keep Stryker, and his mother, Abby, solvent. When his mother needed surgery, medical bills forced the West family into bankruptcy.

Stryker vowed he'd never be poor again. And he'd kept his promise to himself. Recalling the small gifts Minnie gave him, like the Lego police station he'd wanted but his parents couldn't afford, touched him. She bought him books and read to him when he was small. She babysat for him when his father went to visit Abby after her operation.

On their way home from the hospital, The West's car was struck by an eighteen-wheeler. Both his parents died on the spot. Only four years old, Stryker went to live with his only relative, Aunt Minnie. Not long after he arrived, Minnie married Ed Chambers, though they hadn't known each other long. When Stryker hit his twenties, his aunt explained that she did it so he could have a father. When Ed became abusive to the boy, children's services stepped in, and the couple divorced.

Snapshots of outings and adventures with Minnie swirled through his head. Emotion, most often tamped down, blossomed in his heart. Her death would be a bigger loss than he had imagined. Dampness on his cheek surprised him, shocking him out of his reverie. No, Stryker Alexander West didn't cry. He hadn't shed a tear since his parents passed away. And he wasn't about to start now.

"Ready, sir?" Chris asked, standing in the doorway.

"Let's get this over with," Stryker said, stuffing his handkerchief back in his pocket, folding papers, and rising from the chair.

"This way, sir."

Stryker took a deep breath and followed the young man to the large room where people awaited his words.

"Auntie Mame, Groucho Marx, and Charlie Chaplin rolled into one. That was Minnie West Chambers..." he began.

WHEN JESS COASTED INTO the parking space in the back of their apartment house, she switched off the car, patted the dashboard and thanked it for starting on the first try and not stalling. Her mind filled with chores. Start chili for dinner, peel apples for pies, make and freeze dough, the list grew. She plopped her keys in a bowl in the kitchen.

Picking up a mug of hot coffee, she said, "Thanks," to her brother.

"How's Mom?"

"Same." She eased down on a chair at the table.

"I got a call from Dave's Demolition this morning."

"Oh?" she raised her eyebrows and took a sip.

"Someone's hired him to take down that creepy old place."

"Not the mansion on 113?"

Will nodded.

"No! They can't! It hasn't been condemned, has it?"

"I don't know."

"Shit. That explains why the for-sale sign is gone."

"I'm sorry," Will said, squeezing his sister's hand.

"Yeah? We'll see about that. Isn't Grey Andrews the town supervisor?"

"I think so."

After three large gulps, she finished her beverage and jumped up.

"Heading out now." She pushed up from the table.

"Wait," Will said, grabbing her arm.

She stopped.

"There's nothing you can do."

"Says who?"

"Give it up, Jess."

"No. Never. That's my dream. I'll be back," she said, snatching the still-warm keys and heading for the lot.

Nothing was far in little Pine Grove, so Jess barely had time to figure out what to say when the stately Andrews Victorian came into view. She pulled up and parked on the street in front of the gorgeous, huge house that used to belong to the Davenport family. Jess liked the Grey and his family. They'd been generous at Halloween and would make up jobs occasionally and hire Will or Jess, simply so they could earn a few dollars. She appreciated their help. Jess knocked. Grey opened the door.

"Do you have a minute?" she asked.

"Come on in. Pine Grove business?" he asked, stepping aside.

She nodded. Grey led her to a small study and closed the door. He sat on the loveseat and she on a chair opposite.

"What can I do for you?" he asked.

"You're the town supervisor, right?"

"Right."

"No one can take a building down without a permit from you, right?"

He nodded. "Correct."

"Someone wants to bulldoze the lovely old mansion on 113."

"Really? I haven't gotten a permit request yet."

"Good, then I'm in time. Don't sign it."

"What?"

"Please. Don't let them take down that old house." Her voice cracked.

"Why? The place has been falling down for years. Minnie West didn't have the money to take care of it."

"I know. But maybe they'll sell. To me. For almost nothing. To Will and me. Together, we can fix it up."

"It's a much bigger job than you two can handle. Do you have a down payment?"

"I have two-thousand dollars. Is that enough?"

"I doubt it. Though I don't know what the price is, it comes with some land, too. That's probably worth more than the house. On your income, I'd guess a mortgage would be hard to get," he said.

Tears she'd been holding back broke through. She covered her eyes with her hand. Grey rose and put an arm around her.

"Would you like a glass of water?"

She shook her head.

"I don't understand."

"I've wanted that place since before Mom went to jail."

"It's a wonderful old building, but it's in serious disrepair."

"I know. But it can be fixed," she insisted.

"There's a hole in the roof. Who knows what's been living in there."

"With some TLC…" Jess lost control. Sobs wracked her body.

The door opened and Carrie, Grey's wife, entered. "Is something wrong?"

Grey shrugged his shoulders.

"Come with me, Jess," Carrie said.

"No. No this isn't just me being emotional. I want a chance. A chance to save that old house. Can't you help me, Grey?"

"I'd have to have a good excuse not to sign the permit, Jess."

"Please," she pleaded.

Grey stroked his cheek and furrowed his brow. "Well, there might be a way. Kind of a long shot, but I think you can pull it off."

"Tell me, please!" Jess wiped her face with the tissue Carrie handed her and sat up. "I'll do anything."

"Okay. Let me explain..."

TUESDAY NIGHT, JESS made an early dinner for her and her brother.

"Eat fast. I'm going to the town meeting at seven."

"Really? Why?"

"Come along and you'll see."

Will shrugged. "Why not?"

Arriving five minutes before things started, Jess and Will grabbed two seats by the door. Mike Foster called the meeting to order.

"We have one piece of business leftover from last month's meeting. The Landmark Committee."

"I thought we weren't allowed to have one," someone piped up.

"I've contacted the state. The governor's office said we could have one that would be given the task of researching the history of any buildings or land we're considering preserving. Then that committee would make a recommendation to the town supervisor. I have here a folder with the state environmental protection laws. Those could also be used to preserve land. But we still don't have someone to man the landmark committee. Do I have any volunteers?"

Jess raised her hand.

"What the hell are you doing?" Will asked, reaching for her arm.

Jess pushed his hand away and stood up. "I'll do it."

Mike smiled. "Okay, then. We have someone. Jess Lennox is nominated. Anyone second?"

Grey Andrews spoke up. "I do."

"All in favor?"

Everyone, except one person, raised their hands.

"Opposed?"

Will's hand shot up. A titter ran over the crowd.

"Sorry, Will. You're outvoted. Guess you'll have to live with the extra work at your place."

"Like there are any buildings to be landmarked anyway," someone muttered.

"Oh, but there are," Jess replied.

"Like what?"

"Like that big old house on 113," she said.

A murmur ran through the crowd.

"Excuse me, Miss," said an unrecognized, deep voice. Jess turned toward the man.

"Chair recognizes Mr. West."

"Do you mean to say that you are landmarking that house?" he asked.

"Damn right I am. Of course, I will give it further study. But as of right now, my recommendation to the Town Supervisor is that no one bulldoze that building."

"But it's decrepit. It's falling down," the stranger argued.

"Nope. It's completely stable. And it dates back to the early 1800s"

"That building now belongs to me, and I'm planning to take it down."

Jess's heart skipped a beat. Sweat broke out on her forehead. Take it down? Destroy her home, her dream? No way!

"Think again, Mister. No one's touching that house unless it's to fix it up."

"That house has seen a lot of Pine Grove history. I'm with Jess on this," said Laura Dailey.

"Me, too," chimed in her husband, Barney.

One after another, the townsfolks spoke up. Seemed no one cared that the building was an eyesore. Everyone supported keeping it and having it renovated.

"Minnie was my friend. She'd be rolling in her grave if she knew what you planned to do, Mr. West," said Mindy Winslow.

A smug smile of satisfaction spread across Jess's face. Mr. West's brows knit as he scowled.

"We'll see about this," he said, pushing his way out of the building.

Applause went up and Jess took her seat.

"Don't let that rich guy push you around, Jess. Stand your ground, girl," said Marge from the Java the Hut.

Will shot her a look of disgust. "This won't solve anything," he mumbled.

"It's the first step. Gives me some time to figure out what I'm going to do."

"You're going to be a fool, that's what. This is a mistake. That guy's got bucks. He'll destroy you."

"Nobody's gonna destroy me. I've made it this far, Will. And I will prevail."

"Good luck with that," he said, rising from his chair.

She followed him outside. Grey stopped her by the parking lot.

"Well done, Jess."

"I get the feeling this is only the first round," she replied.

"Maybe. Stryker West isn't one to give up easily."

"You know him?"

"We were in school here together. He's tough, inside and out. Stand your ground. You have the town behind you."

"That's a first."

Grey clapped her on the shoulder then headed for his car.

She'd won the first round. But how long could she stall him? A shiver shot through her. Had she bitten off more than she could chew? What would she do if fancy city lawyers came after her? Setting her jaw, her lips in a thin line, Jess headed for her brother's truck. She'd fought against the odds every day for the last twelve years. No reason why this should be any different.

Chapter Two

Stryker Alexander West stood outside the main entrance to the town hall building. Folding powerful arms across his impressive chest, he grinned and blocked her path as she approached Will's vehicle. But his smile didn't make it to his cold, dark eyes.

"Listen, sweetheart, stopping the destruction of that old pile of junk isn't a good idea."

Bristling, she pushed past him, shoving him out of the way.

"Really, honey. Do the smart thing. Sign the demolition permit.

She turned, heat burning in her chest. "I'm not your sweetheart. I'm not your honey. And I don't give a damn how many people bow to your money and power. I'll never, and I mean never, change my mind. I'll never give the okay to sign a permit to destroy that charming old place. Get over yourself and get out of my way."

"We'll see about that," he said, a mocking smirk spreading across his face. He grabbed her arm and whirled her around. "If someone gets hurt in that old place, I won't be responsible. It needs to come down before something bad happens."

"Get your hands off me! No one's going to get hurt in there. Hasn't happened yet."

"Look. I've destroyed men a whole lot bigger and stronger than you. So get out of my way."

"Maybe you've beaten down men bigger, but not stronger. And you're the one who needs to get out of *my* way," she said, placing her hand on the truck's door handle.

He stood so close to her, she could smell his spicy aftershave and feel the warmth of his breath. What was she doing, noticing his broad shoulders and perfect scruff? The man was a menace, a power-hungry monster with no taste and no regard for history or beauty. Still, there was something about him, drawing her. Her nipples tingled. She raised her gaze to his.

"Is there something about the word *never* you don't understand? Now move your sorry ass before I call the police."

He jumped to the side with a slight bow to let her pass.

"This isn't over, blondie. Not by a longshot."

Every curse word she knew sounded in her head, but she opened the door in silence, refusing to give him the satisfaction. Angry? An understatement. Madder than she'd ever been, she couldn't figure out if her temper was a reaction to his uncouth ways or her body's betrayal.

She slammed the door and peered through the window. Their gazes connected.

"How does that guy have Minnie's house?" she asked her brother.

"Guess he's a relative."

"Maybe. The nephew?" she asked, tearing her eyes away from his. Will turned the key in the ignition.

"Don't mess with him. Did you see the car he drove into town? He's got a ton of money. He'll crush you."

"As long as the town is with me, he doesn't stand a chance."

"Pfft!" Will said.

On the way home, Jess checked her messages. There was one from her friend Angie.

"I'm sick. This pregnancy is slowing me down. Can you sub for me tomorrow night?"

Jess dialed. "Sure. What time does your shift start?"

"Five. Thank you so much. You're a lifesaver," her friend replied.

From time to time, Jess subbed at the bar in Homer's Restaurant. It wasn't hard work and she needed the money, especially the tips. She used the twenty-five bucks in tips she raked in for food.

"I'm subbing for Angie tomorrow. I'll leave something in the oven for you, okay?" she asked her brother.

"Fine. Just be careful. Call me when you're leaving, and I'll pick you up."

"Okay." Jess didn't think it was necessary, but she liked her brother's protective attitude. Besides, you never knew what drunken idiot might make a pass and decide not to take "no" for an answer. Will's muscle would settle things down.

After a glance at the clock, Jess made a beeline for bed. She had to be up at five and baking. Just because she'd be bartending didn't mean she could shirk her pie obligations. The Cozy Café in Pine Grove, Teatime in Jeffersonville, The Pine Grove Inn, and Tavern on the Lake bought her wares. Though her earnings per hour were minuscule, she continued to work hard to maintain that steady income that paid their bills.

With Will's odd jobs and her baking, they managed to get along. There wasn't anything left for extras, but Jess had hope. Every week, she placed a few dollars in an empty coffee can under the kitchen sink for the holidays. This year, she vowed they'd have ham, and she'd buy Will something he wanted. The waitressing job provided extra funds to put away.

ANGER FILLED STRYKER'S chest. He drove his Bentley down the dark streets of Pine Grove to the house he'd rented. The furnishings almost made him gag, but there wasn't a reasonably nice hotel closer than twenty-five miles, and he didn't intend to spend his days riding back-and-forth.

He'd let Chris have the night off and had driven himself to the town meeting. Figured it wouldn't look too good to plain folks to be arriving with a chauffeur. Bad enough he drove a spanking new, shiny Bentley. He smirked. Most of them wouldn't have a clue what make his car was, would they?

But that girl, damn her! She stood in his way. All he wanted to do was demolish the house, sell the land, and move on. He had an office in London waiting for him. The last thing he needed was a roadblock.

The fact that it was nine o'clock didn't deter Stryker from picking up the phone and dialing London.

"John, we've got a problem."

"Can't this wait until morning, Stryker?"

"No. And if I'm interrupting sex with your wife, I apologize."

"You're interrupting beauty sleep. But okay, shoot."

Stryker explained the situation to his right-hand man.

"Lay off the threats. What could this young woman possibly want? Money?"

"Ah, yes. Her car looked like it had been through a war."

"Good. She's hungry, offer her money. Sweeten the deal. Obviously, your strong-arm tactics didn't get you anywhere. Try nice. I know it's a stretch for you but give it a whirl. And be generous. She's not going to go away for a hundred bucks."

"You always get insulting when I've interrupted you in mid-fuck."

"Watch it."

"Sorry. But it's true. As usual, your advice is perfect. And I will follow it to the letter."

"Good. I'm hanging up now."

"Give Sarah a kiss for me," Stryker said. But John had already ended the call.

He undressed and slipped into bed with a thriller he'd been reading. When he turned out the light at midnight, an image of the young woman, eyes blazing, pushing him out of her way flashed through his brain.

There was something kind of sweet smelling about her, like spun sugar or honey. And her hair. Speaking of honey, that was exactly the color, wasn't it? He grinned, oh, yes, he'd give her an offer she couldn't refuse. Hmm, he considered amounts and decided to start with five grand and go as high as twenty, if need be. How much was his peace of mind worth? He could go to fifty thousand and never feel it.

Girls like her are so obvious. Her attitude would soften when he waved a check for more money than she could make in a year in front of her face. Of course, if she bit and took the cash, he couldn't sleep with her. That would make it seem like prostitution.

Who wants to have sex with an angry bitch, anyway? Not just angry, fiery. He admitted to himself that her fire turned him on. Women who showed passion in one area of their lives often showed the same heat between the sheets. Many an exhausting but satisfying night had started with that premise.

The girl appeared in his dreams, giving him a restless night. The next morning, he awoke tired and cranky. Chris picked him up for breakfast. They ate at the Cozy Café then headed back to the rental. Stryker opened his laptop, pulled up his schedule, and picked up his phone to call his secretary in London.

"Nigel, clear my schedule for the next week, would you?"

"What about today?"

"I have phone conferences with Dallas, London, and Rome. I'll do those but cancel everything for tomorrow. And the rest of the week. I have business to take care of here. It won't take long."

"Fine, sir. Consider it done."

"Thank you."

He turned to Chris. "I love the efficiency of the British. Now, where were we?"

"I think you were preparing the estimates for the London office," Chris prompted.

"Right, right."

At noon, they returned to the Cozy Café for lunch.

"We got some special chocolate cream pie."

Stryker's eyes lit up. "My favorite."

"Made right here in Pine Grove by Jess Lennox," the waitress, Amy, said.

"Who?"

"Jess. She makes all the pies for all the restaurants around here. It's her gift."

"Okay. Two pieces, please," he said. Turning to Chris, he continued, "I'm assuming you'll join me in this."

"You don't have to twist my arm."

The pie was delectable. Best he'd ever eaten. Indeed, that hostile young woman did have a gift for a flaky crust and a rich filling. What was her problem with the house? He'd have to get the answer before he gave her the money. Would she continue to bake pies once she'd deposited his little bribe in the bank? He'd hate to deprive the town of such an excellent dessert.

He gulped down the last of his coffee, plucked two twenties from his wallet and paid the bill. He dumped the remaining five and change on the table for a tip before making his way to the parking lot.

Stryker climbed into the car and Chris drove them to Minnie's place. Stryker backed up to get a full view of the old house. The roof, missing a dozen shingles, had a hole in it big enough to fit a golden retriever. The paint on the outside walls had peeled off ages ago, leaving raw, weathered wood exposed to rain, snow, and ice.

Every window pane stood broken. Probably teenagers. What was it about a window that tempted a boy to heave a rock through it?

The west side of the house had exterior cellar doors, like in "The Wizard of Oz." The shrubs, once neatly trimmed, had grown unruly, like a child's curly hair. Some had sprouted up five feet or more to partially cover the first-floor windows. Others had had the good grace to die, turn yellow, then brown.

The grass hadn't been mowed in at least six months, maybe longer, clumps bent over, like waves, to cover parts of the slate walk. The mansion had gone to seed, becoming a sorry specimen.

"Well, Chris. What's your take?" Stryker scratched his stubbly chin.

"First, we must repair the roof. Fix that hole, add a few shingles. Then the windows. Trim the shrubs and hedges. Mow the grass, if you can. Might have to take a scythe to it first. Not sure if you should paint or simply re-side the entire building."

"And how much would you estimate that would cost?" Stryker asked, kicking loose stones out of his way.

"I have no idea. Probably a lot."

"Like how much? A hundred grand? Maybe two?"

"Maybe."

"Then there's the inside."

"Of course. Yes."

"If the outside looks this bad, what do you think the inside looks like?"

Chris covered his eyes. "I can't imagine."

"You want me to renovate?"

"It's got great bones. What did you want to do?"

"Tear the damn thing down," Stryker growled in a sour tone, heading for the car.

"Wait!" Chris said, tugging on his arm. "Here's the key. Look inside."

"Do I really have to do this?"

"It might not be that bad."

Stryker cocked an eyebrow at his chauffeur.

"Of course, you're the boss."

Snatching the keys from the young man, Stryker took a deep breath.

"Be back in an hour."

"Right, sir."

With a groan of disgust, Stryker headed for the steps. He shoved the key in the rusty lock and turned. Reluctantly, the tumblers clicked into place. The old wooden door creaked as he opened it.

Before stepping inside, he recalled warm, delicious smells coming from the kitchen. Aunt Minnie had been an excellent cook. Not a gourmet, but she could make a stew that would bring a grown man to tears. His mouth watered as the long-forgotten flavors awakened his taste buds.

Opening the front door, he was slapped in the face by the stench of cat urine. The smell overpowered him, forcing him back a few steps. His eyes stung. Ducking under a cobweb, he strode through the entryway to a once-elegant, long, living room window. Mustering all his strength, he forced the damn thing open. Gulping fresh air, he turned. *What the Hell did Minnie do with the thousands of dollars I sent her every month?* Surely, she had not used one single cent to maintain the house.

Dusty sheets covered the furniture. The braided rug, that had once brought color and warmth to the room, had faded and grown shabby. Paint on the walls cracked and peeled. The wood floor, once polished and gleaming, now scuffed and scratched, had dulled. Where was the chandelier? Old wires sprang from the ceiling like weeds in Minnie's once-tended garden.

His heart squeezed. Did he dare explore the other rooms? Curiosity overcame revulsion, compelling him to forge ahead. One room was worse than the next. Then he came upon his old bedroom. The threadbare, blue chenille spread still covered the bed. A few books lay about the floor, though the small bookshelf stood empty.

Opening the closet, he spied clothes from his teenage years, awaiting his return. A few dusty, mismatched sneakers lay on their sides on the floor. Two pictures of his biggest sports heroes still graced the walls, though the layer of dust on the glass muddied the image underneath.

Tears stung his eyes as he picked up the lone Beanie Baby, a hippo, still perched on his old desk, awaiting his return.

"Herman," he muttered, fingering the tiny, velvety animal.

Stripped of personality and filthy beyond belief, the room no longer resembled the sanctuary he'd learned to love after his parents died.

Corralling his emotions, his resolve to raze the structure hardened. There was nothing left of the place he had called home. Best to take this monstrosity down and hope to erase the memory of the shambles it had become. Settled on the front stoop knees up, like a little boy, his head rested in his hands. Pain seared through him as sweet and sour memories from his childhood resurfaced. He'd worked hard to get away from his early orphaned existence. Could one ever escape where they came from?

"Sir? You all right?"

Stryker raised his head. "Quite. Let's go."

"Made your decision, sir?"

"This place must go. Torn down to the very foundation. Burned. The land sold. And I must move on, spread my airports overseas and never come back here again."

Chapter Three

In the morning, Jess awoke in a good mood. The birds chirped outside on the feeder. The sun burned hot for a morning in June, sending warm air in her open windows. Jess tied an apron around her waist. The bottom edge was a little frayed and the bright pink had faded to an anemic version of the original. Sure enough it was worn, but it had been her grandma's and held a special place in her heart. Jess hummed *Wonderful World* as she measured out flour and shortening.

"Wearing the lucky apron? That means something good for breakfast," Will said as he straddled a rickety chair in the tiny kitchen.

"Nope. Means fresh raspberry rhubarb pie for The Cozy Café," Jess said, pulling a rolling pin out of the drawer.

"Crap."

She smiled behind her hand. "And maybe raspberry pancakes if a certain brother minds his manners."

"Raspberry pancakes? Yippee!" A smile broke out on his face.

"Yeah. I have some leftover. Some of the berries got smushed. You know how fussy Amy is about her pies. They have to be perfect."

"I'll take the imperfect ones. My stomach doesn't know the difference."

Jess melted a small pat of butter. One glance told her she was getting low. She'd have to make do because Amy wouldn't be paying her 'till the end of the week. She remembered the job at Homers. Damn, it hit perfectly—she'd pick up more butter tomorrow.

"We should get a cow," Will said, adding milk to his coffee.

"You want to milk it every day?"

"I would. Then we'd have as much milk and butter as we need."

"Butter doesn't come from a cow. You have to churn it," Jess said.

"Bet you'd get great butter in a couple of minutes in the blender or that fancy mixer you use for bread dough."

She smacked him lightly on the back of the head.

"What was that for?"

"For being smarter than your sister," she said, patting his shoulder.

"I may be smarter. But there's nobody nicer."

She chuckled. "Figure that earns you another pancake?"

"Uh-huh."

"Well, you figured right," she said, pouring batter on the skillet.

After breakfast, Will helped her pack her car and she steered her vehicle toward the Cozy Café. When she finished her deliveries, Jess headed for the broken-down mansion, stopping to look at the old place for the millionth time. She stretched her arms high. Exhaustion crept along her spine. Though only three o'clock, she had been working for ten hours.

She moseyed over to the backyard and eased down on the grass. The June air hung heavy with the promise of flowers and vegetables sprouting in the sun. Leaning back on her elbows, she eyed the building. Picking a tall blade of grass, she stuck it between her teeth, then spoke out loud.

"If the wood's not rotten, I'd repair the back porch. Hang a feeder there. Maybe get a rocking chair."

A short, male laugh startled her. She bolted upright as if lightning hit her.

"Chip? Chip Matthews? What are you doing here?"

"Might ask you the same question." He leaned his tall, lanky frame up against an oak tree, his eyes slowly traveled her length.

Jess scrambled to her feet, brushing the twigs and leaves from her butt.

"Nothin."

"Talkin' to yourself? That's not a good sign, Jess."

"None of your business. I gotta go."

As she brushed past him, he grabbed her arm. "Wait."

"What for?"

"We got some unfinished business."

"Not that I see. Let me go."

He dropped his hold, but his gaze connected with hers. "I'm sorry."

"Sorry about what?" she asked, tossing her long locks.

"Everything. You. Me. Lucky."

"Yeah, sure," she said but didn't move. "You've got Kathy now. Don't worry about me. I can take care of myself."

"I miss you."

"Too bad. You listened to your folks. They busted us up and you let 'em. Nothing to cry about now."

"Ain't cryin'. Just sayin', I miss you." He fingered a curl that rested on her shoulder.

A yearning so strong it almost knocked her down swept through Jess. Memories of disappearing into the warmth and safety of his embrace returned. Chip Matthews had been her refuge during turbulent times in the Lennox home.

Dreams of days on the farm, dinners cooked in the gigantic Matthews kitchen, and stolen moments making love with her strong, handsome boyfriend had haunted her for years. Chip and his family had offered her Lucky, their newest foal when she was only seventeen. She and Chip had been dating for six months. Her father had blown sky-high when Chip brought the foal over.

He'd yelled at him, then at her, and forbid her accepting the horse. She'd cried and begged to keep him. Lloyd Lennox ranted about not having enough money to feed the family, let alone a horse. He'd been right, of course, but his furious slap across her face almost started a beat-down of Lloyd by her boyfriend and her brother.

Things at the Lennox household deteriorated after that. Shortly after her eighteenth birthday, her mother shot her father to death and went to jail for life. Jess's fragile world unraveled, beginning with the Matthews family insisting Chip break off his relationship with Jess. They didn't want a daughter of a murderer in their home or as a member of their family.

A shake of her head brought her back to the present.

"Got a horse fixin' to foal soon. Thought you might like to have it," Chip said.

Her eyes widened, her throat ran dry. Chip cupped her cheek. Tears stung the backs of her eyes, but she refused to give in. She brushed his hand aside and stepped back.

"Pa was right. We didn't have money to feed a horse back then and I still don't. So keep it. Thanks anyway."

She reminded herself that he was a married man. His wife, Kathy, grew angry just running into Jess in town.

"Jess, I—"

"Shouldn't you be getting back to your wife? Aren't you married?" she asked, cocking an eyebrow.

He hung his head. "Married the wrong woman," he mumbled.

"Whose fault is that?" she asked, eyes blazing. Before he could answer or even catch up, she trotted off to her vehicle and roared out of the driveway. Turning down the first dead end street, she stopped abruptly, rested her head on the steering wheel, and let the tears flow.

JESS SLIPPED ON A BLACK tank top and black shorts. Standing in front of the mirror, she brushed her long hair. Will stopped.

"Getting ready for Homer's?"

She nodded.

"Remember, you call me."

"I'm working until one."

"I don't care. In fact, that makes it even more important that I come pick you up."

"Okay, okay."

"Call, you hear? Don't leave without me."

She patted her brother on the shoulder. "Thanks."

When she got to Homer's, the owner, Homer Berryman, handed her an apron. He pointed out which liquor he wanted her to push and where things were.

"Thanks for steppin' in for Angie."

"No problem. Happy to have the work."

"If you ever want to give up pie bakin', I might have a full-time job here for you."

"Thanks, Homer. But I'll stick with what I'm doing, for now."

Jess wiped down the bar. Homer gave her a burger and fries, which she wolfed down while waiting for customers. Two older men wandered in. She filled their beer order between bites. By six, the place was busy. Food and drink orders flowed like cheap whiskey.

Busy nights at Homer's made the hours pass quickly. She didn't mind hard work. Hell, hard work was her middle name. She hadn't had time to count her tips yet. It was only nine, but she had a feeling she was way ahead of the last time she'd subbed for Angie. Laughing to herself, she realized that the snug tank top probably had something to do with the amount of money left for her on the bar. Was that wrong? Maybe. But as long as no one touched her, what did it matter if they looked a little? Not that she showed much, but the top was cut a bit low and when she bent over, the guys at the bar got a healthy peek at the tops of her breasts. Just enough to increase the tips.

Will would be furious if he knew. Over-protective, her brother loved her as if she were his mother, father, and sister. Actually, when her mom offed her dad, eighteen-year-old Jess took on all three roles as she assumed custody for her thirteen-year-old brother.

Suddenly outcasts in the town, they'd become tight. And now at thirty and twenty-five, nothing and no one could come between the siblings. During a breather, Jess wiped down the bar and took a sip of her coke.

"Well, hello," said a deep voice.

Jess looked up. Shit. There sat that arrogant son-of-a-bitch, Stryker West.

"What can I do for you?"

"You can approve my demolition permit," he said with a smile.

"Can't do that. But I can get you something to drink. What'll it be?" she asked, working to keep control of her facial expression. Homer hated it when waitstaff flipped off customers, so Jess corralled her temper.

"Johnny Black on the rocks."

"Sorry. Don't have that brand."

"Oh?" he asked, cocking an eyebrow. "Dewars?"

"Johnny Red," she countered. *Or a shot of arsenic?*

"Fine." He eased his butt up on the stool, never taking his eyes from her.

His probing stare rattled her. She spilled ice and had to clean up. When she got it right, she placed the glass down in front of him.

"That'll be fourteen fifty," she said.

"How are you?"

"What?"

"I mean, you're working hard, aren't you?"

"I always work hard. Money?" She tapped her forefinger on the bar.

He slapped a twenty down on the counter. She scooped up the bill and returned, pushing his change toward him. He eased his hand on top of hers and stopped.

"It's a tip," he said, adding another five.

She'd never gotten a ten-buck tip—not from someone who didn't want sex in return. And she'd always disappointed them. But she'd take the money this time. The jackass could afford it.

"You live a hard life, don't you?" he asked, taking a sip.

"No harder than anyone else."

"That's not what I hear."

She looked up sharply. "Don't believe everything you hear."

"I mean, you drive a rat trap, bake in the morning, bartend at night. Yet you don't make enough to buy a better car?"

"And that's your business how?" she asked, arching an eyebrow.

"Funny you should ask. I'm here to help you with that."

She snorted. "Yeah. Sure." Someone at the other end of the bar raised his hand, and she went to take his order. Maybe that jerk would be gone after she served this joker. She could hope, couldn't she?

"MISS?" STRYKER CALLED. She turned. "Another? This time with soda."

She returned to him. "Coming right up."

"I can make life a whole lot easier for you," he said, his voice low.

"Yeah? Gonna give me the winning lottery ticket?" she asked, cocking an eyebrow.

"Nope. I'm going to give you a check for ten grand."

Jess started, and the glass slipped out of her hand. It crashed to the floor, breaking into a million pieces.

"That'll come out of your pay," Homer growled.

Jess nodded, feeling the color seeping into her face.

"I'll pay for it. Here. Buy a whole new set of glasses," Stryker said, waving a fifty-dollar bill at Homer.

"Thanks," he said, snatching the bill. "You're off the hook, Jess."

She shot Stryker a curious glance. No one had given a rat's ass about her, except Will, in a long time. Or paid for her broken glasses or even bought her a drink.

"Thanks," she said, sweeping up the glass into a dustpan. After she discarded it, she started making his drink again. He waited until she put it down in front of him. Then he trapped her, closing his hand over her wrist.

"You didn't hear wrong. Ten grand."

She arched her eyebrows. "Really? And what do I have to do for that much money?"

"Nothing. Just give your approval."

She tilted her head.

"Just give Grey Andrews the go-ahead to sign the demolition request."

"Hah! Yeah. Sure."

"You will?"

"In your dreams."

"Ten grand," he said, whipping his checkbook out of his breast pocket and plunking it down on the bar. "Right now. Cash it tomorrow. Live like a human being for a while."

The urge to slap that smug grin off his face grabbed her. She clasped her hands together to keep from assaulting him.

"A bribe? Forget it. Never means never." She turned away until his whisper met her ears.

"Then make it fifty. Fifty grand. Enough money to leave this fleabag town and start over somewhere else. Maybe even buy your own place. Or live without working for a year."

Jess stopped. She faced the row of bottles and the mirror behind. Stryker made a thumbs up gesture. Her lungs stopped working. Fifty grand. Oh, shit, fifty grand. How could she say no to that? Visions of the portable sawmill Will lusted after flew through her head, along with the professional stove, a new house, a new car—her mind conjured images faster than she could think.

She hooked her hands over the edge of the sink and took a deep breath. *It's a bribe, Jess. A bribe. But he's not doing anything illegal. Still. It's a bribe. He wants to buy you. No one owns Jess Lennox. But is it fair to Will to refuse?*

The internal war raged. Stryker's stare met hers. She saw light coming into his eyes. He thought he had her. That hardened her resolve. No one bribes Jess Lennox. No one buys Jess Lennox. Whirling around, she met his gaze with her own.

"No sale. Now finish your drink and leave."

He trapped her hand with his. It was warm, dry, and strong. "Are you sure? Fifty grand? It's a lot of money."

"Drop dead. Is that clear enough? Is there something you don't understand about *no*?"

She ripped her fingers from his, ignored the tingling brought on by his touch, and hurried into the back room. Bending over, she gulped air.

"That guy hitting on you?" Homer asked.

She shook her head.

"Because if he is, or he's rude, just let me know, and I'll toss his sorry ass outta here."

She smiled. "Thanks, Homer. No, it's fine. He's fine. I think he's leaving, anyway."

Peeking around the corner, she watched Stryker toss two twenties on the bar and walk out. His jacket pulled slightly across his broad shoulders. He stuffed his hands in his pockets, drawing his pants tight across his butt. Damn, it was perfect. After turning to glance back once, he ambled to the door, opened it, and exited.

Homer accompanied Jess back to her station. He picked up one twenty and tossed the other one to her.

"Big tipper."

"Yeah. Too big."

"You're not meeting him later or anything, are you?"

"Are you asking me if I'm a prostitute, Homer?" Jess rested both hands on her hips, her stance wide. He raised his palms.

"No, no. I'd never say that. It's just. Hell, we don't get no twenty-dollar tippers in here. At least none that don't want something besides food and drink in return."

"Yeah, well the guy's rolling in money. He probably wipes his butt with a twenty. Doesn't mean anything to him. And it sure doesn't mean anything to me."

Another man sat in Stryker's vacated seat. "Hey, honey, how about a beer?"

"On tap?"

"Yeah, fine."

Even with her back to him, she felt the man's stare. She sighed. Another asshole to fend off while she worked. How come she'd forgotten about that part of this job? She slammed the beer down in front of the guy.

"Five bucks," she said.

He slid a five-dollar bill and two quarters over the bar. "Don't spend it all in one place," he smirked, his eyes lit up with lust.

"Don't get any ideas," Jess countered. "Is it one yet, Homer?"

"I'm watching that asshole. Two beers and you send him home."

She nodded. As she worked, she wondered why Stryker wanted to tear down the old house? Why didn't he sell it? Like to her, for a hundred bucks? She smiled. *Dream on, girl.*

STRYKER SLID INTO THE driver's seat of the Bentley.

"Stupid fucking asshole moron," he said, striking the steering wheel with his palm. "I should have known she'd never take a bribe. But, hey, fifty grand? She's a fool. She'll never see money like that again." The moment the words were out of his mouth, something completely new came over Stryker. Sympathy. Empathy. Although he hadn't grown up destitute, he hadn't grown up rich, either. A wave of emotion took him by surprise. Why did he care about Jess Lennox?

She'd berated him, practically took a swing at him, too. He read her eyes perfectly. She wanted to hit him but controlled herself. Hell, he deserved it. He'd behaved badly. Still, a girl who'd opt for poverty over a chance to climb out—well, he'd never seen the likes of her before.

What was it about that house? Why was she protecting it? Sure, he'd loved it, or almost loved it, at one time, but now? It was the biggest money pit in the world. Even throwing bucks at it, he didn't believe it could ever be what it once was—a warm home for a family.

Jess Lennox had the best-looking rack he'd almost-seen in a long time. That top she wore had definitely been designed to up the amount of her tips. He'd sneaked a peek, a very long peek, just like any guy—and liked what he saw.

He put the car in gear and backed out. All the way home, questions about Jess Lennox boiled through his brain. Who was she? Why was she so poor? How come there were people who trashed her? What had she done? But, most of all, why did she protect that house with every-thing she had?

When he opened the front door, he smelled coffee. Chris Toller, his chauffeur and henchman, adored it. Right about now, Stryker could use a cup and some company. He moseyed into the kitchen.

"Hi, Mr. West."

"Please, call me Stryker."

"Want a cup of decaf?"

"Sure. What kind is it?"

"Mocha tonight."

The two men sat at the kitchen table.

"I don't mean to pry, but you get her to change her mind?" Chris asked.

Stryker shook his head.

"That's too bad."

"She turned down fifty grand."

"Wow. Guess she's not too smart."

"It's not that. Just principles, I guess. There's something about that house."

"You haven't given up yet, have you, sir?"

"I know you're anxious to get back to New York and your girl-friend, but no, I haven't. Everyone has their price. We just haven't found hers yet."

"Hmm. Bullying didn't work. And bribing didn't work."

Stryker sighed.

"Maybe you have to try seduction, sir."

The billionaire's eyes widened. "Why, Chris. You're a genius. Se-duction! Yes, perfect."

"How?" Chris asked.

"Hmm," he muttered, stroking his chin. "Good question."

"There's more than one way to seduce a woman." Chris smiled.

"Oh?" he asked, raising his eyebrows.

"Yes. First, the obvious one. The direct way. Put the moves on her. But if that's not for you, then the indirect way. Like through someone she loves. Be super nice to her dog or cat..."

"Or her brother?" Stryker asked.

"She has a brother?"

"She does. And he's a carpenter, I hear. Saw a card tacked up on the bulletin board at the Cozy Café. Probably doesn't get much work or they wouldn't be so poor."

"How does that help?"

"We'll have to fake some kind of project. A high-paying one. And hire him."

"Okay. What kind of project?"

"Don't know. I'll have to think about it. You, too, Chris."

"Oh, I will, sir. I will."

Stryker finished his beverage and headed up the stairs. What could he possibly hire Jess's brother to do? He preferred to think about the first way—direct seduction. Maybe not quite putting the moves on her as Chris suggested, but something much more subtle.

He stripped down and slid between the sheets. Gazing out the window at the moon, he fantasized that Jess was in the bathroom, getting ready to join him. Blood pumped to his groin. Taming her passion in bed aroused him to the point of pain. He'd have to relieve himself.

The idea of Jess relieving him, instead, only made it worse. The sweet, spicy scent of pie that surrounded her returned to his nose and teased him mercilessly. Closing his eyes, he tried to imagine her naked. Though he hadn't had a chance to study her, he conjured up her slim form as she stood for nomination in the town meeting hall.

Ah, seduction! He'd come up with a perfect plan on the morrow. Now, he had to attend to his own needs in order to sleep. His vision of her brought him to completion quickly. He grinned at the idea that what started out as a pain in his butt had morphed into a possibly delightful interlude with a most sexy young lady. Too bad Minnie wasn't there to thank. He thought she'd approve of Jess Lennox. At least for one night. And that's all he'd need.

Chapter Four

When she entered the Cozy Café, Town Supervisor, Grey Andrews, was nursing a cup of coffee. He nodded to Jess. After she placed her pie boxes on the counter, she pulled out a chair and joined him.

"Can I buy you a coffee?" he asked.

"No, thanks. Is the guy who inherited that house on the lake going to sell it?" she asked.

"He didn't say, but I think he's going to keep it."

"Keep it?" Her eyebrows rose.

"Yeah. Tear it down. Sell the land. It's quite valuable. He's already requested a demolition permit. I told him he'd have to get you to sign off before I issue the permit."

"Good. Thanks. I'm declaring it a landmark. There will be no demolition."

"Not sure that will hold up in court."

"There's an ordinance or something about that, right?"

"That's dicey. I know I said you could do that, but I've been rethinking it," Grey replied. "If he turns some high-priced lawyers on you, it could get rough."

"Really?" she asked, her smile dissolving into a frown. "I can't defend that."

"Yeah, I know. Then I did some research. Did you know there are a lot of protected species in New York state?"

"Nope."

"Well, there are. And if some of those insects or birds are living on that property, demolition could disturb their nesting sites. I'd say the Environmental Protection Agency in Albany might have something to say about that."

"Okay. I get it." She nodded.

I'm guessing some searching on the Internet could give you a good list of animals and insects to scout around for on the ten acres surrounding that house." Grey grinned.

"I'm guessing you're right."

"Since you're the landmark committee, I'd say you were the perfect person to do it. And, as the Town Supervisor, I can tell you, I'm not going to issue a demolition permit if it would go against the rules and regs of the EPA."

"Thank you, Grey," she said, giving his arm a squeeze.

Grey reached out and patted her hand. "I get the history of the property, but It puzzles me why you want to save that old place."

"I've got my reasons," she said, smiling.

"Good luck."

"Thanks. I've got this," Jess said, pushing to her feet.

She climbed behind the wheel of her wheezy old car and headed to Tasty Temptations in Narrowsburg to deliver a cake. While she drove, she planned to stop by the library. Having some ammunition to face West with relieved her mind. He could take his fancy lawyers and shove them, as far as she was concerned. She'd find all the species she'd need to block his demolition plans. Tension eased out of her body. She flipped on the radio.

On her way home, she stopped at Pete's Pump to get gas. Jess stood, half-hidden by an oak tree. A fancy car stopped just before the bridge over the Cattail Creek, facing Minnie's place. A man exited the front seat and opened the door to the back. Stryker West got out. *What's the matter? Doesn't he have hands? Can't open his own door?*

West strolled to the center of the bridge, leaving his car blocking traffic. Jess chided herself. There was no traffic at nine a.m. on a Tuesday. As she watched, the corners of her mouth turned down.

Mr. Fancy Pants. Thinks he owns the town. Thinks he'll tear down that house. Well, he's got another think coming. She kept her gaze on the tall, handsome man. Just the way he walked, almost like a swagger, exuded power. She guessed he had confidence to burn.

Checking her wristwatch, she noted she was five minutes late to the Pine Grove Inn but couldn't take her eyes off West. Even though he was wearing sunglasses, he shaded his eyes with his hand as he looked across at the old, dilapidated house. *Pompous. In love with himself.*

Put-down after put-down came to mind, yet she continued to watch him. She had pies to deliver. *Can't be wastin' time gawking at the fancy man here to destroy my dream. Maybe he'll fall in the lake.* She grinned at the image of the big city man, soaking wet, his perfectly-tailored suit, clinging to him, ruined. Water dripping down his face into his scruff.

The mental picture of Mr. Big Shot, all rumpled, and disconcerted, his clothing outlining his perfect body, started a sensation in a place she didn't expect. Yep. The one word she didn't want to admit when conjuring up the image of him wading out of the lake was, sexy. Damn sexy.

She shook her head to clear her mind, then turned away. Jess started up her old rust bucket just as he returned to the back seat of his Bentley. She set her lips in a firm line and steered her car to Maple Street for her next delivery. The sooner Mr. Big Bucks left town, the better.

STRYKER MET A DEMOLITION expert at the house.

"So, what do you think?"

"Takin' down a place this size? Gonna cost a fortune. But you've probably got some real good wood and stuff that you can sell. Won't pay for the demolition, but it'll help."

Stryker rubbed his neck. "What's a fortune?"

"Fifty grand."

"Really?"

"Man, this is a huge house. Might even cost more."

Either way the damn house was gonna cost him money he couldn't recoup. Probably cost two hundred grand to renovate. Now at least fifty to tear down. The house trapped him, his wallet, at least. Not that he couldn't afford it. Fifty grand was practically lunch money to Stryker Alexander West, but he hated to be wasteful. He expected to get something for his money. And paying to raze a house didn't add up. However, paying four times that amount to fix it up didn't make sense, either. How much could he get for it, if he put it on the market?

"Say, Mr. West. Why do you want to take down this beautiful old house?"

"It's a wreck, that's why."

"I've seen places worse than this reclaimed. Turned into fine homes, too. If you've got the dough to fix it up, why not?"

"I hate the place."

"That's harsh. It's built solid. Restore it. Come on. Make it the beautiful place it was once. Nothing like an old house. Lotsa good times there, I bet. I gotta go. Let me know if you get that permit," the man said.

"When. You mean when," Stryker corrected.

"Whatever." The man climbed into his pickup and pulled away.

Stryker opened the front door and went inside. Picking up the dusty sheet from the sofa, he laid it on the floor and sat down. Memories flooded his mind. His thirteenth year flashed back in blazing color.

Stryker Alexander West had made his debut in the local police station when he was thirteen. Hauled in for underage drinking, and disorderly conduct, Sergeant Maguire sat him down hard on a seat in the interrogation room.

"I understand Minnie West isn't your mother."

"Nope." His stomach flip-flopped.

"She's your dad's older sister?" he asked, raising an eyebrow.

"Yessir."

"I hear you been actin' up. Giving her a hard time."

"Old biddie," Stryker muttered.

The sergeant's eyes widened, his nostrils flared. "I can pick up this phone, dial children's services, and have you yanked outta the 'old biddie's' house in a god-damn heartbeat. I can slam your ass in a foster home where they don't give a crap about you. Where they're only in it for the check they get every month. Would that be better? Would you like that? 'Cause I can do it. With one phone call," the policeman said, picking up the receiver.

Even at forty-two, his stomach clenched at the memory and sweat broke out on his forehead.

"No, sir. No. Please don't do that."

"You ma and pa died in a car, didn't they?"

"Yessir."

"How do you think they'd feel if they knew what a dick their son is?" he asked, grabbing Stryker by the collar of his shirt. "Huh? I asked you a question. How would they feel?"

"They wouldn't like it."

"Damn right they wouldn't. They might even say, pick up that phone, Sergeant Maguire. Put him in a foster home. Let him see how good he's got it with Minnie."

He'd trembled in fear. His eyes darted from Sergeant Maguire's face to the phone and back again. By the time the sergeant finished his interrogation, Stryker had been shaking, he'd thrown up, and tears poured down his cheeks.

The policeman laughed as he turned the boy over to his aunt.

"Here you go, Ms. West. If he acts up again, give me a call. Here's my card."

"Thank you, officer, but I'm sure Stryker learned his lesson."

"Did you, son?" the policeman asked.

Stryker nodded at the recollection. At least he'd been smart enough to believe the policeman. At the time, he'd hated Maguire, but now gratitude took its place.

He rose to his feet and walked the first floor. He didn't get what Jess saw in the place. A man with vision who saw profitable ventures everywhere just didn't get it about that old house. The old money pit held no appeal to him. He sighed and dialed Chris.

"Okay. Pick up the usual lunch at Cozy Corner and pick me up. I'll call John. It's time for lessons in seduction," he said then hung up.

It wasn't like he'd need lessons, but, damn, Jess would hardly speak to him. How the hell was he going to seduce her and convince her to give him the okay to demolish the house if she wasn't speaking to him? He needed reinforcements and sage advice.

Brushing dust off his shirt, Stryker stood by the front door. In the heat of July, the house remained cool enough to tolerate. Sadness tugged at his heart. Minnie's house, the home of broken dreams, needed to be taken out of its misery. He walked outside and shut the door.

AFTER HER MORNING DELIVERIES, Jess headed for the library. The librarian showed her how to look things up on the Internet. Jess and Will didn't have the money for a computer and the Internet. They did have phones but were careful to keep the charges down so the service didn't get turned off. A quick study, Jess found the website she needed.

"One hundred and forty-five animals are protected in New York State," she said to herself. "At least one of those has to be on Minnie's property."

Rummaging through her purse, she found an old envelope and a pen. As she came upon creatures she thought might be found on the West land, she jotted the name and a brief description down.

"The Indiana Bat," she murmured, writing. "Tiny thing." She smiled. Scrolling down, she stopped at another mammal, the Allegheny Woodrat. She scribbled that description, too. After checking out a few more species, she exited the page and stuffed the paper back in her purse.

"Thanks, Lucy," she said to the librarian.

"Did you get everything you need?"

"I think so."

On the drive home, Jess smiled. For the first time, victory wouldn't go to the most ornery or stubborn one, like most of her battles in life. This time she had ammunition. She'd surprise Stryker West with facts, as soon as she could gather the data. She sang along with the radio when the song, *We Will Rock You,* played.

In the kitchen, she pulled out ingredients for dinner. With meat in short supply, Jess would stretch what they had with tomato sauce, pasta, and leftover veggies. She called it "kitchen sink", which always made Will laugh. She donned her apron and headed for the refrigerator. Convinced she had Stryker by the short hairs, she hummed a favorite tune.

July days came and went so fast she barely had time to harvest her garden vegetables. Soon it would be August, time for The Corn Festival. Of course, her chocolate chip cornbread would win the baked goods contest again. As for the dance, well, hell, she didn't have anything to wear so she crossed that off the list.

The door burst open and Will strode in.

"What's for dinner?" he asked, yanking open the fridge and pulling out a beer.

"Kitchen sink."

"Again?"

"Anytime you don't like the cooking here, feel free to do it yourself."

"Sorry, sis."

"Bad day?"

"Not really."

"What happened?" she asked, as she tended half a pound of chopped meat browning in a skillet.

"Want one?" he asked, holding out a beer.

"Thanks." She'd worked up a thirst cooking in the hot kitchen.

"Jack Brophy might have some work for me. He's rebuilding his barn."

Will went into detail about the job. Jess listened, proud of her brother. From a snot-nosed teen, he'd grown into a fine young man, a real hard worker.

"Oh, Mrs. Reilly gave me a big tip today for fixing her stairs. Here," he said, dropping a five-dollar bill into the jar under the sink.

"Keep it, Will."

"Nope. I never get a chance to add to your fund. So, this is it. Probably for the year."

"Okay, then. Thanks. Dinner's ready."

They filled their plates and carried them out the back door to the table on the deck. They had the three rooms on the first floor, and another tenant had the three rooms on the second. They shared the back deck. There was no one else at the table. After a forkful of food, Jess broke the silence.

"Think I've found what I need."

"What you need? Hell, we need everything. So which thing did you find first?" he asked, a twinkle in his eye.

"About the house. Got what I need to stop that jerk."

"Are you still on that?"

She stuck out her chin. "Grey Andrews gave me a couple of ideas. I spent two hours at the library, looking up stuff. Seems that old SOB West might have some endangered species living on his land. That would mean he couldn't do demolition. Might disturb their nests and stuff. It's not me sayin' it. It's the New York State Environmental Protection something. It's the law. And fancy city lawyers can't do a damn thing." A triumphant smile spread across her face.

"Damn. I should have known. You're like a dog with a bone. You just don't give up, do you?"

"It's my dream, Will."

"I know, I know. Why don't you marry this guy, instead of trying to destroy him?"

Jess spit out food. "Marry him? That bastard? Are you kidding?"

"You might get a lot farther if you were nice to him."

"Typical male response. Why don't you ask me to sleep with him?"

"Been a long time for you. Might do you some good." Will smirked.

Jess's mouth fell open. She bolted up out of her seat.

"Don't get your panties in a twist. I don't think you should do that. But bein' nice never hurt anything. And being nasty'll get you nowhere."

Jess closed her mouth and sat down. "Can't be nice to a guy without him expectin' sex."

"Never know 'til you try."

Jess ate in silence. Sometimes Will came up with a good idea. Couldn't hurt to stop yelling at West. Especially since she had this in the bag. No reason to be mean. After all, she'd won. She'd be gathering evidence of those critters on his property, then he'd be hog-tied. She'd outfox the billionaire and his army of expensive lawyers. Might as well be charitable, since he's gonna lose the fight anyway.

"You know, you're right." She picked up her fork.

"What?" he sputtered.

"You're right."

"You're gonna sleep with him?"

"I didn't say that. But it can't hurt to be nice to the man. After all, with the information I got today, I'm only one step away from winning anyway. Nobody likes a sore winner, right?"

"Charity is your middle name," he said, shaking his head.

"That's right. Don't forget it either."

"Never thought I'd live to see the day when you admitted I was right," he said.

"Me, too. Guess you're growing up. Thanks for the advice."

"I just know guys. Nasty never gets you anywhere with guys."

She smiled. "I'm turning over a new leaf. Maybe I can sweet talk him into selling me the building cheap without having to find an Allegheny Woodrat or an Indiana Bat after all."

AFTER BREAKFAST, STRYKER and Chris headed back to their house. The phone rang.

"It's John, sir."

"Put it on speaker." Stryker settled down on the sofa.

"Stryker. How are you?"

"Fine, fine. Now about this seduction thing." Stryker got to the point.

"I thought you'd nailed this by the time you were eighteen?" John asked.

"For an ordinary seduction? Hell, yeah. I could do that in my sleep, and have on occasion." He chuckled.

"Then why are you calling?"

"I've never used seduction to get something, like this. I mean to get sex, sure. No problem. But to get this bitch to back off and let me demolish the house? Not so easy."

"You're right. It's not the same. Sex is easy, this, not so much," John replied.

"Do you have any ideas?"

John laughed. "Well, you might start by being nice to the girl."

"Nice? To that nasty bitch who bites my head off?" Stryker rose from his seat.

"Maybe that's because you're always badgering her about signing the demolition permit?"

"Well, okay. So maybe I do."

"First thing—stop badgering her. Stop bullying her. Stop asking her to approve the permit."

"Okay. You're right. It won't be easy, but I'll do it."

"Being nice is never easy for you, Stryker," John said.

"Now wait a minute. I can be nice. Very nice."

"Prove it."

Chris shrugged. "Try it."

"You, too?" Stryker sniffed.

"John's right, you know. Don't fire me, but you do come on a little strong."

"It's just my personality."

"No, it's you wanting something you're not getting," John piped up.

"She's being unreasonable."

"By your standards. Have you even considered why she's standing in your way?" John asked.

"Yes, and I have no clue!"

"Have you asked her?"

"Ask her?" Stryker's voice rose.

"Go to the source," Chris put in.

"Chris is right. Come out and ask. Don't be a wimp."

"I'm no wimp," Stryker said, jutting his chin out.

"Speak to her. Ask her. Nicely! And don't demand she sign the demolition papers."

"Okay, okay. But where do I start?"

"Where do you always start your seductions?" John coaxed.

"At the dinner table. People are more open to your ideas..."

"Manipulations—" John put in.

"Whatever. As I was saying, people are more open to your ideas when they've been fed. Hunger makes people disagreeable."

"Some people are like that even when they've just finished a meal," John said.

"Don't go there. I'm not disagreeable."

"Not when you're getting your own way. I've got to go. Things are heating up here in London. I have possible office plans from the architect and a contract with the broker to work out. Take my advice. Good luck. You know, Stryker, I think you can accomplish anything you set out to do."

"Thanks, John," Stryker said, and the conversation ended. "So where do I start, Chris?"

"You might ask her to dinner."

"No, no, she's too smart for that. She'll see right through it."

"How about with her pies?"

"Excellent. Yes. Hmm. Let's see. Get the manager of The Meadow on the phone. We'll order pies for the whole place for dinner tomorrow."

"That should get her attention," Chris said, opening the laptop.

"And put a few cents in her pocket. The poor girl. She doesn't have a dime to her name."

"Not everyone is as lucky as you are, sir," Chris said while his fingers flew over the keys.

"Luck? Luck had nothing to do with my success. I started early and worked my ass off for years to get here."

"I'm sorry. I didn't mean to offend you."

Stryker patted his chauffeur on the shoulder. "That's okay. You made the same mistake everyone makes. You think this happened by the swish of a magic wand. It didn't. I'm forty-two. It's taken me years to build this."

"I get it. Okay. Here's the number. Dialing."

Stryker cleared his throat. "Mrs. Reilly? I'm Stryker West."

"Oh, yes. Minnie West's nephew."

"Right. After the unfortunate demise of my aunt, I'm now a property owner in Pine Grove."

"That old house. Such a wonderful place."

"Isn't it? I thought I'd like to do something for the residents here."

"Oh? What did you have in mind?"

"I'd like to sponsor a pie night. I'll buy enough pies from Miss Lennox to feed your residents."

"We have twenty people living here. That's a lot of pie."

"No worries. I can handle it. Would that be acceptable?"

"They'd love it. Now we have some very strong opinions about pie here."

"Give me your order, number of pies and the type, and I'll take care of the rest."

"That's awfully generous of you."

"Nothing's too good for the people of Pine Grove."

After jotting down the pie flavors and number, Stryker cleared his throat and called Jess.

Chapter Five

Jess wiped the flour off her hands onto her apron and picked up her phone.

"Hello?"

"Hi," said a deep voice she didn't recognize.

"Who is this?" she asked.

"Stryker West."

"You really don't understand no, do you? I guess you don't hear it very often…"

Will stood next to her, gesturing. He whispered, "Nice! Be nice!"

Jess stopped to take a breath.

"What do you want?" she asked, shooting an evil grin at her brother.

"Ah, this isn't about the house. It's about pies."

"What about pies?"

Will's gestures got bigger. "Nice!" he hissed.

"I mean. Is there something I can do for you?" Her free hand clenched into a fist at her side.

"I'd like to order some pies."

"I don't…"

Will jumped up and down.

"I don't usually take orders for individual pies, Mr. West. But in your case, I might make an exception."

Will nodded his head so vigorously, Jess worried it might fall off.

"That's very kind of you. No, I want to order seven pies."

"Seven?" she asked, her eyebrows heading to her forehead.

"That's right. I have a list of the fillings requested. Do you take requests?"

"For an order that big, I sure do. Wait a sec. Let me get a piece of paper. Where do you want them delivered and when?" she asked, looking around on the table.

Grinning, Will handed her a pen and a piece of paper.

Jess scribbled quickly, punctuating her writing with nods and mumblings of agreement.

"Is it too late to get them delivered by five o'clock tonight? They eat early at The Meadow."

"Tonight? The Meadow? I see. Yes, I can do it. No problem. Thank you so much."

"And how much is that per pie?"

"Twenty-five dollars," she replied.

"Fine. I'll have a check in an envelope, waiting for you. Do you accept checks?" he asked.

"I do. Sure. Thanks again."

"No, thank you, Miss Lennox." The line went dead.

"Seven pies?"

"Yep."

"You're charging him more."

"He can afford it. Besides, he's not reselling them."

"A hundred seventy five bucks for one afternoon. Not bad."

Jess checked her watch. "I'd better get going."

"Can I help?"

"Come back at four thirty. You can help me pack them up."

"Will do."

She shot him a questioning glance. "How'd I do?"

"Fine, just fine." Will patted her shoulder. "You dialed it down. You were nice."

"I didn't think I could do it." She smiled.

"Neither did I." He chuckled on his way out the door.

Jess took out the pie ingredients and measured into her biggest mixing bowl. A chickadee landed on the bird feeder outside her window.

"What do you think Stryker West wants?" she asked the bird, who quickly flew away. "Yeah, I don't know either.

Two male goldfinches, their iridescent gold feathers almost providing as much light as the sun, replaced the feisty little black-and-white bird. They stayed on perches to feed. Jess directed her conversation to them.

"I don't care what Will says. That guy's up to no good. I don't trust him. He wants something. Probably the demolition permit. He'll never get it. He can buy a thousand pies. I'll never change my mind."

After wiping her hand with a paper towel, Jess turned on the radio. She sang along with her favorite country music station as she rolled dough and prepared filling. Thinking about the seniors at The Meadow, she smiled to herself. She knew all of them and their tastes. Once a month, the manager would buy a pie or two and portion out small slices.

They loved her pies and often complained about the size of the pieces. The manager explained that their food budget limited the number of special treats they offered. Seven pies meant the residents could have generous portions and even enjoy more than one kind.

She refused to give Mr. West credit for his charity and kept her suspicions alive. A man like that didn't give anything away unless he wanted something in return. Well, the payment for seven pies didn't buy her, and he'd not be getting a change of heart and a signed demolition permit for his efforts. Still, it warmed her heart to be delivering her wares to The Meadow.

She hummed as she rolled, filled and baked. At four forty-five, Will rolled in. Jess noticed a lipstick smear on his cheek.

"A little early in the day for that, isn't it?"

"What?" he asked, putting together a box for a pie.

She reached over and wiped away the color. Will blushed.

"Oh. That. Naw. Never too early." He finished one box and tackled another.

Jess put a warm pie in the box and sealed it. Then she wrote "blueberry" on the top.

"Who's the lucky lady this week?"

"What difference does it make?"

She cocked an eyebrow.

"Don't distract me."

"Yes, we're behind because you're late."

"You could have started this without me."

"It's not like I've been sitting around all afternoon reading."

"Okay, okay. I'm sorry. Let's get this done."

They worked together in silence until all the pies were packed, then toted them carefully out to his truck. Will tossed the keys to Jess. She put it in gear and headed for The Meadow.

THE NEXT DAY, JESS slapped a twenty and a ten on the table.

"Your cut. For helping me yesterday."

"Cash? Nice," Will said, stuffing the money in his wallet.

"Don't spend it all in one place."

"I'm taking Jennie to the movies tonight." He shot her a shy grin.

"Not Jennie Matthews?"

"Yep."

"That's a mistake. A big mistake." Jess cut a generous slice of strawberry rhubarb pie and pushed it across the table to her brother.

"Just because it didn't work out with you and Chip," he began.

"Didn't work out? Bullshit! His parents got in the way. And our mother, bless her twisted little heart, did, too."

"But it's been years. I'm sure they've gotten over it by now." He fished a fork out of the drawer.

"You think so? I don't." Jess filled the coffee maker. Will pulled a beer from the fridge.

"Beer and pie?" Jess made a face.

"Beer goes with everything."

"You can date her. Just don't get serious. I'm telling you, they'll put a stop to it."

"I'll get serious if I want to. Jennie's an amazing girl."

"I'm sure she is." She took milk out of the fridge.

"She was just a kid when you were engaged to Chip. You don't know her." He shoveled a forkful of pie in his mouth.

"I know the family. They're bad news."

"You didn't think so when you agreed to marry Chip."

"I was marrying him, not the whole family." Jess grabbed a mug from the drying rack.

"This is different."

"Look, if you get serious and they put a big ole roadblock up, don't come crying to me."

"So, I'm supposed to pick my girlfriends by their family?"

"I'm just sayin' the Matthews family is trouble."

"I've never met a girl like Jennie," he said, his voice low and soft.

Jess put her head in her hands. "Damn. Should have known."

"I'm happy. Why can't you be happy for me?"

"Because I can see the handwriting on the wall. No murderers in their family."

"That's ancient history." He took a swig of his beer.

"Is it? I just don't want you to get hurt," she said, giving his shoulder a squeeze.

"I know. I won't. Girls like Jennie don't come along every day." He shot her a grin.

"Okay. It's your funeral. Good luck."

"I want you to meet Jennie."

Jess frowned. "Why?"

"Because I love her, that's why."

"Oh, shit. Damn." Jess closed her eyes.

"Stop. Can I invite her to dinner?"

There was a long pause.

"Please?" he asked.

"Friday," she said.

"Make something special."

"Beef stew?" Jess mentally put aside some of the money in her pocket for meat.

"Yeah. I love your stew."

"You're my best customer."

"And chocolate cream pie?"

"You got it," she said, smiling.

When they finished eating, Will helped clean up. Stealing a few minutes to herself before starting the evening meal, Jess grabbed her book and hit the hammock. She put the novel down to watch the little finches at the feeders. They had been her friends when folks in town had shunned her. Gratitude for their presence warmed her heart.

The brilliant goldfinches contrasted with the stark black-and-white of the chickadees. A nuthatch arrived and jockeyed with the others for a perch. Life seemed so simple for these little creatures. Why couldn't her life be simple, too? Jess sighed. She made plans to hunt for threatened species on the West property at the end of the week.

Getting back to her book, she read for an hour, then picked squash, cucumbers, and lettuce from her garden. Time to whip up a veggie pasta dish and a salad. A knock on the screen door startled her. It was Chip. He opened the door without her permission.

"What are you doing here?" she asked, tying her apron behind her back.

"Though you might like this," he said offering a brown paper bag.

"What is it?" she asked, eying the gift.

"Chicken. We had an extra. Thought you could use it."

Emotion closed her throat. Never one to ask for charity or be willing to accept it either, Jess didn't know what to say. His gesture touched her heart.

"Thanks," she choked out, taking the bag.

"You're welcome." He turned to go. She put her hand on his upper arm.

"You don't have to do that, you know."

"I know. Just being neighborly."

"This doesn't fix anything—between us."

"I know that ship has sailed. I regret it every day."

She dropped her hand and let him leave.

"Thanks again," she called after him. He raised a hand to her and kept going.

Jess returned to the kitchen. She put the bag on the counter. Then, bracing herself with her hands on the edges, she hung her head down and let the tears flow.

THURSDAY NIGHT, JESS subbed again for her friend at Homer's. She served dozens of beers to the usual crowd.

"Well, hello there," came a familiar voice.

Ugh. She glanced up in time to see Stryker West slide his choice butt on the seat in front of her.

"Hi." *Nice, Will said to be nice. Be nice. Be nice.* She forced a small smile. "Thanks for the pie order."

"I heard they loved them. Lady there told me there wasn't a crumb left the next morning."

"Yeah. They don't get much fresh pie over there. Thanks, again," she said, wiping a glass dry and moving down the bar.

"Excuse me," he said.

Damn, he's being polite. That still won't get him the permit.

"Yes?"

"Can I get a Vodka Collins?"

"Collins? Let me take a look," she said, peering under the bar. Sure enough, a bottle of Collins mixer stared back at her. "No problem."

"Tell me something," he continued, watching her work. "Why do you care about that old house? It's not like you grew up there or anything."

"It's personal."

"Oh?" He arched an eyebrow. "Now I'm intrigued."

She plopped the drink down in front of him. "Personal is just that. Personal. I don't discuss it with strangers."

"But we've met. I've introduced myself."

"Sorry. Can I get you anything else? A burger?"

He hesitated, his gaze never leaving hers. "Sure. Why not? Medium, please. And with cheese."

"Coming right up."

She disappeared around back to place the order in person, rather than use the POS system. She'd log it in after. Anything to get away from his stare and his questions. Unable to stall for long, she returned to the far end of the bar, avoiding him.

He picked up a pretzel, took a bite, and washed it down with his drink. Since his gaze was on the television screen, she could study him in private. He had a strong profile. Perfect nose, slightly squarish jaw. His dark scruff and hair had been shaped to perfection. He wore a perfectly-tailored navy sports jacket over snug-fitting jeans. His white shirt emphasized the dark chocolate of his eyes and his tanned complexion.

She'd never seen a man so richly clothed, so handsome. Reminding herself how evil he was, she corralled her emotions. Still, staring at him made her breath come a little faster and warmth spread through her. And his lips, damn. He licked salt from the pretzel off his lower lip, and she grabbed onto the bar to steady herself.

How could she be attracted to the man who wanted to kill her dream? Kill, how apt was that word—as if he'd be executing it, putting it in the electric chair and turning on the juice. She shivered.

"Burger up!" the cook called from the kitchen.

Damn, she'd have to face him again. She picked up the plate, grabbed a napkin and silverware and headed toward him.

"Looks good. Wish you could join me." He smiled at her.

She smiled back. How dumb did he think she was? Nice went out the window.

"Look, Mr. West—"

"Stryker, please,"

She sighed. "Okay. Stryker. Turning on the charm isn't going to work. Never means never."

"I'm just being polite."

"Sure you are. Yeah, right. That's almost insulting. How you think buying my pies and a few nice words are going to make me roll over like a trained dog." She glared at him.

He laughed. "Honey, if I could get you to roll over, the last thing on my mind would be that old house."

She wanted to slap his face. Color heated her cheeks.

"You're a pig, you know that?"

Homer moved behind her. "Did I just hear you call a customer a pig?"

Stryker raised his hand. "She's right. I shouldn't have said that. I apologize. My honesty got the best of my better judgment."

Homer smiled. "Have one on the house." He pointed a finger at Jess. "It'll come out of your salary," he said, then walked away.

Anger pulsed through her. "Why do you come here? Just to torment me?'"

His smile faded. "That's not my intention."

"Then what is?" she asked, throwing a rag on the counter.

"To make peace. Why are we enemies?"

"You're an idiot, you know that?" she said, her voice lower.

"It's hard to make up when you keep calling me names."

"I have no desire to make up with you. Why can't you leave me alone?"

She raised her gaze to his. His warm eyes mesmerized her. She dropped hers to his lips and her nipples hardened. Crap, yes, it had been that long.

"Because you intrigue me. You're beautiful, poor, hard-working, and in love with my aunt's house. Do you think I can walk away without finding out why?"

"Force yourself. Do just that. Walk away. Put the *for-sale* sign back and let it go."

"Aha! Now we're getting somewhere. The *for-sale* sign? Did you want to buy the house?"

Though she avoided his eyes, color still flowed to her face. No way would she admit it, only to be laughed out of the bar. Jess busied herself with the rag, wiping down the counter, moving away from Stryker. He grabbed her wrist.

"You do, don't you?" he asked, trapping her.

"I never said that."

In defiance, she raised her gaze to his, only to find sympathy there.

"But you can't raise the cash, right?"

At his simple, true statement, tears stung the backs of her eyes. She refused to give in, but, instead, yanked her hand away from him, knocking into another patron's glass. His beer spilled and the man, leapt up off his stool, yelling.

"Oh, God. Tom. I'm so sorry. Really. I'm sorry. I'll get you another. On the house." Jess scrambled over to the growing puddle and mopped it up with several rags.

Tom glared at her. "If you'd stop flirting with this dude, this wouldn't a happened."

"She wasn't flirting with me. We were having a conversation. I'll be happy to pay for your beer, and any damage to your clothes," Stryker said, tossing a fifty-dollar bill on the bar. The man snatched it up and left.

"Thank you." God, she hated being beholden to Stryker West—now twice in two days. Or was that three times?

"Look, you don't owe me anything. I was a jerk. Sometimes guys get like that around pretty girls. I'm sorry. Won't happen again. I don't mean to hound you. I'm just curious. But, hey, if you don't want to tell me, fine. I'll leave you alone." He whipped out another fifty and slid it across the bar to her.

"That's too much."

"Keep it," he said, sliding off the stool and heading for the door.

Well, finally! He said he'd leave her alone. Didn't she get what she wanted? Then why did an aching emptiness grip her guts?

Chapter Six

"Well, you sure did *that* perfectly didn't you? Now she loathes you even more than before. And you promised to leave her alone. Great job, Stryker, you fuckin' idiot," he mumbled shaking his head as he made his way to his car.

He stepped on the brake and put the car in gear. As he drove back to the house, he thought about what had transpired. Jess Lennox sure got it from all sides, didn't she? Homer deducted mistakes from her salary. He'd bet a bundle she didn't make a living wage working there. Customers were rude. How many hit on her and shaved their tips down or didn't tip at all when she didn't give in?

He blew out a breath. He'd been shielded from this side of the working world for years. But his memory didn't fail. When he first started out, he'd encountered plenty of bumps in the road. When he was thirteen, Stryker delivered newspapers. He remembered the house where the next-door neighbor stole the papers. The subscriber accused him of not delivering them, and the paper had fired Stryker.

He spent several mornings hiding out until he caught the thief. He took pictures and got his job back, but his boss never trusted him again. The recollection of the injustice burned anew in his chest. What must that be like for Jess? A beer spills and she's docked. Hell, a kid delivering papers isn't supporting a household, isn't feeding a family. But Jess is.

He shook his head as he exited the car. The light in the kitchen was on. *Chris must be up.*

"Well, how'd it go?" Chris asked. He sat in shorts and a T-shirt, sipping a beer.

"I blew it. And now she hates me more."

Chris's eyebrows shot up. "She hates you more?"

"I didn't think that was possible, but she does."

"What happened? What did you do?"

Stryker straddled a chair, leaning on his forearms.

"It's like this. When she said roll over..." he said, spilling his story.

When he finished, he filled the coffeemaker and pushed the "on" button.

"What are you going to do now?"

Stryker shrugged. "Have a cup of coffee, I guess."

"If you'll pardon my saying so, that's a loser attitude."

"What?"

"You're not a man who accepts defeat," Chris continued.

"It's over. The chick hates my guts. Every time I get near, something goes wrong."

"So change that."

"How?"

"I don't know. But drinking coffee, sulking, and feeling sorry for yourself isn't going to get you there."

"True," Stryker said, filling a mug. "You want one?"

"Beer's fine. Thanks."

"What do you suggest?"

"Take her out to dinner. I heard the restaurant The Waterfall in Oak Bend is real nice. And expensive, too."

"Take her to dinner? How about starting with getting her to speak to me again?"

Chris laughed. "You're funny. You wipe the floor with your opponents in every business deal, but this woman, with nothing, who's no one, has got you floored. I never would have guessed."

Stryker stared at his chauffeur. "You're right. I can't throw in the towel. Not yet, anyway."

"Go down with the ship."

"But how do I cross over that bridge?"

"Nice. Be nice."

"I tried that. Either it didn't work, or I'm not very good at it."

"Probably the latter," Chris said, then, when his boss glared, he raised his palms. "Just being honest here."

"Sometimes the truth hurts."

"It always hurts. But the truth is the truth. Can't get away from that," Chris replied.

"You're right. I can't let her win. I need to take that stupid house down and get to London."

"Oh, an email came in from John. Seems there's some trouble with the architectural plans for the London space. He said the drawings won't be ready for two months."

"Two months! I have to spend two months here?"

"You could go back to your office in New York."

"Too hot in the City. I hate air conditioning."

"Then it's the country life for you."

"Okay. Now, what's my next step?"

"Ask her to dinner. Do I have to walk you through this? You've got way more experience than I do."

"Yeah, maybe. But you have more experience in being nice," Stryker admitted.

Chris laughed, then made some suggestions.

"Might as well do this now," Stryker said, checking his watch. "I think she leaves in fifteen minutes."

"I agree. Why wait?" Chris asked.

"I'll never be able to sleep if I don't." He finished his coffee, picked up his keys, and headed for the driveway.

"LAST CALL. WE'RE CLOSING in fifteen," Jess announced to the bar.

"Okay. Another shot," said a fat man, about forty-five, wearing shorts and a T-shirt. His flab hung over the barstool.

"You've had enough, mister. I can't serve you anymore. It's the law."

"Aw, come on. I'm okay. I can drive. I'll touch my nose, see."

She tried to smile. "I'm sorry. Those are the rules." She turned away, but he grabbed her forearm.

"Come on, honey. Let me drive you home. I'll show you I'm not drunk," he smirked, wagging his eyebrows.

"Look, mister. I'm tired. Please, just settle up and go home. I'm sure your wife wonders where you are?"

"Nah. She's asleep by now."

"Go home."

"Not unless you come with me."

"Fine. Then sleep on the floor. I'm going home."

"You got a boyfriend."

"Bye," she said, heading for the back room.

Homer had developed a fever and left early, giving the keys to Jess. Jose, the cook, had cleaned up the kitchen and returned to his home. Three steady patrons paid their bills and shuffled through the door. The wise guy scooted out without paying.

"Hey! Where's that guy?" Jess asked. But the place was empty.

Swell. He ran up a tab of twenty-five bucks, which would come out of her pay. Then except for tips, she didn't make a dime. She took a deep breath, fished her car keys out of her purse and turned off the lights.

Recalling her experience earlier with Stryker West, Jess shook her head.

"Nice? What do I know about nice?" She truly did not know how to be nice anymore. She'd been nasty, he'd returned it with a dickhead response, and then she'd picked up the gauntlet. Why couldn't she let it alone? Why couldn't she tell him about the house and how much it meant to her?

Confusion and anger warred with desire. Did she want to sleep with him or kill him? Maybe both. She turned the key in the lock. Then she picked up her phone and texted Will.

Locking up. On the way home.

She smiled. He was a protective, pain-in-the-ass little brother. Gratitude filled her heart. What would she do without him? Words rang out in the still of the night, chilling her blood.

"Hello, sweetheart. Ready for that ride home?"

A shiver of fear ran through her. She turned. There was that fat, nasty man, grinning. The lot was empty and so was the street. She swallowed. Will had warned her.

"I saw that guy give you the keys."

"You knew I'd be here alone?"

"Yep. Just my lucky day, I guess."

"You guess wrong. Don't come near me. I'll scream."

"No one to hear you out here. Look around. No lights on in the houses. No cars on the road. Just you and me, sexy lady."

Jess backed toward her car. Feeling for the unlock button, her hand shook. The sound of her house keys jangling seemed loud in the silence of the night.

"No need to be afraid. I ain't gonna hurt you. You be nice to me, and I'll be nice to you." He stepped closer.

Jess followed his gaze. He stared at her keys. She shifted them behind her back. As she tripped on a stone, they slipped from her hand.

"That's right. You don't need those. You're gonna take a ride with me, right?"

"Wrong! Get back." Fear spiked through her. Her heartbeat pounded in her ears, but she kept moving. Damn it, where the hell was her car? It wasn't locked. If she could just get in and lock the door, she could call Will.

"I'm afraid I can't do that," he said, advancing. His voice dropped an octave. "Get in the car."

The crunch of tires on gravel drew their attention. A car stopped abruptly, and Stryker West jumped out.

"What the hell's going on?"

"This is none of your business, mister. This pretty lady's gettin' a ride home from me."

"No!" she hollered.

Stryker stepped in front of Jess, pushing her behind him with one arm.

"Get your ass out of here before I call the police. Jess? Snap his picture. Smile asshole."

She whipped out her phone and did as told.

"Wait, wait. What are you doin'?"

"Getting your picture so we can give it to the police. You were threatening this woman. I'm a witness. You'll go to jail."

"Gimme that phone!" The fat man lunged with hand outstretched, but Stryker kicked him in the shin and joined his hands together to clock the assailant on the back of the neck, sending him down.

"Call 911," Stryker said.

Though her hands shook badly, she dialed.

"Give me the phone," Stryker said. While he spoke to the police, explaining what had happened, the phone dinged. The man on the ground groaned and attempted to stand up. "Better stay down there if you don't want more of the same."

"I didn't touch her," he moaned.

"But you would have. You were going to. Even though she told you not to. You're a piece of slime and belong in jail."

The sound of a siren in the distance released Jess's tightly held control. She burst into tears. Stryker took her in his arms, holding her against his chest with one hand and stroking her hair with the other.

Clinging to him, she sobbed into his shirt, pushing her face against his hard muscle.

"It's okay. Here come the police. It's all right now. You're okay."

"Thank you," she blubbered.

Right after the police car, another car pulled up. Will jumped out and ran at Stryker, fists raised.

"No! Don't! Will! It's okay. He saved me." Jess said, pushing between Stryker and her brother.

Will glared at the tall man.

"The bad guy here is this asshole," Stryker said, pointing.

Stryker greeted the police. They called Jess over.

"What's your name?" Officer Jones asked.

"Jess Lennox."

"Say, aren't you Betty Lennox's kid?" the second officer, Sergeant Parker asked.

Officer Jones shot his partner a look. "It's okay, Sarge. Murder doesn't run in families."

"Okay. Wanna tell us what happened?" the sergeant asked.

After questioning Jess and Stryker, the police took the man into custody and drove away. Too rattled to drive, Jess sank down on a large rock.

"Come on, sis. I'll take you home."

"What about my car?"

"We can get it tomorrow."

"Can I talk to you for a minute, Jess?"

"Sure. I'll meet you at the car, Will."

"Thanks for helping Jess out, Mr. West," Will said.

Stryker smiled. He and Jess walked over to the street lamp, lighting up the parking lot.

"What were you doing here? Not that I'm not grateful, believe me, I am. Very. But you just happened to drive up? At this hour? A coincidence?"

"Nope. I regretted the things I'd said earlier. I came back to ask you to dinner. To plead with you to give me another chance—over a nice meal."

"Yeah?" Her heart jolted.

"I didn't hold out much hope. But I suppose this idiot helped me out, didn't he?"

"Do you mean will I have dinner with you? Yes, I will. And maybe you do have him to thank for it."

"Would you have gone if I hadn't been here to intervene?"

She shrugged then lied. "Not sure."

He chuckled. "Very politic of you."

He looked so strong standing there in the shadows, the planes of his handsome face emphasized by the soft light. She leaned against him for a moment.

"Saturday good for you?"

She nodded.

"What time?" he asked.

"Six?"

"Perfect. Put in your address," he said, handing her his phone.

"Come on, Jess!" Will called.

"I've gotta go," she said, stepping toward the car. Stryker followed. She stopped and faced him. Standing on tiptoe, she kissed his cheek. His eyebrows shot up.

"Thank you. You're my hero," she said softly.

"You're welcome. Anytime." He chuckled, running his thumb along his whiskers.

Jess got in the back seat, as Jennie Matthews sat beside Will.

"See? It's dangerous to be here alone. Now maybe you'll stop thinking I'm crazy," her brother piped up.

"Stryker West came along and saved me. Amazing." Jess gazed out the window, watching Stryker get back in his car.

"You're just damn lucky. Next time, I'm coming."

"I can't believe it was him. Of all people," Jess said, more to herself than her brother.

STRYKER STOOD ALONE in the parking lot, waiting for Will's car to pull away. He glanced up at the moon then back at the quiet street. His body had ratcheted up to high alert. Then she was in his arms, sending a different signal through him. He took a deep breath, let it out slowly and headed for his car.

As he steered along the quiet roads, he worked at pushing unwelcome thoughts from his mind.

"Stop thinking. Keep alert. Watch for deer on the road." Able to divert himself for a while by looking for deer, he couldn't keep his mind still.

When he pulled in to the driveway and turned off the ignition, he sighed. Resting his forehead on the wheel, he moaned.

"No, no, no, no, no."

Feelings shot through him like arrows. How the hell did he let her sneak under his defenses? No way would he care about this chick. She was simply another obstacle to getting what he wanted. He'd sweep her out of the way using any method that worked. All that bravado about bullying then seducing her—who has actually been seduced?

He did not want to care about her, but her plight touched his heart—or whatever was left of it. He'd lived in his ivory tower for so long, he'd forgotten about the struggles so many go through each and every day. He'd grown up with that. His father didn't make much working for the post office. And his mother was a teacher. But when they died, and he went to live with Minnie, his standard of living dropped.

Minnie had been a seamstress. She worked for a tailor in bustling Oak Bend and never made much money. The house had been her mother and father's place. But they were gone by the time young Stryker arrived.

He remembered hand-me-downs and clothes from the thrift store. Life had been hard. Jess brought it all back. Watching her work night and day, yet still struggle, reached inside him to a place he'd locked away. Memories of living poor flooded back. Her predicament took his breath away. And when she leaned against him, all vulnerable and soft——well, hell, he was only human, wasn't he?

He dragged himself inside and turned on the light in the kitchen. No way would he get to sleep yet, so he popped a beer. He'd classified Jess as a bitch, hard, intractable, determined to have her own way and for no logical reason. But now, seeing the fear in her eyes, feeling her body tremble with emotion. Touching her hair, her warmth mixing with his, desire for more than a roll in the hay sprang up in him.

No! He would not fall for that pathetic creature. Talk about gold diggers—she was probably the queen of the lot. He smirked and swigged. Yet that image didn't gel with reality. Jess appeared far too independent to want to get her claws into his money.

"What's going on? Why are you still up?" asked a sleepy Chris, rubbing his eyes.

"Jess almost got abducted."

"Ab what?" the chauffeur plopped down on a chair.

"She could have been raped and killed."

"Holy hell!"

"Yep. Alone, closing down the bar."

"And you were there? Did you stop it?"

"Yep. I knocked the asshole down," Stryker said, then went into a detailed explanation.

"Just lucky you happened along," Chris said.

Stryker finished his beer. "Damn right."

"This should get you big points with her."

"She's having dinner with me Saturday."

"Great! So, you prevailed?"

"I did," he said, rinsing out the beer bottle.

"And the next step should be easy. She's already disposed to like you now."

"I suppose."

"Where are you taking her?"

"Oak Bend. John said they have a nice restaurant there."

"Sounds good. Are you feeling okay?"

"I am. Why do you ask?"

"You look a little flushed."

"I've got a business to run. I can't get trapped in this hole. I need to okay the plans for London. Get papers filed for an airport outside of Paris. I have a life, a business. I can't get dragged into this Podunk shit."

"Okay."

Stryker glanced out into the darkness. His words were as much for himself as for Chris.

"I'm not going to get involved with her. I don't have time to care. I don't want to fall for her."

"I'm going back to bed," Chris said, pushing up from the table. "Leave the light on?"

"No?" Chris flipped the switch. "Goodnight."

Stryker stood in the dark, still staring. He'd keep cool, guard his heart. He'd avoided entanglements with women ten times as beautiful and accomplished as Jess Lennox. But there was something about her—so soft against his chest, something so real, naked, and raw And he had responded, not wanting to, but he'd been swept up by her vulnerability, her need. He'd put the brakes on now—first thing tomorrow. Dinner, sure, but that was all. And then loosen that permit from her tight little fist. The heart shit had to stop, he had to end it, nip it in the bud, immediately.

Stryker had saved Jess, but could he save himself? As he turned toward the stairs to his room, he prayed it wasn't too late.

Chapter Seven

With frayed nerves, Jess returned home after her second trip to the police station. Will had heated up leftovers and dinner awaited.

"How'd it go?" he asked, popping open a beer.

"That sergeant. He gives me the creeps. He thinks I'm a criminal because of Mom."

"Asshole. Why do people do that? Why do they think it's contagious or something?"

"I don't know. Some are okay. But guys like this cop? Geez, they're suspicious and ready to assume you're in the wrong."

"What? He thought you led that creep on?"

She nodded. "He didn't say so, but he asked questions like he thought I did."

"You'd have to be damn desperate to want to go off with that pig."

"I know. Yuck! Gives me the creeps."

Will hugged his sister. "It's over now."

"I hope so."

They sat down to eat.

"You going out with that rich guy?"

"Just dinner. To apologize for some stuff he said to me." Jess loaded a portion of the casserole on her plate.

"Oh?" Will raised an eyebrow.

"Don't get upset. I handled it. No worries."

"I think he likes you."

She choked on the pasta dish. Will pounded her back.

"He hates me."

"Didn't look like hate to me," Will said, taking his seat.

"What do you know? You don't know him."

"I know guys. And it looked like the opposite of hate."

"He just wants that permit. That's why he's taking me to dinner. 'Softsoap', as Mom would say. Buttering me up, hoping I'll give in. I keep telling him never is never. But he doesn't believe me."

"Looks to me like he might have a whole different reason for taking you out. And the after dinner question might be one you're not expecting."

"That's never, too."

"Really? Then why are you going out with him?"

"A free meal?"

Will snorted. "Right. Like you'd ever go out with a guy for a free meal."

"There's always a first time."

Will put down his fork and stared at his sister.

"What?" she asked, shifting in her chair.

"Don't mess with him. Don't lead him on. And, whatever you do, don't lead yourself on."

"Lead myself on?"

"Fall for the guy. He's filthy rich. He can have any woman he wants."

"Not this one." She cast her gaze to her plate.

Will closed his fingers over her wrist. "That's what you say now. But I saw you hugging him. Stuff was going on. I'm not a little kid. I know all about sex and stuff. I'm not a virgin. I'm warning you, Jess. I don't want to see you get hurt."

"And you think he can't like me? Love me?" she asked, snapping her gaze up to meet his.

"I didn't say that. You're the most lovable person I know. But he's a player. He'll take advantage and take off. Leave you crushed. I've already seen you like that once. It wasn't a pretty sight. I don't want to see it again."

"I can take care of myself."

"You're not the badass you think you are."

"Oh, yes I am."

Will laughed. "You're a complete wimp."

"How can you say that?"

"Because I know you. You take in every stray cat that comes by. Including Chip Matthews."

"He wasn't a stray cat."

"Face it, Jess. It's nothing to be ashamed of."

"You mean because I have a heart."

"That's right. A big one. You go out of your way for the folks at The Meadow all the time. Even the ones who can't pay."

"Not everything is about money."

"It is to Stryker Alexander West."

"It wasn't tonight."

"I'm sure that's the exception, not the rule."

"You sure don't like him, do you?" she asked, taking a forkful of food.

"I don't really know him. But I know his type. Silver spoon kinda guy. Expects the world to fall at his feet. And every chick to want to sleep with him."

"Not this chick."

"Good. Stay away from him. He's trouble."

"Maybe he'll make me a good deal on the house."

"Jess. You've got to give that up."

"You said you'd help me fix it up. When I get it."

"When? If, Jess. If. A big, fat if. A whopping Empire State Building if."

They finished the meal in silence.

"Can you clean up? I've got a date."

"Sure. Jennie?"

He nodded.

"Have fun. Don't knock her up, okay? Two mouths are all I can afford to feed."

While she washed the dishes, Jess watched birds at the feeder. It was still light out and they occupied all the perches. Summer was her favorite time of the year. The song of a chickadee came through the open window.

Was Will right about Stryker? He seemed so different last night, not at all the wise-guy, take- no-prisoners man he'd been before. Unwilling to trust her instincts, she decided to keep an open mind. The dinner would tell her what she needed to know.

When Will had asked her why she was going, she'd lied. No way could she admit her attraction to West. Will would throw a fit. Attending the dinner with the billionaire for all the wrong reasons, she'd keep her thoughts to herself.

Perhaps she'd conjured up another kind of dream. *Careful!* She'd tread softly, fear of emotional pain ruled, but curiosity gnawed at her. She had to find out more about him. That's what dinner dates were for, weren't they?

SATURDAY MORNING, JESS faced her closet with trepidation and a frown. Nothing to wear on the date with Stryker. Wait a minute! She didn't even know where she was going to dinner. She ruled out Herbie's Hot Dogs and Java the Hut. Maybe to The Waterfall in Oak Bend? It was the classiest restaurant within fifty miles.

And she had no clothes. Nothing good enough. Jess dialed her closest friend, Jory.

"I'm going out to dinner with a...a friend tonight. I have no clothes. Help!"

"Let me finish up these dishes and I'll be right over."

"Thanks."

Jess pulled down a couple of tall glasses and filled them with ice. Jory loved Jess's mint iced tea. The garden provided a bumper crop, keeping the pitcher full day in and day out. When the doorbell rang, Jess poured and hollered out, "Come in! In the kitchen."

She handed Jory a glass as soon as she entered.

"Great! How did you know?"

"Good memory. Steel yourself. This is going to be brutal."

As they climbed the stairs, Jory asked, "who's this date with?"

"It's not a date."

Jory cocked an eyebrow. "Really? Come on. We're best friends."

"Honestly. It's an apology dinner."

"Oh? And what did he have to apologize for?"

"How do you know it's a *he*?"

"Because you wouldn't care about clothes if it was a she." Jory put her drink down and sat on the bed. "So, what have you got in there?"

"Nothing. That's the problem."

One by one, Jess held up tops, skirts, and dresses. Since she didn't own much, it didn't take long to go through her meager wardrobe.

"Come on. We're going to my house."

"Why?"

"I have the perfect thing. It's a dark green sundress."

Jess hung back. "I can't. I can't take your clothes."

"It's only for one night. And yes, you can. We're friends, Jess. You'd do the same for me."

Mulling over her friend's words, she gave in to temptation. She knew the dress Jory referred to, and she was right, it would look perfect on her.

"Okay, but just this once."

"Not so fast." Jory blocked the bedroom door. "There's a price."

"I'm broke, as usual."

"Not that kind of price. You have to tell me who you're going out with tonight." Jory grinned.

"You blackmailer!"

"Yep. Give."

"Stryker West."

Jory's mouth fell open. "Holy Hell! That guy? He's got the bucks to fly you to Paris for dinner."

"And the airplanes, too, from what I've heard," Jess added.

"Wow, Jess. That's amazing. What's he like?"

"Well, he hates me. And, then again, I hate him. So, it's a stand-off."

"A level playing field?"

"You could say that."

Jory burst out laughing as the two women piled into her car for the short ride to her house. They disappeared into Jory's bedroom and tore apart her closet. After trying it on, Jess agreed that the forest green dress with small flowers outlining the sweetheart neckline and the hem suited her best.

"Hmm, no bra," Jess said, examining her reflection in the mirror.

"That's right. Tantalize him."

"I have to remember not to bend over."

"Oh, don't be like that. Drop your napkin on the floor. Give the guy a thrill for the price of dinner," Jory replied.

Jess gathered up her long locks. "My hair might look better up."

"Perfect! And I have just the thing," Jory said, fishing around in her dresser drawer. She pulled out a small box. "Wear these."

Jess examined the earrings in Jory's hand. "Trent gave you those for your anniversary. They're solid gold. I can't. Really. They're too special."

"Yes, you can. And you will," Jory said, pressing the gold hearts into her friend's hand.

"No, no, no. What if I lose one?"

"You won't. They have their own clasp, see."

After some arguing, Jory convinced Jess to wear the jewelry. She put them on, so they wouldn't get lost in transit. She'd never worn anything as elegant and expensive before. The responsibility made her nervous. One glance in the mirror confirmed Jory's opinion. They were the right touch and made the outfit perfect.

After a hug, Jess returned home. Will breezed in.

"Don't make dinner for me," he said, grabbing a bunch of grapes from the fridge.

"Why not?"

"I'm taking Jennie to Java the Hut then a movie."

"And when did you get so rich?"

Will pulled out the coffee can from under the sink and waved three twenty-dollar bills in her face before stuffing them in with the others.

"I painted a fence for MacGregor."

"Oh? That's great."

"He gave me a hundred twenty. So, I'm splitting it. Sixty for the fund and the rest for a Saturday night out." The fund had been expanded to include saving up to buy the house.

"Go. Have fun."

"Watch that guy tonight, Jess. I don't trust him."

"You don't trust anyone I like."

"Yeah? Well, I know guys. And you can't trust 'em."

She laughed. "You're right about that. Be good. Use a condom."

Will colored. "I'm a grown man, Jess. Stop with that kind of advice."

"Okay. If you say so."

"I'm hitting the shower. Just dinner with the bozo, right?"

"Bye, Will," Jess said, heading upstairs.

STRYKER BUTTONED HIS shirt and tied his tie. Chris told him no one wore ties in the country, but Stryker donned one anyway. It's who he was, dressing formally for a formal dinner. Nerves on edge, he licked his lips. What could he expect from Jess? She'd kissed his cheek after the confrontation with that moron at the bar. Would she still be nice to him?

Or would Jess return to hating him? If he brought up demolishing the house, that might set her off. But, hell, regardless of what he'd told her, that was his reason for taking her to dinner. He stared at himself in the mirror. He'd always said, "Never lie to yourself."

He watched his cheeks color. Yep, he'd lied. That wasn't his only reason for taking her to dinner. Facing the fact that he found her extremely attractive stimulated his heartbeat. Not even sure he'd bring up the permit thing tonight, and he looked forward to their date.

Yes, it was a date. After slapping on his signature aftershave, he picked up his sports jacket and headed for the car.

"You don't need me, do you?" Chris asked.

"Take the night off."

"Thanks." Chris shot him a knowing smile.

Did he think Jess would jump into bed with him? All he had to do with most women was wave his wallet in their faces and they'd start undressing, but he doubted that would carry any weight with Jess. Of course, you never knew with women. Hell, the ones who didn't want his money, scorned him for making so much. Go figure? He guided the Bentley over the road to the dirt and gravel driveway that led to the rundown building where she lived. She waited on the sagging front porch. Stryker pulled over and got out.

Stepping out of the shadows and into the light, her beauty took his breath away. The dress hugged her figure perfectly. The spaghetti straps telegraphed that she was braless, tempting him to slide them down off her shoulder and reveal her luscious flesh.

Her hair was done up in a knot with loose tendrils framing her face. He'd never noticed how long and graceful her neck was—so ripe for kissing. Small clusters of golden hearts hung from her delicate earlobes. While he figured they were probably fake, their shimmer added the perfect touch. When his gaze made it to the teasing glimpse of her breasts visible at the neckline of her dress, blood rushed to his groin. Oh, no, that would never do. He could not get an erection now.

He took a deep breath, willing himself to calm down. A vision of loveliness, all soft and touchable with no hint of the hardness he'd seen in her before, she swept him off his feet. He coughed and strode up to meet her.

"You look amazing," he said.

"Thank you. You clean up well, too," she replied.

He grinned. The spunkiness still lived under that alluring exterior.

"Where are we going?" she asked.

"The Waterfall. In Oak Bend. Is that okay?"

"Perfect. I've always wanted to go there."

A pain shot through him. The girl had lived here thirty years but never been to that restaurant? He reminded himself that poor people didn't dine at expensive restaurants and to stop being such a snob. If it had been there when he lived in Pine Grove, he would not have dined there either. He opened the door for her.

Jess put her rear end down first, then swung her legs in, giving him a peek at beautiful, slim, calves. Damn, she could be a top model, earning millions.

"This is a beautiful car. The seats. Wow. So soft," she said, pushing her palm into the leather.

"Agreed. A Bentley is less showy than a Rolls."

"I wouldn't know a Rolls if it ran me over," she said, laughing.

For a moment, embarrassment at having such a wildly expensive car shot heat to his face. No, Jess Lennox would never waste this kind of money on a car. He got the message. Maybe she had a point.

"I'm not knocking this. It's a treat to ride in something that still has functioning shock absorbers."

He laughed.

"AC or fresh air?"

"Always fresh air. If you don't mind. You're wearing a tie and jacket. I have a lot less on, so it should be your call."

"I noticed. And less looks great on you."

She covered her eyes with her hand. "Leave it to you…"

"Sorry. But you leave these great openings. I can't resist. Fresh air, it is," he said, lowering all the windows in the car.

"Ah. It's cooling off. We don't have air conditioning in the apartment. Only ceiling fans. I don't miss it."

"Really? That wouldn't work for me. But New York gets hot in ways it never does up here."

"Right. If you just slow down. Or jump in the pond, or take a cool shower, you're fine."

Was Jess content with her lot or just making excuses because she couldn't afford an air conditioner? He didn't know for sure but expected the former.

IMPRESSED BY THE SWANKY car, Jess kept her observations to a minimum. She'd try like hell not to sound like a hick by going on and on about the expensive car. Of course, if she had that much money, she doubted she'd spend it on a car like this. Having a car in good running order with shock absorbers that worked, and no wheezing, clanking, or stalling would be enough of a gift.

From what she'd read and heard, the price of this car, a couple hundred thousand, was a drop in the bucket for Stryker Alexander West. She couldn't imagine being so rich—it was obscene. She had to remind herself not to feel jealous or like a have-not. Stryker's life experience had been different than hers, that's all. Besides, he was older than she. When she reached his age, she'd be sitting pretty, running a successful bed and breakfast and living the good life in Pine Grove.

He found a parking spot near the entrance. Inside, they were greeted by an older man.

"Hello, I'm Joe Palermo. I own The Waterfall. Do you have a reservation?"

"Yes. Stryker West."

"Oh, yes. Right this way, please." The man picked up two menus and led them to a table in the corner. The dining room was half full already. Jess didn't see any faces she recognized. Stryker held her chair for her, then sat himself.

"Your waitress will be along in a moment to take your order," Joe said.

"Thank you," Stryker responded.

Jess looked around. The room had dark wood paneling on the walls. Muted lighting gave Stryker a handsome glow. The tablecloth was white and the napkins a claret color. Two small candles in glass holders burned in the center of the table for two. She sighed. Such a romantic setting. Should she be sitting there with her mortal enemy?

"What do you like to drink? Wine? A Martini? A Cosmopolitan?"

"Are you trying to get me drunk?"

"Never. Just asking."

"A Cosmo on the sweet side sounds good." She couldn't take her eyes from his face. Dark hair, a hint of dark scruff, sharp, penetrating eyes, so dark as to appear black, that examined every inch of her. Damn, the man gave her goosebumps. She rubbed her arms.

"Are you cold? The AC here is cranked up high."

"A little. I'll deal with it."

He rose from his seat, taking off his jacket and laying it across her shoulders. "How's that?"

"But what about you?"

"Guys are always hot," he said, then blushed at the double entendre. "I mean, our body temperature runs higher. I've got a long-sleeved shirt on and a tie. I'm fine."

"Thank you."

Wow, would he pull out all the stops just to get that permit? She stopped. Maybe that wasn't fair. Could he simply be acting nice, being attentive, like a date? She had to acknowledge to herself that might be true. She shot him a grateful grin.

"Is that better?"

"Much."

"You know you don't always have to put up with things the way they are," he said.

"Sometimes accommodating is easier."

He nodded. The waitress approached. "The specials are," she began, then stopped and took a long look at Jess before continuing. "The specials tonight are—roast duck with cherry sauce and fresh trout almondine. The soup is butternut squash, and the salad is romaine with cucumbers, tomatoes, and Greek olives."

"What appeals to you, Jess?" Stryker asked.

"Say, don't I know you?" the waitress asked Jess.

"I don't think so."

"Those earrings are nice. They're just like Jory Walker's," she said. "She and her husband come in here all the time. He gave 'em to her on their anniversary. They did it here. I waited on them, too. He's ex-military."

"Very nice. Jess?"

"The trout sounds good."

"Wait! I've got it now. You're Jess Lennox, Betty Lennox's daughter. And those are Jory's earrings. Did you steal 'em? They're very distinctive. Different, like. Never seen another pair like them. Did you swipe them?"

"What?" Jess's pulse kicked up.

The waitress turned to Stryker. "Do you know who you're having dinner with? Her mom's a convicted murderer."

"What the hell?" he said.

"Are those your earrings?" the waitress asked, her tone sharp and accusing.

"No, their Jory's."

"See? I told you. I think we should call the police."

Stryker stood up. "What's going on here. This is the most outrageous behavior I've ever seen in a restaurant."

"I borrowed them from Jory."

"A likely story."

"Miss, you'd better shut up. Stop accusing her."

The owner came over. "What's the problem here?"

"Those earrings are stolen. She admits they're not hers. I think we should call the police."

"How dare you?" Stryker said, his hand fisting at his side.

"Is that true, Miss?"

The blood drained from Jess's face. "No. I borrowed them."

"Her mother's a murderer. What would you expect, ya know? I bet if we called the police, they'd say the earrings were stolen and they're lookin' for them. Maybe there's a reward."

"Shut up, Mary," Joe said, but his brows knitted.

"If Jess says she borrowed them, she borrowed them. It's none of your business. And I don't give a rat's ass what her mother did. This is a witch hunt!" He threw down his napkin.

Lightheaded, Jess tried to stand but wobbled. Stryker was by her side in an instant. Everyone in the restaurant had stopped eating and stared.

"Would you mind if we called Jory, Miss?" Joe asked, wringing his hands.

Unable to speak, Jess nodded. Tears flooded her eyes. She clung to Stryker's hand. He slipped his arm around her shoulders and pulled her to him.

"I'll be right back."

"I'll stay here. Make sure she doesn't escape. People like them Lennox's. Can't trust 'em, ya know?"

Struggling to breathe, Jess thought she'd dreamt this nightmare.

"It's all right. I'm sure you'll be vindicated. What a bitch! I'm so sorry you had to go through this. I believe you," Stryker said.

"Thank you," she croaked out, unused to having anyone in her corner.

Although it was only five minutes, it seemed like hours to Jess before the owner returned.

"I'm so sorry. Please accept my apology. Ms. Walker confirmed your story, Miss."

"What? That's a lie!" the waitress bellowed.

Joe turned to her, his face stormy. "Mary, you're fired. Take off your apron and leave immediately."

Stryker kissed the top of Jess's head. "We're getting out of here," he whispered.

"I'm so very sorry. Please don't leave. Dinner's on me, if you'll just stay."

Stryker looked at Jess, who shook her head. "I don't think so. You've insulted my friend beyond belief. There's no way we could enjoy a meal here now."

Jess took a big gulp of her water then tightened her grip on Stryker's hand. The other diners had returned to their meals. Humiliation burned in her chest. She had to get away.

"Come on. Let's go. We'll find somewhere else," Stryker said.

Chapter Eight

Once they hit the fresh air, Jess's knees gave out. Stryker caught her in time. She clung to him, forcing herself not to cry, hiding her face in his shirt.

"I'm so sorry. Ignorant, nasty people. If she'd been a man, I'd have punched her lights out."

The cloth muffled her laugh.

"Is there somewhere else you'd like to go?"

She shook her head, took a deep breath, and stepped back. "Seems like every time I see you, lately, I'm in tears."

He waved his hand. "Forget about it. Let's find somewhere else."

"Saturday. Hmm, It's ribs night at Homer's. Let me make a call," she said.

"Do we have to eat there? Too many idiots at the bar," he whined.

"How about takeout? I've got an idea."

She called and placed the order. By the time they arrived, the food was ready.

"It's all on the house tonight. Even threw in a salad and cheesecake. Cause I heard about that guy the other night. Geez, Jess, I'm so sorry. He's banned from here. That was a close call. I'm glad you're all right," Homer said, handing her a big bag.

"Thanks, Homer," Jess gave him a half-hug and passed the food to Stryker.

He placed it in the trunk. "Okay. Where to now?"

"It's still light. Not too hot. Let's swing by my place for a minute."

They stopped at Jess's for five minutes, then headed for the lake. He pulled in to Minnie's house.

"Here?" he asked, raising his eyebrows.

"Uh huh. A picnic," she said, heading for the trunk. Slinging a blanket over one arm and holding a large candle, she grabbed his hand. "Follow me." He picked up the bag.

Jess led him away from the house to a grove of trees by a large pond.

"I used to go skinny dipping here when I was a kid," Stryker remarked.

"Don't get any ideas," she responded.

He chuckled and followed her.

"Right here. You can see the house, but no one can see you from the street." She spread out the blanket under a maple tree.

"Okay to no skinny dipping—for the moment—but I've gotta take off this tie," he said, ripping it from his neck and stuffing it in his pocket. He removed his jacket and rolled up his sleeves, revealing powerful forearms sprinkled with brown hair.

While he unpacked the bag, Jess sat with her legs stretched out, crossed at the ankles, staring at the sky.

"The moon is out, sort of. It'll be sunset soon. Then we can light the candle."

When he finished laying out the food, Stryker joined her on the blanket. "This is the perfect spot," he said, picking up a rib.

"Homer's is known for their ribs," she said. "I love it here. Most peaceful spot on Earth."

"Except for the frogs. Seems like someone is having an active social life tonight."

She laughed. "Frogs never stop. They're like background music."

They ate in silence for a while.

"Do you mind me asking you something?"

"I don't know until you ask, do I?" she replied.

"I guess not," he said, chuckling. "Did you, do you still, get a lot of grief over what your mother did?"

"Not so much these days. It's been twelve years. But there are a whole lot of people who still won't talk to me. I lost a lot of friends and one fiancé."

"A fiancé?"

"Yep. His family decided they didn't want murderer genes in the family gene pool."

"That's terrible. Did he break your heart?"

"Into a million pieces."

They dug into the sweet potato fries and the gorgonzola salad.

"This is delicious," Stryker said.

"My favorite," she replied.

"How come you didn't move away after?"

"I didn't have any money. Besides, I didn't do anything wrong. Why should I leave my home? Will was in junior high. Didn't want to put him in a new school."

"How old were you?"

"I was eighteen when Mom went to jail. I took over custody of my little brother."

"That's a helluva load for someone that age."

"Yeah, well, I was an old eighteen. Always been the responsible one in the family."

"I'm impressed."

"I'm not trying to impress you. Those are just the facts."

He leaned over to kiss her, licking a smudge of sauce off her lower lip. She backed up. "Don't."

"Sorry. Couldn't help it. You look so beautiful out here, in the evening light."

"I'm not going to sleep with you."

"I don't think I asked you," he said.

She felt color sting her cheeks again. "I'm sorry. I didn't mean to be presumptuous. Just want to be clear. I like to be direct so there are no misunderstandings."

"I appreciate that. But a simple kiss is harmless."

"I doubt any kiss from you is either simple or harmless," she replied, raising her gaze to his.

Damn, with the top button of his shirt open, and the sleeves rolled up, his hair wind-blown, he was the most attractive man on Earth. Heat shot through her body, landing in a place it had no right to be. Being honest with herself, she wanted him. And that's exactly why she'd spoken up. Get it right out there that she wasn't giving herself permission to make love with this man, no matter how irresistible he appeared. At least not yet.

"If you won't sleep with me, will you answer me one question. Honestly?"

"Okay. Shoot."

"Why won't you let me knock down Minnie's house?"

STRYKER EXECUTED SUPREME willpower to keep from taking Jess in his arms and making love to her. Of all the things he'd seen in women through the years, he'd never seen such a vulnerable one relying on her inner strength. In that skimpy dress, clinging to her curves, inviting his touch, she oozed sexiness.

Respect. That lit his fire. He hadn't met that many hot women he respected. The combination made him dizzy with desire. Of course, he'd abide by her wishes and keep his hands to himself, no matter how hard that might be.

He put down the rib bone and turned his attention to Jess. She smiled at him and put her hands behind her, palms flat on the blanket. Her head tilted backward, and her gaze met the sky. He guessed he'd finally get the answer to the question that had been bugging him for weeks. He sat completely still, riveted.

"Well. Hmm. I guess you sort of have a right to know."

"I'm listening."

"During my growing up time, things were tense at home. Actually, that's an understatement. I left the house whenever I could. Rain, shine, snow, or heat—I'd hit the road, roaming around looking for a place to hide from my life."

He nodded, watching her.

"And when I found Millie's house, well, it intrigued me. I'd never seen anything so big. The house is enormous. And it's old. Nothing up here has columns like that."

"Did you ever go inside?"

She nodded. "Millie discovered me hiding in the shrubs, staring. She invited me in for tea and cookies. She made great cookies. Gave me the recipe, too."

"She was a kind woman."

Jess nodded. "That's true. She'd put up a bench nearby. See?" she said, pointing. "That's it. Over there. She put that in for me. At least that's what she said."

"No reason to doubt it."

"Nope. She gave me the tour. The house is grand. I'd never seen anything like that. Still haven't. And I fell in love. I wished that someday I could live there, away from all the anger and hate in my life."

Emotion rose in his chest.

"The dream began to take shape when I was in high school. I took a couple of cooking classes. Then it hit me. If I could own that house, fix it up, I could run a bed and breakfast there."

"Ah. I see."

"I'm a hard worker. I'd make a success of it."

"I bet you would. But you need money for a dream like that."

"Dreams aren't built on money. They're built on what-if's and wishes."

Stryker's throat closed. His only dreams, of a new airport here or there, had been built by money, not wishes. They weren't dreams really, they were aspirations, springing from ambition. Shame filled him.

"I don't expect you to understand. That's why I haven't told you before. Will and Grey Andrews are the only ones who know. My brother has the ability to fix the place. We've been saving. Over the years we've managed to put away two thousand dollars. It isn't much, but by now, that old house isn't worth much, is it? Not to somebody else. I've watched people come, look, and leave shaking their heads. You've been trying to sell that house since Minnie went into a nursing home, with no luck."

"That's right."

"So that's it. If you demolish it, you tear down my dream."

"Dreams aren't worth much."

"How do you know? Did you ever have a dream?"

He laughed. "You think you're the only one? I learned early that dreams are a waste of time."

"How so?" she asked, sitting up.

He waved his hand. "It's water under the bridge." No way would he tell her about his dream. No sir, and have her laugh in his face?

"I told you mine."

"It's stupid. Silly. You'll laugh."

She inched closer to him. "No, I won't. Tell me."

Although he tried, he couldn't avoid her stare. The sun sent a blaze of color through the sky, drawing his eye.

"Look. The sunset is magnificent."

"Oh," she said, moving back. "I see. You're one of those."

He wrinkled his brow. "One of what?"

"One of those who thinks it's okay for other people to reveal their secrets, but never to reveal your own. Don't want to be vulnerable? I doubt you'd care what an inconsequential person like me would think of anything. So, go ahead. Keep your dream to yourself. I get it. I'm finished here." She moved to her knees.

"Wait! No. Wait. Please. Don't go. This is so nice."

Jess slumped back down. "Tell me."

"All right, all right. But you have to promise not to laugh."

She crossed her fingers over her heart. "I promise."

"When I was four, my parents were killed in a car accident, returning from the hospital. That's when I went to live with Aunt Minnie."

"And your dream was?"

"I'm getting to that. Every night, when I got into bed and the lights were out, I'd make a wish, a dream, really." Emotion flooded his chest, cutting off his air. His chin quivered.

Jess moved closer. She eased her arm around his shoulders. "Deep breath."

He took in air and looked away. "Okay. I dreamt that my parents would come back. I wished so hard, that I actually believed it. I was convinced that there had been some mistake and they would come through the door any day. That was my dream. That they weren't dead. Go ahead. Call it foolish."

Turning to face her, he saw full eyes. He cupped her cheek, wiping away the wetness with his thumb. "I held on to that dream until I was ten. At day camp, a boy named Bobby told me that dead people don't come back. That I was an idiot, a baby, then beat me up. That was the end of the dream."

"Oh my God," she whispered, stroking his face. She moved closer, winding her arms around his middle. He took a deep breath, closed his eyes and leaned into the hug.

"On that day, I decided dreams are stupid. A waste of time and energy. I've never had a dream since. I live in the real world. Dreams are for people who can't deal with reality. At least that's what I thought."

"And now?" she asked, releasing him from her embrace.

"Your dream is different."

"Aren't all dreams escapes?"

"Maybe," he said.

"Mine is possible. Not very likely, maybe, but possible."

"It would take a ton of money to fix that old house. Even if you could buy it for a few bucks. Where would you get the money to renovate?"

"Will would do the work. Maybe a bank loan?"

"Not after a bank takes a look at the place."

"Really?"

He hated to step on her hopes.

"Maybe a local bank would take pity on me. They might see the potential."

"They might," he said, against his better judgment. He didn't have the heart to tell her that banks are cold, they're only interested in return on investment.

"You didn't get where you are from having dreams, did you?" she asked.

"I worked my ass off and made good investments. Some of them lucky, some from good decisions. I never let anyone or anything get in my way."

"I wish I could be like that." She lit the candle.

He inched closer and snaked his arm around her waist. "Don't change. You're amazing just the way you are."

The sky turned pink and orange as the sun sank below the horizon. A soft teal blue followed, preparing to take over the sky before the sun went to sleep. One lonely hand closed over another. Jess raised her gaze to his.

"It's horrible, what happened to your dream. I'm so sorry. Please don't give up on dreams. Mine has kept me going through all kinds of crap."

His gaze roamed from her forehead to her chin and back. Her eyes, large and luminous shone with understanding. Her lips tempted him beyond control.

"You're lovely," he said, as his lips brushed hers.

JESS'S HEART HURT FOR Stryker. She couldn't imagine what it must be like to lose everything at four, then cling to hope, only to have reality pounded into your head at ten. He spoke softly, all swagger and arrogance gone. She hadn't expected him to open his heart. She touched his face and met his gaze. Surprisingly, they had something in common—an understanding that life can be hard and sad.

His revelation made him sexier. When his lips touched hers, it was like a match to gasoline. She responded, sliding her hand around the back of his neck and opening her mouth. His tongue plunged in, seeking hers. She didn't disappoint.

Stryker crushed her to him, her breasts flattened against the hard muscle of his chest. Inside her, heat grew. He put his hand on the side of her head, steadying her, keeping her close. When they finally broke for air, his eyes glowed with lust.

"Sorry. I shouldn't have done that."

"It's okay. I wanted you to."

"I don't want to start something you don't want to finish."

"I appreciate that." The sun disappeared. They sat bathed only in the light from the candle and the moon.

While her body ached to make love, her mind reined in her emotions. Letting go physically might open her heart. Did she trust Stryker? Not one little bit. Time for a test. Let's see if he still wants me.

"I have to confess something." She pulled away, moving closer to the pond. Her body cooled where air replaced the feel of him next to her.

"Oh?" he asked, raising an eyebrow.

"I searched your property and I found three species of mammals and frogs here that are endangered, protect by the EPA."

"You did? Why are you bringing this up now?"

"Just to let you know. I've filed the information with the state. They will prevent you from demolishing the house, as it might disturb the habitat of these protected critters."

The look of shock on his face surprised her. *Yeah, see. It's all about the permit. Seduction and then you sign. Uh, no. Never means never.* The heat in her body ebbed, replaced by cold reality.

"You didn't think I'd go that far did you?" she asked.

"I didn't."

"Surprised?"

"Absolutely," he replied.

"So now what are you going to do?" she asked, folding her arms across her chest.

"I don't know. I'll worry about the house later."

"Let's have our cheesecake and go. It's getting late."

"It's nine o'clock on a Saturday night!" he exclaimed.

"I work tomorrow. I work every day but Tuesday."

Stryker narrowed his eyes. "Even so, you don't need to go home yet. What's up?"

"I figure you'd want to break this up. Once you realized I wasn't going to sleep with you or sign the permit."

"Ouch. Geez. You think I'm that shallow? That kiss was just about the permit?" he frowned.

"Well, wasn't it?"

"You're right. Forget the cheesecake. You can have mine. Give it to Will. Let's go," he said, gruffly, pushing to his feet and gathering up the dinner things.

"Wait," she said, grabbing his arm.

"What for? You dropped the bomb you'd been waiting to drop. You've stymied me, probably permanently. You won. I concede defeat. What more is there to say?"

"I didn't want things to end this way."

"Really?" he asked, cocking an eyebrow. "You've been holding on to that little tidbit until the proper time."

"I figured you'd come on to me to get the permit."

"You figured wrong. But what does it matter? You're not interested in me. Or the truth. Fine. Let's go."

She could hardly believe her eyes. The great and mighty Stryker Alexander West had his feelings hurt. Could she have been wrong? Does he truly care for her? No way would a man that wealthy want a girl like her. She had nothing but the shirt on her back and her half of two thousand bucks. Stryker West would marry a rich woman, with connections, who could help his business. That sure wasn't Jess Lennox. Wait. Marriage? Who said anything about marriage?

As she picked herself up, something magical happened. Her dream morphed. It became Jess running a bed and breakfast, with Stryker West—as her spouse. She blinked several times. No, no, this new dream was not a good idea. More preposterous than the original, it would only intensify her heartache.

"I'm sorry," she said, touching his shoulder.

"Don't be. I had a great time, found out what I wanted to know, and now have a resolution to the house situation."

"What are you going to do?"

"Put it back on the market and go to London."

"London?"

"I have business there."

"Oh."

"Disappointed?" he asked, a note of hope in his voice.

"Of course. Sort of." Jess refused to reveal her feelings.

He laughed. "Sort of. That says it all."

"When are you coming back?"

"Not until there are purchase papers to sign. Then I'll give this little town the brush."

Sadness washed through her. "I'm sorry."

"Don't be," he said, opening the car door for her. "You've proven something to me."

"What's that?" she asked, getting in the car.

"That women lie. You never know what one's thinking. They make you think they want you, then they dump you. And as soon as you have your back turned, they stab you."

"I didn't mean to."

"Oh, yes, you did. You absolutely did. You set me up and shot me down. It's okay. That's not the first time it's been done. But, and believe me on this, it will be the last time."

Chapter Nine

They drove to Jess's house in silence. She searched for something to say but came up empty. He parked, opened her door, then retrieved her articles from the trunk.

"I'm so sorry," she said, folding the blanket over her arm.

"You keep saying that. Why don't I believe you?" he said, tossing a sharp glance her way.

"Thank you. It was, the evening was—"

"Unforgettable? You betcha."

"Memorable," she responded.

He laughed. "You could say that. It's one I'll never forget."

Jess approached him, laying her hand on his arm. He shook it off.

"Look, let's not pretend. You manipulated the situation to get what you wanted. You got it. Stop making like you're sorry you stomped on my face, okay?"

"But I am. I had no idea about you, your, your dream, your life."

"Please do me one favor. Forget what I told you. Sometimes I don't know when to shut up."

"How could I forget that story?" she asked, reaching for his cheek. He stepped back, thwarting her gesture.

"Goodnight. Thanks for, well, an entertaining evening."

He got in the car, slammed the door, and put it in gear. When he glanced in the rearview mirror, he saw her standing forlornly, watching him drive away. God, she tempted him on every level. But she was poison, like most women he'd encountered. Lovely Jess had turned out to be just like the rest, only out to get what she wanted.

And she had succeeded. Sure, he could bring a lawsuit against the state, but it would be costly, engender tons of bad publicity, and he'd probably lose anyway. Little Jess Lennox, nobody from nowhere had defeated the great and mighty Stryker Alexander West. He laughed at the irony.

His humiliation couldn't compare to his broken heart. He didn't mean to care for Jess. But she'd ceased to be simply an obstacle to his wishes and had become a flesh and blood woman. He applauded her gumption and hard work. Not one to complain about her lot, she'd simply gone about her business of baking and working and saving. He admired that.

Somewhere along the way, admiration had melded with attraction and turned into something more, something he didn't want, but couldn't stop. Was it too soon to call it love? Maybe. Hell, what did he know about love? Nothing.

He slowed down, glancing from side to side, looking for deer. So what could he do now? He was back to square one with that damn house nobody would buy, and now his heart had been broken. He shook his head. *I should know better than to get involved in something I'm totally ignorant about. Love is not for me.*

He pulled into the driveway. There was another car next to where he parked his and the living room light was on. Wouldn't that cap it all if Chris was in the living room having sex with some female? He shook his head, then made sure to make a ton of noise as he entered the garage and climbed the steps to the kitchen.

Not moments after he poured a whiskey, Chris bustled into the room, all sweaty and flushed, buttoning his shirt.

"Didn't expect you back so soon," the young man said.

"Obviously." Stryker chuckled.

"I'm sorry. I've met someone here. Her name is Molly."

"At least one of us has scored a home run."

"Not exactly. But if you'd been a little later, that might have been true."

"Should I go to a movie or something?" Stryker asked.

"It's okay. Hey? What are you doing home so early?"

"While you were batting a thousand, your boss was striking out."

"Oh, damn. I'm so sorry."

"Please!" Stryker said, holding up his hand. "I don't want to hear that word again for a long time."

"Okay. Do you want to talk about what happened?"

"I want to down this drink and go to bed. The house is yours."

"Thanks."

"Oh, I'm leaving for London tomorrow. Email John to have everything ready and get me a flight, will you?"

"Of course. What about this place?"

"The rent is paid for a year. I don't know when I'll be back. Why don't you stay here, keep the place from getting broken into? Drive my car, too."

"Really? That would be wonderful. I can work from here via computer."

"Exactly. No reason to have two broken hearts, is there?"

"Oh, God. I'm—"

Stryker held up his hand. "Don't say it!"

"Oops. Well. You know."

"I do. Goodnight, Chris. Good luck," Stryker said, heading for the stairs.

He undressed quickly and slid under the sheet. The room was warm, but not unpleasantly so. With the windows open, a cool breeze caressed his skin. He laced his fingers behind his head and stared out the window at the moon.

"London. Get the office there up and running."

The perfect antidote to unhappiness would be a new project. Being busy would divert his mind, ease his pain. When he revealed his dream,

Jess had seemed so sympathetic, then she wielded the knife and shoved it in, with a twist. Why did she have to bring up the fate of the house?

After hearing her dream, he'd mentally scuttled his efforts to get the demolition permit. Half in love with her, he couldn't destroy the house and her dream with it. Did he have another solution? He didn't. If she'd have waited, just until the next day, he would have told her it was safe. But, no, she had to have her way right then and there.

He sighed. Best thing to do would be to go to London, not return to Pine Grove at all, and forget Jess Lennox. At least try to forget her. He closed his eyes. Tomorrow, he'd get a grip on his life and forge ahead to conquer new challenges and leave love behind forever.

JESS STOOD IN THE DRIVEWAY, clutching the large candle and blanket, watching Stryker West drive away. Pain seared through her heart. What had she done? She'd let her brain rule, hah, what a mistake! Her comment about the EPA wrecked the mood and destroyed the entire evening.

"The man opens up to you, which he probably doesn't do often, and what do you do? You bring up the stupid house! You best him. Were you not listening to his dream thing? Did you not hear his pain? Jess Lennox, you are one cold bitch," she said, turning to walk into the house.

Regret filled her. She chewed her lip as she put away the blanket and pulled out a pitcher of mint iced tea. How could she fix this? His goodbye sounded so final. Maybe it was too late. The sound of the crunching of gravel in the driveway drew her attention. Peeking out the window, she saw her brother stop the truck and begin smooching with Jennie.

"It's so easy for him," she muttered.

Of course, Will had had her shielding him, fighting for him, and protecting him when he was growing up. No one protected her from the violence in their home. Her mother had blamed everything on her father's drinking, but Jess knew the truth. Her mother hated her father and baited him into fights. Betty always took the first swing. Not that she approved of her dad taking a swipe at her mom, but if she'd just leave him alone to be drunk and fall asleep in peace, it would have been a different story.

After every incident, her mother would call the police and lie about it. Afraid of the authorities, Jess told the truth. So, when Betty finally shot him, declaring years of abuse, the police records showed that her bruises, minor at best, had resulted from fights she had started. While the legal aid lawyer said that nothing excused her father smacking her mom, the jury didn't buy it.

When the prosecutor made the case that her mother had started things with the idea of finishing off her father, the jury found her guilty. And she got forty years. Jess had testified against her mother. It had caused a rift. For three years, Betty had refused to see her daughter.

Jess stopped going until she received a letter one Christmas begging her to come and bring candy. So, the daughter took a bus to see her mother once a month. Betty talked the whole time, and Jess pretended to listen. Did she hate her mother? She felt sorry for the woman. She'd made bad choices and had no life.

"At least one of us turned out normal," Jess said to herself, proud of Will.

The truck door opened, and he and Jennie entered the house.

"You're here?"

"Surprise!" Jess said.

Will's face fell. "Oh."

"Sorry to spoil your little whatever-you-want-to-call-it." Jess filled her glass. "Tea?"

Will and Jennie shook their heads.

"What happened to Stryker?"

"I wrecked it. It's over."

At the sound of her words, the reality of the situation penetrated. Her eyes filled, and she sank down on a chair. Resting her forehead on her arms, she sobbed.

"I did it. I drove him away. I destroyed it, like I destroy everything."

A strong arm circled her shoulders. She looked up to see Will's concerned face.

"I'll wait outside," Jennie said, shooting a sympathetic glance at Jess.

"What happened?" Will asked, taking a sip from his sister's glass.

Between bouts of tears, she recounted most of the evening, leaving out Stryker's dream. Will listened.

"So right after making out, you hit him with the EPA thing?"

She nodded.

"Damn! Jess. Bad timing."

"He thought the whole dinner thing was just a ploy to spring it on him."

"Was it?"

"No! No. I wasn't going to tell him yet. I was waiting to see what he did next. But he was so, so...well, you know. I needed to make sure it wasn't all done to get to me sign the permits."

"Why don't you think a guy would like you for you? You're pretty, you're nice, you're smart. Most guys'd be lucky to have a girl like you."

"Thanks," she said, lowering her gaze.

"You didn't believe him? So now he's gone?"

"That's what he said."

"Well, as a guy, I know one thing. If he meant it, he'll be back."

"I don't think so, Will."

"Trust me. He will. And if he doesn't, then you were right in the first place. And it was all done just to get you to sign the fucking permit."

"It sounded final. He's going to London."

"He'll be back. I saw the way he looked at you. And that had nothing to do with a permit."

"I hope you're right."

"When he comes back, just don't blow it again, okay? 'Cause a guy'll come back once, but not twice. Got it?"

"Got it." She kissed her brother on the cheek and graced him with a small smile. "What would I do without you?"

"Don't know. But you might have to find out soon."

"Really? That serious between you and Jennie?"

"Might be. Gotta go. She's waiting."

"Have a good night, Will. And thanks."

"No worries. Goodnight."

Jess trudged upstairs. Could her little brother be right about Stryker? She doubted it. A man like him, used to getting his own way, would never come crawling back to her. That ship had sailed. But she could dream. She undressed got into bed and closed her eyes. In her mind's eye, she pictured the house, looking beautiful, and Stryker heading the table in the dining room on Thanksgiving. With a sigh, she drifted off to sleep.

THE MORNING WAS ONE big blur for Stryker. He packed quickly, grabbed an egg sandwich to go at Java the Hut, and hustled to the airport. Chris pushed the speed limit to get his boss there on time He made the plane with only seconds to spare.

Settled in his first-class seat, he promptly fell asleep. Over the Atlantic, he awoke and got online. John would meet him at the plane and take him to Claridge's. The old-world elegance of the hotel suited Stryker perfectly, and his favorite suite was available. Finally, something was going right.

After a day of adjustment to the time difference, Stryker awoke ready to face the day. He breakfasted in the luxurious living room of his suite. His right-hand man, John Sweet, joined him. They dined together as John went over the schedule for Stryker's visit.

"Rafe can send the plans to Pine Grove," John said, spreading jam on his scone.

"Really? How? By fax?"

"No, no. Rafe Pelletier, our architect, is from a firm in Pine Grove. His partner is still there. Rafe can email him the plans for the London office and his partner, Charlie, will produce it on paper to go over with you. I thought I'd made that clear."

"I thought you meant he could fax the plans. I couldn't imagine how that'd work. I mean architectural drawings are big."

"Right. Charlie has the equipment to print out the plans."

"So, I didn't need to come? Well, I'm here now. When can I meet with Rafe?"

John finalized their schedule for the week, then faced Stryker.

"What the hell are you going to do with that damn house?"

"Dunno," Stryker said, shaking his head.

"Sell that damn thing and be rid of it."

"I would if I could. Chris is putting the *for-sale* sign back up. No one has shown any interest in the past, and I doubt that'll change."

"The cost to fix it up is astronomical," John said.

"Yes. And now I can't destroy it, either."

Stryker filled in his associate about the EPA filing.

"Swell. What the hell? I thought you were supposed to sweet-talk that chick into signing the permit."

"Forget it. It'll never happen."

"Hmm. The only person with enough money and foolish enough to invest it in that house is you. So we're stuck. That's valuable land, too. It's a shame."

"What did you say, John?"

"I said you're the only one with enough extra bucks to renovate."

"That's it!! Exactly! You're a genius!" Stryker pushed to his feet and began to pace. "I can't sell the damn place the way it is. So, I'm going to renovate it myself. Then it will be salable."

"Brilliant! Once it's fixed up, you'll get a bundle for it."

"It'll make the perfect B and B," Stryker said.

"Bet you could get at least half a mill for it. Maybe more."

"Of course! Sell it as a business property. We'll have to have it zoned that way."

"Can you pull some strings?" John asked.

"Someone on the town council owes me a favor. I'm sure I can get that done."

"Perfect. Hey! Hire Rafe's firm. If you like his work here in London, let his guy in Pine Grove handle the reno."

"Excellent idea. Let's get them started right away."

"I'm on it."

"Oh, wait. One minute. Tell this guy, Charlie, that I want them to hire a certain contractor. Will Lennox. Yes. Tell Charlie to hire Will Lennox, and anyone else he needs to do the work."

"You know this guy?"

"I've met him. He needs the work. I'm betting he's qualified."

"Charity case, huh?"

"Not exactly. More like someone who needs a helping hand."

"Stryker, that's not like you. You're getting soft."

"Just do it, okay?"

"Aye aye, Captain."

"While you're at it. Let's have more tea and scones. I'm still hungry."

John picked up the phone next to the sofa. Stryker strolled over to the window to catch the lovely view of the city. He smiled. While she might not love him, he could still help her, even in this round-about way. Warmth flowed through him. Will would make a fair wage and have more work than he could handle. Jess could sneak over there and get a look at the place as it returned to its old glory. While it might not be hers, at least it would still be standing and looking fine once again. Wasn't that what she wanted?

Once it was completed, it would be snapped up quickly by savvy business folks, bringing him a tidy sum. Sounded like a win/win.

AT THE END OF THE WEEK, Stryker and John sat down to dinner.

"You're going back to Pine Grove tomorrow?"

"Yep. Got some unfinished business."

"Plans for the house won't be ready yet."

"I know. It takes time. That place is huge."

"Why don't you stay here? Someone needs to sign off on the changes for the plans for the office here."

"You're capable of doing that. You don't need me."

"I appreciate the vote of confidence, but you should have the final word."

"Okay. I'll be back."

"Quite a jet-setter. Back and forth to London all the time."

"Whatever it takes."

"With these two projects, you'll be a busy man." John peered at him.

"Just what I need."

John shook his head. "I wasn't going to tell you, but Chris filled me in. You're going back for her. Admit it."

"And if I am? So, what?"

"If you can't be honest with me, at least be honest with yourself."

"Okay, okay. And I repeat, so what?"

A grin broke the stern lines of John's face. "It's about time."

Stryker laughed.

John drove him to the airport. They went over details about the office construction in London as they wended their way through traffic. Ten times more excited to be returning to little Pine Grove than he had been to land in London, Stryker smiled. He had no idea what he'd say to Jess if he saw her again. Would she even speak to him? She'd saved the house and had no more use for this self-centered, arrogant rich guy, did she?

He wanted to tell her about the renovation. Of course, Will had probably already spilled it. He hoped she'd be happy the house would stand proud, brought back as close as possible to its original glory. He didn't do it for her, he did it for the money and to get rid of that thorn in his side. At least that's what he kept telling himself.

Chris met him at the airport.

"How's your girlfriend?" Stryker asked.

Chris turned bright red. "Fine."

"It's nice that one of us can handle romance. Have you seen Jess?"

"Nope. She delivers her pies early. They're always there when I hit the Cozy Café. For breakfast."

"Thought so. How early do they open?"

"Six thirty, I think."

"Damn! I'm not getting up that early to run into her."

"Your call."

"Have they started work on the house?"

"Not yet. I called Charlie. You have a meeting with him tomorrow afternoon."

"Good. I need to know exactly how much this is going to set me back. Set up a meeting with three real estate brokers. Wait two weeks. By then I'll have a better idea how much I'll be laying out to turn this sick puppy into a show dog."

"You're gonna sell it once it's fixed up?"

"Damn right. I'm not going to throw away two hundred grand on the place. And that's just my rough guess. It'll probably be more. But when it's done, we should be able to earn that back plus a nice profit."

"Sounds like a plan. What about Jess?"

"She got her wish. I'm not going to take it down. In fact, I'm going to bring it back to life. She'll be able to have afternoon tea there and feel good about saving it."

Wearing a frown, Chris nodded.

"What? What's wrong?"

"Nothing."

"Come on. I know that face. You don't approve?"

"It's none of my business."

"I asked."

"If you want my opinion? I don't think she's going to be happy that someone else will own the place."

"Hey, I may be a little bit dizzy. But I'm not stupid. I'm not going to throw away a fortune for a crush or whatever this is."

"You asked," Chris replied.

"I appreciate your honesty. But this is real life. People don't do things like that."

"Right. I get it."

But the expression on Chris's face stayed the same. After he unpacked, Stryker got behind the wheel and drove to the old house. He wandered over to the tree where he and Jess had had their picnic. How could something that started so great, end up so badly? He shook his head.

Jess had been on his mind from the moment he took her home. Afterward, he'd kicked himself. Then, John and Chris had piled on. They'd been right, of course. Seemed like he was never right anymore. Where was his head? Why couldn't he figure things out?

Maybe because it wasn't about dollars and cents, but about feelings and emotions. When he was at Yale, if there had been a class in that, he'd have flunked. He feared the only one glad to see him back in town was Laura Dailey at the Cozy Café.

The next morning, he headed to the little eatery for an early breakfast. Yep, it was six thirty and he was dressed, through the door, and stifling a yawn.

"Stryker! Welcome back. You're just in time for the corn festival. Having your usual?" she'd asked, adding half a teaspoon of sugar to his coffee. "Your table is free."

He smiled and took the seat he'd occupied every morning at the Cozy Café during his stay in town. How could it feel so good to be back? This tiny hamlet, barely a blip on the map, had crept into his blood. Or was it Jess Lennox? As he sipped his brew, she came through the door, her arms loaded down with pies.

When she saw him, she almost dropped the boxes. He'd rushed to help, putting two of the containers on the counter.

"What are you doing here?" she'd asked, her eyes brightening.

"Good to see you, too."

"Sorry. It's not that I'm not glad to see you. I am. Glad, I mean. I am glad. Not, not glad."

"I get it," he said.

"I didn't think you were coming back."

"Neither did I," he replied.

Chapter Ten

When she laid eyes on Stryker West, Jess's heart skipped a beat. Wil had been right on the money—the man had come back. Why? Will had told her he'd been hired to work on the renovation of Minnie's place. Thrilled and relieved to have some additional steady income for a few months, the pair had treated themselves to ribs at Homer's.

When she asked Will why Stryker had decided to repair the mansion, he'd shrugged.

"No clue. I got a call from Pelletier and Grand, Architects. You don't question that, just say yes and get your butt on the job."

"Hmm. I guess. Odd, though. Right? Why would he fix it up? To live in it himself?" she asked, trying to control her pulse. Damn, if he was moving back to town, she'd have a chance to make up with him, to repair the damage she'd done. Her heart lifted.

"Really, Jess? Get real. A guy like that doesn't live in a one-horse town like Pine Grove, no matter how big the house."

"You're probably right."

He grinned. "I'm right about everything."

"Watch it. I'm still older than you."

"So, what? You gonna beat me up? I don't think so." He chuckled.

"I bet Jennie has something to do with that swelled head of yours."

"Maybe, maybe not. Not telling. I've gotta go. I gotta repair the walls in the living room and paint before I start sanding that floor. Geez. I hope I can get the stink out."

"Me, too. Good luck." She patted him on the shoulder and watched him leave.

Now eight o'clock, she refilled her mug with coffee and sat on the deck. Stryker had invited her to breakfast, but she had other deliveries to make and had begged off. When she suggested lunch, he'd jumped at it. They'd meet at Homer's at noon.

Watching the birds, she noticed warmth. Was it the temperature or her own body heat? Thinking about Stryker West tended to jack it up. Their lunch date loomed large in her mind. What would she talk about? How many times could she apologize? Nope. She'd ask him about his plans for the house. She had to know what he was up to. Relief flushed through her. At least the house was safe. Maybe Will would let her take a peek inside as he worked on the place.

Victory. Did it taste sweet? A sense of satisfaction filled her. Now that the house was safe, she might have to let go of her dream. She sighed. Once it was fixed up, there's no way in hell could she afford to buy it. The *for-sale* sign had reappeared, as if by magic, after Stryker left. It tempted her. Now, she'd have to control her emotions and see how this played out.

To divert her worries, she'd help the seniors with their grocery shopping. Finishing her coffee, she watched the birds. August heat would dissipate soon. September and autumn loomed, waiting to change everything. She loved summer, warm days, cool nights, swimming in the lake. She sighed, remembering evenings she and Chip would steal down to Cedar Lake at midnight to go skinny dipping. They'd make love and sneak home before dawn, keeping their secret. He'd been so fun-loving, full of laughter, and affection.

Chip had been her anchor, helping her cope with her difficult life. Hours spent with him brought happiness. She'd help him feed the goats, set the sheep out to pasture, and groom the horses. When that foal was born, Chip had promised it to her. But her father had dragged her away, kicking and screaming. She'd been heart-broken.

It wasn't long after that when her mother instigated a showdown with her father who was too drunk to stand. She'd fired, killing him in cold blood. That was the day life ground to a halt for Jess. As soon as her mother was put on trial, Chip broke their engagement. Days darkened for Jess as she accepted the responsibility of taking care of her brother and paying the bills. Misery arrived on her doorstep and never left.

Emotion choked Jess. Things were better now. Will's work on the house would lighten the heavy load she carried. Stryker must have arranged that. Pelletier and Grand had never hired Will before. She doubted they even knew he existed. She smiled. An act of incredible faith and kindness from Stryker surprised her. Maybe her luck was about to change? She didn't even dare to hope.

STRYKER HEADED FOR Homer's. What would Jess think of the work on Minnie's place? Would she be angry? When the house sold, her dream would be over. Would he want to substitute a different dream for her? He shook his head. That was ridiculous. Hadn't he figured out yet that he wasn't marriage material? Marriage? Hell, he couldn't even make it through a two-week relationship. He cringed at the memory of his time with his previous girlfriend.

Stryker excelled at making money, not falling in love. He'd accepted that, long ago. Or thought he had. A new need grew in him, one almost similar to the hunger for money and financial security that started when he was a boy. This new yearning—for acceptance, damn it—for love, had been ignored. It didn't go away, instead, it grew, crowding every waking thought.

Although he had everything, and she had nothing, they were alike. They'd struggled and dealt with the blows life rained on them. Two survivors, in different ways. Drawn to Jess like a moth to a flame, Stryker thought about her all the time. New feelings threw him. He'd lost control, his cool, detached, businesslike demeanor disappeared. Left in its wake? A blithering, drooling idiot who could hardly string words together when in the presence of the woman he loved. Who was this Stryker Alexander West? He had no idea.

He parked the car, entered, and secured the best table on the deck, overlooking the lake. Arriving early, he ordered a beer and watched the jet skiers. The sound of the door opening drew his attention. Turning, he faced a vision in a flowered skirt and teal blue tank top. Her hair loose and flowing tempted his fingers. He pushed to his feet and pulled out her chair.

"You look beautiful," slipped out of his mouth.

"Thanks," she said, sitting. A slight blush colored her cheeks.

His gaze swept over her. Could she possibly be more beautiful than before? His gaze drawn to the neckline of her tank top, he smiled. She revealed enough to pique his interest and get his blood circulating.

"Menu?" he asked.

"I work here, remember? I'll have a burger. Next to the ribs, that's the best."

"Then why not have the ribs?"

"Too messy."

"Ah," he said, nodding.

They ordered two burgers and a beer for Jess. She watched him, making him sweat. What did he know about being a hero without using money? He'd always bought whatever he wanted, dangled jewelry, expensive trips, and once, even a car, in front of a beautiful woman to get what he wanted. Did he get their love? No. They may have shared their bodies but kept their hearts behind stone walls.

Buy Jess? Impossible. His money would be no good in wooing her. Her strength protected her from men who only wanted to lure her, buy their way into her bed. She'd be too savvy to fall for that. Maybe a lack of trust from being knocked around by life did serve to protect one? Stryker had been using it for years. Being the most untrusting soul he knew had served him well in business. But now? When it came to love, he might as well be twelve years old for all the experience he had with feelings. And yet, love is what he wanted from Jess. But how to get it escaped him.

The waiter came with their food. As Stryker prepared to take a bite, Jess spoke up.

"So," pause, "what do you plan to do with the house?

"Will's fixing it up. But you know that."

"Yeah. He's got a couple of guys working with him. Said the job was huge and that it needed to be done before the holidays."

"Right. Deadline is November first."

"Why?"

He shifted in his seat. "As much as I might like to, I can't give you the house, Jess."

She bristled, sitting up straighter in her chair. "Never asked you for it."

"Of course, you didn't. There are tax issues. No way would the attorney general accept that the house, even in its sorry condition was worth less than thirteen thousand five hundred dollars."

"And so?"

"So, any value above that would be considered taxable income. If they valued it at sixty grand, which might be right considering the land, too, then you'd have to pay income tax on forty-eight thousand dollars."

Her face fell. "Really?"

"The gift maximum that isn't taxed is thirteen five."

She nodded. "So why are you fixing it up?"

"As you know, there's no way I can sell it the way it is. Damn thing's been on the market for years with no offers. I decided to renovate it and then sell it. If it's in good condition, it will be easy to sell."

"Sell it," she said, toying with a French fry.

"That is the plan." He covered her hand with his. "My sweet Jess, you've never run a bed and breakfast. There's a whole lot more to it than changing sheets and scrambling eggs."

Again, she nodded. Leaving her hand joined with his, she munched on a fry and directed her gaze away from his.

"Please, sweetheart. Try to understand."

"Don't talk down to me. I understand just fine," she snapped, shooting him a fiery glance.

"It's business."

"I get it. I'm not experienced. And probably too dumb to learn. Anyone with blonde hair and nice boobs obviously doesn't have a brain in her head."

"I didn't mean—"

"I know exactly what you meant. Let me tell you something. You think I don't understand business? I've been running my own business since I was eighteen. Yep. That's when they handed over my brother and said 'take care of him'. That's when I became mother, father, sister, breadwinner, and cook. I've kept our heads above water for twelve years. We've never had the gas turned off or been late with our rent. And that's all because of me. So don't you dare talk down to me. I know all about running things. I've been doing it half my life." A tear splashed on her plate as she pushed to her feet and strode out of the restaurant.

"Jess, please. Don't. I didn't mean. You're right. Don't go. Please, don't go," he said, hustling after her. He managed to grab her hand, but she ripped it out of his grip and was through the door in an instant. He heard the wheezy cough of her car's engine as she roared out of the parking lot in a cloud of dust.

"Damn it. Damn it. Damn it. When the hell am I going to learn?"

JESS PULLED ONTO PARSON Street, turned into the church parking lot, and cut the engine. Then she put her head down on the steering wheel and cried. How could she have lost it like that? Screaming at him? Why didn't she keep her cool—convince him she had business experience—talk him into arranging a way for her to pay off the house?

There probably weren't enough years left in her life to pay off a loan as big as she'd need to buy the house renovated.

Still, maybe they could work out something. What did she do? She yelled at him, got all offended and high-and-mighty. From where he stood, she was just a poor baker, a floor-scrubbing female who didn't know a balance sheet from a piece of toilet paper.

But she did. She'd figured out real quick that she had to make a profit on her pies. She'd realized bargaining for the ingredients, or using cheaper, in-season fruits for pies would give her a bigger profit. Paying the rent was all about profit. In the winter when fruit wasn't as plentiful, she'd baked cakes. Getting flour and sugar in huge bags to save money made sense. But it had become a challenge to keep little critters out of the bags. She and Will spent days at the beginning of each month, re-bagging the dry goods to keep them safe.

Jess made her own balance sheet, adding up the cost of the pie ingredients, then calculating how much to charge. And she wasn't afraid of math. Her high school teacher had taught her, "math is your friend," and Jess agreed.

How would a man as high up as Stryker Alexander West have any idea about what she did or what she knew? He wouldn't. But what cut her the most was not his ignorance, but the fact that he didn't seem to think she could learn what she needed to know to run the place.

When she'd cried out all her anger, she headed home. What would Will say? He'd tell her she'd been a fool and that she should show Stryker how smart she is, not tell him. She pulled down her ledger. She kept all her costs, profits, and losses in that black-and-white book.

She didn't use fancy systems, like on the computer, maybe because they didn't have one. But she excelled at math, so a pencil and her book were all she needed to keep track of her little business.

After humiliating him in public, Stryker probably wouldn't speak to her again. She needed to apologize. Jesus, why was she always apologizing to that man? What was it about him that brought out her bad side? The door banged open. Will had arrived.

"You're home early," Jess said.

"Taking a break. I needed to pick up a Phillips head, too. Thought I had it in my toolbox. Have you seen it?"

"I borrowed it. It's on the counter."

"Geez, Jess. Put it back, why dontcha?"

As he turned to leave, she grabbed his arm. "Do you have a minute?"

"Is it important?"

She nodded.

"Okay. What is it? Make it fast." He sat at the kitchen table.

"Why do I always fight with Stryker West?"

Will laughed. "You're just like a guy. 'Cause you like him."

"Like him?"

"You know, in that way I'm not supposed to talk about because it embarrasses you?"

"You mean because I want to sleep with him?"

"Hey, Jess, TMI!" He held up he hands.

"I mean *if* I wanted to sleep with him."

"Yeah. Guys are like that sometimes. Then they wonder why the girl doesn't like them."

"When did you get to be the smartest man on Earth?"

"Just born that way. Is that it?"

"No. How do I stop?"

Will blushed. "Sleep with him. But you didn't hear it from me," he said, rising quickly and scooting out the door.

Jess laughed. Was Stryker West simply an itch that needed to be scratched? Could she get him out of her system by having sex with him? She doubted it. Spending more time with him without talking about the house might be a good idea. But how to break the ice?

Will returned at six for dinner. Jess had to step up the amount of food she prepared because, since he'd started working fulltime, his appetite had blasted into outer space. She broached the subject, again.

"You want me to tell you how to get together with West? Jess, I'm no pimp. Besides, this is way too much information for me."

"No, no. Not to sleep with him. Just spend some time with him without talking about the house. Maybe we can call a truce or something?"

"Good idea. The corn barbecue is Saturday. Why don't you invite him? Bet he's never been to one of those."

"Great idea. But I have to make the first call."

"Word is he has breakfast every morning at the Cozy Café."

"Yeah. I ran into him there. Okay. That's perfect. I owe them a blueberry pie anyway."

"Good. Now handle your love life yourself. I've got all I can deal with on my own."

"How are things with Jennie?"

"Great. She's real nice."

"Yes, she is. She was a cute little kid, too."

"Maybe we can double date sometime," he said, a twinkle in his eye.

Jess threw a sponge at him. "Right. Like that will ever happen."

AFTER REFUSING TO CALL Jess, Stryker accepted that the only way to make sure to see her, outside of stalking her home, was to get up at the ungodly hour of five-thirty and drag his sleepy body into the Cozy Café and await her arrival.

Yawning as he opened the door, he raised his brows when he spied Jess. She sat at the counter, sipping coffee and chatting with Laura Dailey. Last time she breezed in an out. Hmm, she couldn't be waiting for him, could she? Nah, he'd never get that lucky.

"Good morning, Mr. West. Coffee?" Laura asked.

"Stryker, please. Yes."

"The usual?"

He nodded. "Good morning, Jess," he ventured.

She shot him a warm smile. "Morning."

What the hell? Where was Hurricane Jess? Who was this young woman? He took a sip of the coffee.

"Scone?" Laura asked.

"I think I need something stronger."

"Bacon and egg sandwich?"

"Perfect," he replied, taking his coffee to his favorite table.

"Mind if I join you?" Jess asked.

Her words shocked him so badly he almost dropped his mug.

"Sorry about that," Jess said, helping him to steady it.

"I didn't expect you to speak to me again, let alone want to join me," he confessed.

"Hah, really? I thought the same thing. I want to apologize."

"No, no, it's I who should apologize."

"I shouldn't have lost my temper," she said.

"I shouldn't have condescended to you," he replied.

They laughed together. "How about this? We make a pact to sit here and not discuss the house."

"Perfect. Excellent. I agree," he responded.

"Good. Do you know about the Corn Festival?" she asked.

"Laura mentioned it the other day, but I'm not familiar with it. Tell me about it."

"Corn is a big thing here. It brings in a lot of money, and no one has better corn than we do. The festival runs for a week. The corn barbecue at the firehouse on Saturday night kicks it off. Then we have a corn cooking contest, and a corn baking contest, and a scarecrow contest for kids. A dance winds up the celebration on the following Saturday night."

He smiled. "Kinda sounds like fun."

"It is. Some people look forward to it all year."

"Do you ever submit anything to the corn baking contest?"

"My chocolate chip cornbread wins or places every year," she said, beaming.

"I'll have to try some."

"Would you like to go to the corn barbecue with me?" she asked, her brows knitting.

"Sure."

"Oh, good. I'm so relieved." She smiled.

"Did you think I'd say no?" he asked.

"I didn't have a clue. I figured you'd probably be pretty mad at me after our lunch fiasco."

"Actually, I was mad at myself. You were right. I was condescending. Pretty stupid. I mean I don't know that much about you and yet I jumped to conclusions. Wrong conclusions."

"Thank you." She slid her hand over his. He laced his fingers with hers.

"What time should I pick you up?"

"It starts at six. Why don't you come at five thirty?"

"I'll be there."

"See you then," she said, leaning over to kiss his cheek. He stood up, slipped his hand around her waist, and pulled her to him for a real kiss. Jess leaned into it.

"If you're going to kiss me goodbye, make it real," he said.

"Aye, aye," she replied, clearly breathless as she headed for the door.

"Here you go," Laura said, delivering food to Stryker's table. "I didn't want to interrupt," she confided.

"Good thinking." He sat down and picked up the sandwich. The bacon, done perfectly blended with Laura's special scrambled eggs. He'd closed his eyes for a second to savor the delicious breakfast concoction, his favorite item on the menu.

When he swallowed, he dialed John.

"Well? How'd you do?"

"She asked me out."

"No shit?"

"No, uh, right," Stryker said, eying Laura.

John laughed into the phone. "You're making progress. What'd you do to get her to do that?"

"Admitted I was wrong."

"That gets 'em every time. If a man could admit he was wrong more often, he'd get laid every night."

Stryker laughed. "I did get a kiss."

"See? If you were in a private place with her, I bet you'd have gotten more."

"Maybe. I just want her to stop hating me."

"Bullshit. Be honest. You want a lot more than that."

"I admit nothing."

"You can't fool me. I've worked for you for ten years, Stryker."

"I suppose you do know me best."

"I'm glad things are moving along. How's the house coming?"

"I'm going over there to inspect the progress after breakfast. I'm meeting with the architect this afternoon."

A ding alerted him that he had another call.

"I've got to go. That's them on the phone now."

"Talk to you later," John said before ending the call.

Stryker switched calls. "Good morning, Mr. West."

"Please call me Stryker."

"This is Charlie from Pelletier and Grand."

"Yes. We're meeting this afternoon."

"That's what I was calling about. Could we meet this morning instead?"

"Sure. Something wrong?"

"Nope. One of our contractors had an idea and I wanted to run it by you before we went any further."

"Should I come over now?"

"Perfect. You have the address?"

"I do. See you in a few."

By the time he'd finished his food and paid Laura, Chris was outside with the car.

"Off to see the architects."

"Did you see Jess?"

"I'll fill you in on the way."

Chapter Eleven

"That was Charlie Grand. He wants to see you," Will said to his sister before putting down his phone.

"Me?" she asked.

"Yep. Today. As soon as possible."

"Really? Why?"

Will shrugged. "Dunno. Gotta go. Just go over there, will you?"

"Okay." She picked up her car keys and headed to the beautiful renovated building that now housed the architectural firm's office. Every time she drove by, Jess noticed it. She itched to see the inside. Today, she'd get her wish.

Charlie Grand opened the door.

"Jess Lennox?"

"That's me."

"Please come in. Coffee?" he offered.

"No, thanks. What's this about?"

"Have a seat," Charlie said, gesturing to an upholstered chair opposite a loveseat. He eased down and opened up a long cardboard tube.

"We're working on the renovation of Stryker West's aunt's house. But you probably know that because your brother is handling much of the work."

"I do."

"He told us that no one knows that house better than you. You spent time there when you were young?"

"I did. But Mr. West knows it much better than I. He lived there for years."

"True. But he doesn't want to have anything to do with this project, outside of a few approvals. He's given us carte blanche. The only caveat was that he wants it done as the perfect, turnkey bed and breakfast."

"He does?"

"That's what he said. He plans to set it up as a B-and-B, making it easier to sell. Hell, up here no one could afford to heat that mausoleum in the winter. It's gotta be a business."

"I see."

"Will said you have lots of good ideas how a B-and-B would work there. We wondered if you'd share them with us. We'll pay you for your time."

A lump formed in Jess's throat. Stryker selling the place as a ready-made bed-and-breakfast hadn't occurred to her. Once it was done, he'd have plenty of offers for the old place, and it would be gone for good.

"I...I..." she stammered.

"You don't have to decide now. Take a day or two to think it over. I'd be glad to show you the plans for the house and share some of our ideas."

"Thank you, Mr. Grand," she said.

"Charlie. We can pay twenty-five bucks an hour for your consultation," he said, standing and extending his hand to her.

"I'll let you know."

"Soon?"

She nodded. Damn, she had to get out of there and think. Driving home, she focused on the pies she had to make for the next day. When she arrived, she lost herself in the dough, lining each pan and stacking them in the freezer.

She couldn't bear to think about the renovation. But even elbow deep in flour and butter, the house crept into her thoughts. It could be such a fabulous place. A real mansion, stately, regal, with the right touch. And she had a chance to make that happen. Didn't she owe it to the old place to help it get back on its feet and show the world it's beauty?

She finished at five, cleaned up and started dinner. Will blew in about a quarter to six.

"What's for dinner?"

"Chicken and rice casserole."

"No one makes a casserole like you do. Did you see Charlie?"

"I did."

"Did you take the job?"

"Not yet. He said I could think it over."

"What's wrong with you? Makin' twenty-five bucks an hour for your spare time? What's to think about?"

"It wouldn't be fulltime, right? I have my pie customers."

"Nope. Part-time."

Jess sank down on a chair and tears flowed. "I'd be helping Mr. West sell that place."

"Yep. And finally get it out of our hair."

"I thought you loved it, too?"

"I do. But not enough to wreck my life and yours. Jess, it has to happen. You have to let it go. At least this way, you'd have a hand in makin' it pretty. I thought you'd like that. You'd get to be there, see the plans, watch the renovation. And know you'd been the one to set it up right."

His words touched her. Yes, there would be all kinds of pleasure before the final pain of loss.

"You're right, you know."

He grinned. "And yet again, the little brother shows who's smart."

She smacked him in the shoulder.

"Ow!"

"And big sister can still subdue him."

"So, you gonna do it?"

"I have to. I know I'll be bringing about the end, but I can't stand by and just watch. I want to be involved. I know it can never be mine, but maybe, for a little while, it can. Sort of. You know?"

"Yeah, I know. Kinda like babysitting. For a while, the kid is yours."

"Exactly. That's better than nothing."

"Should I call Charlie?"

"Nope. My job. I'll handle it. I'll stop by tomorrow after I finish delivery."

"Good decision. Where's the casserole. I could eat a whale."

Jess brought the bubbling dish to the table. Will scooped out a huge portion.

"Take it easy. It's hot."

"You're such a mother, you know that?"

"Somebody had to do the job."

He squeezed her hand. "I'm grateful. You've been a great mom."

"Eat," she said, tamping down the emotion in her chest.

They chowed down in silence. After dinner, Will went to meet Jennie. Jess took a glass of mint tea out to the deck. The air had cooled and the sun had lost much of its heat from the day. She sat in her daddy's old rocker and watched the birds at the feeder.

Once the house was renovated and sold, there'd be no reason for her to stay in Pine Grove. She and Will could finally pick up stakes and make a fresh start somewhere else. He'd been begging her to leave for years. Soon, she'd be ready. The trees sighed, as if in sympathy with her mixed emotions.

She vowed to be happy during this process and stop dreading the end. Her mind turned to curtains. "Hmm, lace ones for the first floor where you don't need privacy, but solid ones for the rooms upstairs," she said to the birds. At once, her mind took off, making a mental list of the things that needed to be done to create the perfect bed-and-breakfast.

JESS RANG THE BELL at Pelletier and Grand. Charlie answered.

"You're here. That means you want to do it?"

"Yep."

"Come in, come in. Have you eaten lunch yet? We were just sitting down to chicken salad my wife made. Join us. This is Selena." Charlie made the introductions.

Pulled into the warmth of Charlie's greeting, she sat at the small table and shared their food. The unexpected meal quieted her nerves regarding her decision.

"We want to hear your ideas. Charlie's handling the renovation, but I'm helping with the decoration. Mr. West wants a totally finished product, down to the silverware and napkins."

"Oh, good. Because I had some ideas about the china and silver."

"Let's talk about the house first," Charlie said, bringing his plate to the sink in the small kitchen. He picked up a notebook and pen on his way back to the table.

"I don't mean to rush you. Take your time. Eat. I'll make notes while we talk."

"I was thinking, the house is so big and imposing. It might scare people off a little. So I'd make the entryway cozy. Warm colors, a bench with a nice cushion against the wall shared with the living room. A couple of old-fashioned hooks hanging on the opposite wall. And a painting. I think the right artwork is important."

"What kind of décor did you envision," Charlie's wife asked.

"That's tricky. At first, I thought kind of Victorian, or like that era. Then I thought kind of country, maybe even country French. But finally, I decided to blend both—country and Victorian—wherever I could."

"You've given this a lot of thought, haven't you?" Charlie asked.

"Oh, yes. When I was young, I'd go over to the house, sit outside so as not to disturb Mrs. Minnie. I'd dream about how it would be when it was mine someday."

She lowered her glance to hide her emotion. The room was still.

Selena leaned over and squeezed Jess's forearm. "This must be hard for you."

"At least I get to have a say in what the place will look like. Better than not being involved."

"You're brave," Charlie muttered.

"No. Just foolish. I've let that house occupy my mind for too long. It's time to make my peace and move on."

"Let's take a ride over there. Better to discuss ideas on site, don't you agree?" Charlie said, pushing to his feet.

"I do," she said. They piled into their cars and drove to the mansion. Selena stayed behind. The sounds of construction greeted them. A huge floor sander screamed, and an electric saw buzzed in the background. Drop cloths were everywhere.

"Let's start at the beginning," Charlie said, stepping over thick electrical cords.

"First, you have the dining room and the kitchen. I mean, those can be used even if you don't have guests. You can make it into a beautiful restaurant, too. So, I thought those places should be done first," Jess said.

Jess took them to the huge kitchen in the back.

"Since there are thirty-six rooms, the house probably had a large family here plus servants. Everyone had to eat. The kitchen runs the entire width of the house."

She ran her finger through the dust on the long, cracked wooden table. "This is probably where the help ate." There were long, faded, stained counters and ancient appliances.

"We need a professional stove, two sinks, and a professional refrigerator and freezer," Jess said, stepping over broken tiles on the floor.

"This room could take a month to rebuild all by itself," Charlie murmured, making notes.

"I see this as the hub of the house. Once it's ready, everything flows from here."

"Let's check out the dining room," he said, wiping dusty hands on his jeans.

She followed him. "I love this room. We don't need much furniture here. A long table, chairs, a hutch, or a sideboard. A corner cabinet would be nice."

"That should be easy."

"They need to be wood. Dark, beautifully finished wood. To give warmth to this room. It faces north, making it colder than the rest," Jess said.

"Maybe we should add a fireplace?" Charlie asked.

"Wow, you can do that?"

"We can do anything. It's just money."

"My money," came a deep voice from the archway.

"Hi, Stryker. We were just discussing adding a fireplace," Charlies said.

"Maybe we don't need one. People aren't going to be in here for long periods. A fireplace needs tending. Whoever is running this place"—she stopped and swallowed—"won't have time to do that. A fire in the living room and the study, where people will sit for a while would be more useful."

"A study?" Stryker arched an eyebrow.

"Of course, a study. Or a library. Call it whatever you want. A cozy room with a sofa, a rocker, a wing chair, a fire burning, a window seat, drapes, and some landscape paintings."

"You have a clear vision of this place, don't you?" Stryker asked.

"It's been my favorite fantasy for years," she said, almost in a whisper.

"I've got it. Let's move on to the living room," Charlie put in.

"I didn't know you'd be here," she said to Stryker.

"I'd have been here earlier, but I had a phone meeting with London. So, you took the job?"

She nodded.

"Good. I'll get out of your way. Looks like you, Charlie, and Selena are knee-deep in this thing. You don't need me."

He raised a hand in farewell and left. Jess took a deep breath to slow her pulse. Standing in the dining room, even the wreck it was, with Stryker sparked desire. She'd much rather have been discussing her ideas with him, tucked safely into his shoulder, resting her head against him. When the hell was she going to stop dreaming about things so far above her pay grade? She might as well be thinking about building a house on Mars.

"Ready?" Charlie asked, breaking into her thoughts. Time to get back to work. She was on the clock now.

"Ready," she said, following him into the living room.

SATURDAY AFTERNOON, Stryker stepped out of the shower, dried his body, then wrapped the towel around his waist. Soon he'd be heading to the Corn Barbecue. Even though he had no damn idea what the hell a corn barbecue was, he'd be there with Jess. Not knowing about the event bugged him, so he opened the door and hollered downstairs.

"Chris! What the fuck is a corn barbecue?"

As he heard Chris making his way up the stairs, Stryker slipped on boxers before he combed his hair.

"Are you going to the corn barbecue?"

"Yes. Now what the hell is it?" Stryker asked, facing the mirror.

"It's a social gathering where they grill a whole lotta corn, eat it with butter and salt, or plain, drink beer, wine, or sweet tea and talk."

"What? They grill corn?"

"On the cob. I'm told it's great. I love corn."

"Me, too. Boiled and at the table. Are you going?"

"I am."

"Taking your girlfriend?"

"I am. She said they grill the corn in the husks. So, you grab the long end of the corn and peel back the husks. Almost like corn on a stick. She said it's better than corn cooked on the stove."

"I'll give it a try. I don't really give a shit about the corn. Jess is going with me. Otherwise, I could care less."

"Don't think Jess is going to like your attitude."

"You're probably right."

"Try to get with the program, won't you?"

"Okay, okay. I'll smile. Be nice."

"Excellent. Then you might even have a good time," Chris said and huffed out of the room.

Stryker stared in the mirror, rubbed his face and picked up his razor. He needed to look the best he could tonight. And dump his sour mood. What did the amazing, filthy rich Stryker Alexander West have to be unhappy about? John had moved the expansion to London along perfectly—the space reconstruction was underway and he was in negotiations to buy a townhouse.

He had the perfect life. What man could want more? The renovation of that old house, such an albatross around his neck, would bring a handsome price. What would he do with an extra half-million-dollar profit? He rubbed the back of his neck. He'd find something.

What was the problem? What could he possibly put on his Christmas list? Love, marriage, family—maybe those were missing from his life. He'd crossed those off ages ago. Why would they crop up now, destroying his good mood? Had he changed his mind? Did he want to find a wife? No, not just a wife, but a woman who would love him for more than his money. He'd been unable to find any such woman, until now, maybe.

Is Jess a diamond in the rough? Just out of his reach, she tantalized and teased him. Had he finally found something he wanted that all his money couldn't buy? A rueful smile crossed his lips. One in a million, what would Jess want with him if it wasn't about his money? Surely not his warmth and good nature. He laughed. Perhaps it was Stryker Alexander West who needed renovation—even more than that old house. There's a project Jess Lennox could handle with ease.

He shrugged his short-sleeved sports shirt over his broad shoulders, added jeans, socks, and sneakers, checked in the mirror one more time, and then descended the stairs.

In an attempt to brighten his mood, Stryker played country music in the car. It worked. Still humming "Here You Come Again," by Dolly Parton, he exited the car. Lighthearted and smiling, he approached the old, saggy porch.

"Be right out," she called from inside.

He stopped but continued singing. At the squeak of the rusty hinges, he turned to face her. His jaw dropped. Wearing a simple white skirt and aqua ruffled off-the-shoulder blouse, she looked stunning. Her hair pulled up on the sides and held with a barrette in the back kept it out of her face but flowing around her shoulders. *If angels walked the Earth, this is what they'd look like.*

"You look...gorgeous," he choked out.

"Thanks. You look pretty good yourself."

He extended his hand and she slipped her fingers through his. He opened the door for her, then got behind the wheel.

"You didn't have to pick me up. I live close enough to walk. I could have met you there," she said.

"I wanted to. Wanted to walk in with you on my arm," he said.

"You're first corn barbecue," she said, changing the subject. "Are you excited?"

"I'm blown away to be going with the prettiest girl in town."

"Considering the size of Pine Grove, that's not saying much." She chuckled.

"You're not serious?"

"Just kidding! Loosen up, Stryker. This isn't a merger, it's a corn barbecue on a Saturday night. And there's going to be music, too."

"Oh?"

"Yep. Dwayne and Wayne will be playing banjo and guitar."

Stryker cracked up. "Dwayne and Wayne? You've got to be kidding me."

"Nope. Wait 'til you hear them."

"Okay. I'll keep an open mind."

"Gotta love Pine Grove people," she said.

At least one, he thought as he rounded the bend and pulled into the parking lot.

Chapter Twelve

Jess had never seen Stryker in such casual attire. Secretly she had wondered if he even owned a pair of jeans. Damn, dressed up or down, the man looked good. His shirt fit snug across his chest, outlining a well-defined set of pecs. A tad bit tight across the shoulders, the garment emphasized the power in his muscles. A tuft of dark brown hair peeked through the unbuttoned placket on the front. A tingle shot through her as she imagined him shirtless. Restless, her fingers itched to touch him. Barely able to control the urge to bury her hands in his hair, she babbled on about the huge pile of unshucked corn and the musicians.

Taking his hand, she led him over to the three barbecues where corn cooked, releasing a bit of smoke and a mouth-watering aroma into the air. They stopped at a table where Nancy Collins from the veterinarian's office sat with a metal box to her left.

"Well, shear my sheep! If it isn't Mr. West!"

"Nancy, meet Stryker West," Jess said.

"Everybody knows who he is. Welcome, Mr. West."

"Stryker, please."

Nancy blushed a bit. "Well, now, gettin' familiar so quick."

He chuckled. Jess squeezed his hand.

"You don't gotta be embarrassed for me, Ms. Lennox. I can do that for myself!" she said, giving out a hearty guffaw.

"How much?" Stryker asked.

"Everything's a donation. We're asking for five dollars, but you can give whatever you want. It's for the fire department. We run a volunteer one here."

Stryker retrieved his wallet from his back pocket and pulled out two fifty-dollar bills."

"You don't have to give that much."

"But it's for the fire department, right?"

"Yes, sir."

He added another forty dollars and put the money on the table. "It's the least I can do."

"Well, thank you, sir! That's mighty generous." Nancy put the money away and handed them each a ticket. "Hang on to this one, Jess. He's a keeper."

Sensing heat in her face, Jess turned away. Did this happen to Stryker often? Did people judge him by his generosity, by his ability to slap big bucks on the table? She wondered how he felt about it. One glance at his frown and she knew. He didn't like to be known as Mr. Filthy Rich. Who could blame him? But would he be throwing around fifties if he made an ordinary income?

"Come on," she said, pulling him toward the side. "We've got to get in line."

As they waited for corn, he rested his arm around her shoulders.

"Does that happen to you often?" she asked, snaking her arm around his waist.

"All the time. I should be used to it by now."

"I'm sorry."

"It's not your fault," he replied.

"No. But I'm sorry just the same. Guess it's not always easy to have a ton of money."

He laughed. "That's putting it mildly. I get hit up by everyone who needs a helping hand, legit or not. If I come across, sometimes they sneer at the amount. Or simply say that it doesn't dent my wallet." And scam artists? They buzz around me like flies."

"Wow. I never thought..."

"Everyone thinks having money solves every problem on Earth. It doesn't. Sometimes it creates more."

She hugged him tighter. "Nobody thinks that, do they?"

"Nope. Nobody." He leaned over and kissed the top of her head. "Now I know."

"You're not like that," he said.

"Maybe I was, at least a little bit, until now."

The wariness that shone in his eyes when he talked with Nancy, melted away, replaced by warmth. As she gazed into them, the world fell away. For an instant it was only the two of them, standing there. Her heart swelled.

"Next!" called one of the chefs tending the grill.

"Smells good," Stryker said, nudging Jess ahead of him.

"It is. Plain? Butter? Salt? Condiments over there," the man said, pointing to a big side table.

"I take it with the works," Stryker said, closing his fingers around the corn and following Jess.

"Me, too," she said.

They applied butter and salt, then picked up sweet tea, and headed for a long table on the side of the firehouse.

"It's family style here. At least the seating is," she said.

They sat facing each other at the end of the table.

"Hmpf. Too good to sit with the rest of us, huh? Too rich to mix with the poor folks?" an older man said.

"What?" Jess asked.

"What are you doin' with Mr. High-and-Mighty? Think he'll give you some dough?"

"Shut up, George," Jess snapped.

"Look, Mister. We're none of your business. Please leave the lady alone, okay?" Stryker said, peeling back some of the husks on his ear of corn.

"It's a free country. I can say what I want."

"Come on, Stryker. There's room over there," she pushed to her feet and led the way to an empty table.

"I could have punched his lights out with one hand."

"I know. He's not worth it. You'd probably get arrested, and he'd sue you."

Stryker laughed. "You've got the drill down, don't you?"

"I know some of the slimier people in this town."

"I see. Protecting me?"

"Someone's got to," she said, trying to hide a grin.

He leaned over and planted a kiss on her lips. "Thanks."

When they finished their corn, they moseyed over to another grill where hot dogs were cooking. Stryker ate two. Then they hit the bake sale table where he laid down twenty bucks for two brownies.

"Let's go to my place. I've got cold beer, and we can watch the birds from my deck," Jess said.

He nodded.

"We can walk. Did you know that Will is a volunteer fireman?"

He shook his head.

"We live so close, he decided to join up."

"That makes sense."

"Let's go," she said, taking his hand.

STRYKER'S BIG HAND engulfed Jess's small one. They meandered, stopping when she spotted two redwing blackbirds chasing each other through a meadow. Sheep grazed on a hill, while goats played in a pen. The air smelled of freshly mown grass and farm animals.

It brought back earlier days for him. Some good memories mixed with bad. Riding bareback with a friend. Skinny dipping in the lake. Aunt Minnie's chocolate cupcakes with buttercream icing. He'd made friends with a few other misfits in his class.

Through the years, he'd wondered what had happened to Ralph and Eddie. Never curious enough to attend a reunion, Stryker shied away from events that included his past, who he used to be, and where he came from.

It wasn't that he was ashamed that he came from Pine Grove, more that the pain of losing his parents never left. How proud they would be of what he had achieved. Stryker took pleasure in taking care of Aunt Minnie in her old age. Grateful for her warmth and caring, and taking him in without a second's hesitation, he'd paid for everything in her life. The second he could afford to send money home to her, he did.

At first, she objected, but as he built his empire, she'd quieted down, accepting his generosity. Not until a week ago did he discover what she had done in the last five years with the money he sent.

Rather than tend to the house, she'd donated the excess beyond her barest living expenses to the ASPCA and various animal rescue outfits. He'd laughed when he found out. Of course, Minnie spent her life taking care of strays, like him. It made perfect sense.

"Whatcha thinkin'?" she asked.

"Nothing really. Just about what Minnie did with the money I sent her to keep the house in good condition."

"You did?"

"Of course. Minnie had the deed, but I paid the upkeep."

"You did?"

"You're repeating yourself."

She giggled. "I had no idea."

"I owed my very existence to Minnie. I made sure she could live in comfort."

"You loved her."

"She was mother and father to me."

"Do you still miss your parents? Do you think about them?"

"Every day. I have a few pictures."

She stopped to hug him. "It must be hard."

"I'd guess you know all about that."

She nodded. "I do. Dad tried, but alcohol was his mistress. He couldn't stop. And Ma? I go see her once a month. We don't have much to talk about, but someone's got to do it."

"Are you mad at her?"

"I was. For a long time. But not anymore. You can't stay mad forever."

"She left you with a ton of responsibility."

"She did. But the arguing and the fighting stopped. After she left, we lived in peace. Still do."

"That's something."

"I suppose. Still. Two adults. You'd think if they couldn't get along, one would leave. But no, they were too stubborn."

"Your mom left a big stigma on you when she did...what she did."

"You mean when she killed my dad? Might as well come out and say it. It's a fact. Yeah. I lost most of my friends. My fiancé. And my babysitting jobs dried up. Seems no one trusted a murderer's daughter alone with their kids."

"That's terrible," he said, drawing her to him.

"It was hard. But Will and I managed."

"You did. Made you super strong."

"Hah! Don't let looks fool you. I'm not nearly as strong as you think."

They stopped at the rear of her small apartment house. There were a few sturdy-looking chairs on the back deck and a small, round table. Three bird feeders hung from a nearby tree.

"I'll be right back," Jess said, disappearing into the house. She returned carrying two sweaty bottles of beer. Stryker joined her on the deck. They took seats and watched as the birds jockeyed for positions on the feeders.

"Which is your favorite?" he asked.

"I like them all. The nuthatch is funny when he hops down the tree. The chickadee is feisty. But the goldfinch is gorgeous. The male, that is."

"Not as pretty as you," he replied.

She blushed. "You don't have to do that."

"Do what?"

"Lavish compliments on me. I like you well enough without that."

"It was merely an observation."

"You're a player. I get that. With your lifestyle, it fits."

"I'm not. Really. I haven't had a relationship in a long time."

"See? That's what I mean. But you haven't gone without a woman for a long time?"

Now it was his turn to be embarrassed. "Well, it depends on what you mean by a long time."

She laughed.

"Okay. Sure. I take what's offered. But I don't manipulate. Or bribe or pay for sex," he said.

"Good to know," she said, sitting back in her chair and raising the bottle to her mouth.

He joined her in taking a drink. The cool liquid slaked his thirst. But watching her drink, hell, he couldn't keep his gaze from her mouth. Damn. Simply sitting there, drinking beer and bird-watching, she oozed sex. He wanted her. But this would have to be done carefully. He'd have to tiptoe or she'd get the wrong idea. It wasn't just about sex with Jess. How could he get that across without opening up?

"What about you? You've only mentioned your ex-fiancé. Is there no one else?"

She shook her head. "I've gone out on a few dates. A very few. Mostly new guys, who don't know my family history. Some take off when they find out. Others think I'm desperate, and they don't want to take no for an answer. Most of the time, I get bored or turned off. Things rarely last beyond two or three dates."

"That's a shame. A woman like you should be kissed long and often."

She pushed to her feet. "Maybe we'd better get back to the barbecue."

He followed, mentally kicking himself. He'd done it. Said the wrong thing. Scared her like a deer in the headlights. At the side of the house, he took her arm and turned her to face him.

"We've danced around this for a long time." He stepped closer, then pulled her to his chest. "I like you, Jess. More than I like most women. A lot more. I want you. I think you want me. We're adults."

She flattened her palm on his chest, raising the temperature in his body. Blood pumped to his groin. Her gaze connected with his, and he didn't see anything stopping him.

"You're right. It's just that—"

"I promise, I won't hurt you. I won't make love to you and take off. It's not like that with you, Jess."

She softened against him. "Can I believe you?"

He chuckled. "I may be a lot of things but a liar's not one of them."

SLOWLY, HE LOWERED his mouth to hers. She tilted her chin up to receive his kiss. His lips were soft and warm. It had been too long since she'd slept with a man. Damn, Stryker knew how to stoke the fire. Resting her hands on his rock-hard biceps, she felt their power.

Should she resist? Impossible. She melted under the warmth of his kiss, wound her arms around his neck, and pressed her hips to his. His arm tightened, drawing her closer. The heat from his chest penetrated the thin fabric of her blouse, ratcheting up her body temperature. God, desire flashed through her, settling between her legs. Jess wanted him with every fiber of her being. Inside her—now!

He read her signals perfectly, sliding his hand up over her breast. His fingertips dipped over the neckline of her dress, coming in contact with her skin. With no bra to get in the way, he made quick work of exposing her flesh. When his fingers pinched her nipple, a zing shot through her. She squirmed under his expert touch.

"Do you want me?" came the rough whisper, vibrating against her neck. She cupped his smooth cheek. Arching her back, Jess closed her eyes and muttered, "God, yes." She slid her hand under his shirt, combing her fingertips through his chest hair. Contact with his skin spiked her need. She wanted more.

Jess raised her leg, hooking her foot behind his calf. He eased his hand from her chest, slipping it under her skirt to stop above her knee. First, he gripped her, then moved up to take possession of her flesh. His long fingers wrapped almost all the way around her slim leg. He ran his hand up and down, his thumb pressing against the sensitive skin of her inner thigh, then back to rest on the edge of her panties.

She gulped air as he neared her core. Faster! More! She wanted to scream, "Take me!" but no matter how she nudged his growing erection, he kept to his own pace. Finally, he slipped one fingertip under the lace edging, down her slit, and into her, for a second, before withdrawing it.

"Quit teasing," she breathed into his ear.

A soft chuckle was his reply.

"What are you doing?" came a loud, masculine voice.

As slowly as the seduction began, it ended in a nanosecond. Stryker withdrew his hand. Jess pushed down her skirt. He yanked up her bodice, then turned to the intruder.

"Who the hell are you, and how is this any of your business?"

"Chip Matthews. Her ex-fiancé. And it is my business."

"Chip?" Jess straightened, put her hands on her hips, and faced him.

"Ex is the important word here. Why don't you run along, sonny," Stryker said.

"Sonny!" Chip hollered, his hands fisting at his sides. "Bring it on, old man. You wanna fight? I'll punch your lights out."

"Old man? I'm afraid you're mistaken," Stryker said, his eyes cold.

"Stop. Okay? No fighting. Chip, this is my life. Not your business. You should leave."

"Leave? Leave you to this...this predator? Never."

"You're married. Go on. I don't need you here. Stryker and I are seeing each other."

"Biggest mistake of your life, Jess," Chip said.

"Hey!" Stryker took a step forward before Jess stopped him, flinging her arm across his chest.

"Biggest mistake of my life? Getting engaged to you was the biggest mistake of my life! At the first sign of disapproval from your parents, you caved. You threw me under the bus, Chip. Deserted me, when I needed you. You were the biggest mistake of my life. Stryker wouldn't do that. Would you?"

"Never. I don't care what people think. Jess is an amazing woman. And as long as she wants to see me, I'll be there. Get over it, asshole," Stryker said.

Chip charged, like a bull in the ring. Stryker crouched down.

"Stop! Wait!" yelled Jess, but the men didn't listen.

Chip bounded toward the older man, who dove for the knees. Stryker took Chip down, put him in a wrestling hold and held him there.

"Done?"

"I'm gonna punch your lights out," Chip growled.

"Chip. Go home to Kathy. She's your wife. Not me." Jess tugged on Stryker's arm. "Let him up. Please."

He did as she asked. Chip took a swing, but Stryker ducked.

"Hey, the lady asked us to stop."

"Okay, okay," Chip muttered, frowning.

"You have to leave me alone. Stop checking up on me, Chip. Kathy must be mad as hell."

"I don't care. I never should have lost you. It was a mistake."

"That was forever ago. It's ancient history. Forget it, will you?"

"Okay, okay. But I don't trust this guy. He's old enough to be your father. How old are you, anyway?" Chip directed his question to Stryker.

"Forty-two. So what?"

"Exactly," Jess echoed. "So what?"

"It's your funeral, Jess. When he can't get it up in five years, don't come crawling to me." Chip lumbered off, shaking his head.

"Don't worry. I won't." She turned to Stryker. "You okay?"

"Of course."

"Where did you learn to fight like that?"

"Yale wrestling team."

She laughed. "You sure surprised me. I thought you were going to get creamed."

His brow knit. "Don't worry about me, Jess. I don't roll over. I don't give up. I prevail. It's what I do."

She raised her palms. "Okay, okay. No offense meant."

"I don't need you to protect me. I've been doing it, successfully, myself for many years."

"I'm sorry."

"It's okay. Where were we?"

"About to get another cupcake," she said, lacing her fingers with his.

"That's not the way I remember it." He chuckled.

"The mood is ruined."

"Okay. Besides, taking you against the side of a house is not the way I picture our first time."

"Oh, really? And how do you picture it?"

"Come with me, and I'll tell you." He snickered, pulling her arm through his. She smiled and measured her gait to his as they returned to the festivities.

Chapter Thirteen

While Jess buttered another ear of corn, Stryker chowed down on his third hot dog.

"Damn, these are good," he said.

"It's the grill. Makes everything taste good," Barney Dailey, Laura's husband, said.

Jess stood to one side, munching, watching Stryker absorbed in mundane conversation with a couple of the older men. Will wandered over and joined in. Stryker asked questions about the renovation and Will answered. He was patient with the older man who didn't know a hammer from a Phillips head screwdriver. Jess turned her back to hide her smile. Finding Stryker ignorant about something pleased her. Will totally outclassed the rich man on the subject of house renovation.

Finally able to control her laughter, she moseyed on over. Before she could speak, Stryker's phone rang. He looked at the display and frowned.

"Gotta take this," he said and stepped to one side.

Jess sharpened her ears and listened in.

"What? No. I wasn't planning—"

Silence.

"I know. Do I have to?"

Silence. Jess discarded the empty ear of corn.

"It's not about her. Stop. That's not funny."

Silence.

"All right. Two days. But that's it. Two. Only. Yes. I'll fly out tomorrow. Right. Thanks, John. I think."

He hung up. A pang of curiosity mixed with jealousy in Jess. "Her who?"

"You were eavesdropping?" he asked, cocking an eyebrow.

"Hell, when you talk out in public, it's not eavesdropping." She stiffened.

"Her was you."

"What about me?"

"John is demanding that I go back to London. He says they have a problem with the office renovation there that only I can solve."

"And how do I fit into the equation?"

His face pinked. "When I said I didn't want to go, he accused me of staying because of you."

"Really? Oh. Okay."

"I told him it wasn't true, but I never could lie to John and get away with it."

"You're staying because of me?"

He nodded.

"Why?"

"Isn't that obvious?"

The idea that a wealthy, powerful man like West would want to remain in tiny Pine Grove to be with her struck her as hilarious. She burst out laughing.

"What's funny?"

"You don't expect me to believe you'd blow off London to stay here with me?"

"Of course I do. That's the truth."

The smile melted off her face. The back of her eyes stung with sudden tears.

"Really?" Her voice, almost a whisper, shook.

"Yes, really." He took both her hands in his, drawing her closer.

She bowed her head, stepped up to him, and rested it on his shoulder. Stryker circled her with his embrace. *It's stupid to cry.* But the tears came anyway.

"Oh, honey, don't cry," he whispered. "That's a good thing."

She nodded slightly, fighting to control her emotions. Clouds rolled in, cooling the air. Jess shivered.

"You're cold. Let's go." Stryker led her to the car.

Following his lead, she eased into the front seat of his luxurious Bentley and lay back, wiping her face with her hands. Opening her bag, she rummaged through searching for tissues and lipstick.

"Glove compartment," he said, popping it open, revealing a small box.

"Thank you." She took one and dried her eyes.

"How about a hot coffee or an ice cream?"

"How about both?"

"Or a piece of pie. What did you drop off this morning?"

"The Cozy Café has the last of my blueberry pie. Berries are done for this year."

"Well, hell. What are we waiting for? Blueberry is my favorite. Along with chocolate cream, and coconut, and maybe apple?"

Jess laughed. "You're my best customer."

"In every way," he said, shooting a warm smile at her.

Embarrassed, she turned her face to the window. The clouds had thickened.

"Might be a storm coming," she said. "We're due for some rain."

He pulled into the parking lot and the two headed for the café. Laura Daily greeted them.

"Damn clouds! I've put up a fresh pot. How about coffee?"

"And pie?" Stryker asked.

"And pie."

"Blueberry?" he asked.

"I've got two pieces left. They're yours."

The couple sat at his favorite table, savored the dessert, and drank steaming hot house brew. The drink warmed Jess. She glanced out the window, watching clouds form over the lake.

"You're flying out tomorrow?"

"Yep. I'm taking the puddle jumper from Oak Bend to Kennedy airport. Then on from there."

"How long will you be gone?"

"Two days there, then flying back on the third. You'll be here, right?"

"I will."

"And you won't find anyone else before I return?"

"I'm not planning on it."

He laughed. "That's reassuring."

"You're not worried, are you?"

He took her hand. "Not really."

"Don't get too comfortable."

"I'm sure you won't let that happen."

"You can count on it." She chuckled.

WITH STRYKER FLYING to London, Jess headed to jail to visit her mother. She picked up *Red Carpet Romance,* slipped on jeans, a thin sweater, and a jacket, then drove to the bus stop.

Rusty Evans pulled the big vehicle up to the curb.

"Goin' to see your mom?"

"Yep."

"You're my first passenger."

"It's a nice day. Folks are probably having picnics and stuff."

"Not that nice. Weatherman's predicting rain. Might even be a storm."

"Really?" she asked, looking up from her book.

"Yep. There's a hurricane coming. Or at least that's what Joe Small said on the radio this morning."

"Hurricane?"

"Yep. By the end of the week. They're thinking about postponing the corn festival dance."

"Oh my God. Really?"

"Never can be too careful," Rusty said.

Jess returned to her reading. Rusty had asked her out several times, but she'd turned him down. Didn't seem to discourage him, though.

"Got a date for the dance, in case it isn't rained out?"

"Uh huh."

"I should have figured. Pretty girl like you."

"I'm seeing someone," Jess replied. And for the first time, it wasn't a white lie. She sat back and closed her book, letting her mind wander. Jess turned her gaze toward the window. Was she seeing Stryker? They'd almost had sex, so, yeah, they were seeing each other. She smiled. He didn't want to be gone, because of her. Her heart swelled.

As the bus bumped along, making its way to the highway, Jess sat back and continued to read. The story drew her in and she finished two chapters by the time the bus pulled into the parking lot.

"Should I wait?"

"I won't be long."

"Okay. I'll get lunch and be here when you get out."

"Thanks."

Jess turned her handbag and book over to the guards, went through the metal detector, and headed down the long hall to the visitation area. Because her mother had committed murder, she was isolated and had to sit across from Jess behind protective plexiglass.

A few minutes after she sat down, the door opened and her mother shuffled in. Jess picked up the phone.

"Hi, Ma."

"Hello, Jess."

"How are you?"

"How can I be? Stuck in this hellhole."

Jess listened for ten minutes while her mother complained. Then the guard stood up on her side. "Ten more minutes, Miss," she said.

Jess nodded. "Only ten minutes, Ma"

"You got a boyfriend?"

The question took Jess off guard. Her mother rarely asked Jess anything about her life. The visits were all about Betty. Unprepared, the truth slipped to her lips, color heated her cheeks.

"Ah, so you have?"

"Sort of. Nothing serious." *Right. Like I couldn't settle down with him in that old house in a heartbeat.*

"Sure, sure. You sleepin' with him?"

"Ma!"

"Well?" Betty grinned, raising her eyebrows.

"I gotta go, Ma."

"Wait! Give me a thrill, will ya? I got nothin' in here. Makes me happy to think you're gettin' some."

"I'm not sleeping with him. Okay?"

"Too bad. I hope you'll change your mind. Life's short. Take the good stuff where you find it. What's his name?"

Jess breathed a sigh of relief when the guard stood.

"That's it. Time."

"Bye, Ma."

"When are you coming back?"

"Move along," the guard said, getting between Jess and the desk.

"A month, Ma," she called over her shoulder.

The guard shot her a dirty look. Jess moved quickly own the hall, picked up her things, and scooted out the door. Her head pounded.

Once she hit the outside, she took a deep breath. Jess hated the stench, the visits, the confiscation of her belongings, even if just for twenty minutes. The metal detector, the pat down, the suspicion annoyed her, and then there was her mother. Convinced she'd been railroaded by a corrupt judge and an incompetent attorney, Betty did nothing but bitch her heart out during Jess's visits. The wall of negativity sapped Jess's strength, surrounding her like an evil cloud, clinging to her like cat fur or a bad smell.

Fresh air cleared her head. Closing her eyes would help. Rusty opened the door.

"You don't look so good," he said.

"I'll be fine. Just close my eyes for a while."

"I got seven stops to make on the way home."

"No problem." Jess didn't have anywhere to go until six o'clock when she'd be doing a stint at Homer's. Work, work, work—her days were spent toiling with little respite. Only difference now was that she and Will were saving money. Always good to have something in the bank, in case of emergency. That's what her dad used to say, on his sober days.

JESS TIED THE APRON around her waist. She took a sip from a glass of seltzer. Wouldn't it have been nice after leaving the jail to settle into the front seat of Stryker's car and have him whisk her away to a nice dinner by the lake? Ah, she could dream.

Surprised at how quickly she'd grown accustomed to his attention, she confessed to herself that she missed him. By six thirty, Homer's was jumping. Folks filled the dining room, and there was only one empty seat at the bar.

Jess made drinks, delivered food, and chatted briefly with the patrons.

"When's your chocolate chip cornbread coming out, Jess?" one man asked.

"Not 'til tomorrow."

"Whatcha doin' here? Shouldn't you be home cooking?"

"I'll get up at dawn and get it done then."

"Two drafts, Jess," Homer said.

"Coming up."

The freelance work with Charlie Grand allowed Jess to cut back on her time at Homer's. She preferred to spend time making renovation plans for the house and what the rooms should look like. The architect proved to be a good listener, taking down her suggestions and discussing ways to make them real.

Still, she'd promised Homer to pick up the slack on busy nights. Busy for a Thursday night, Jess kept in motion for hours. By eleven, most of the patrons had gone home. She leaned back against the wall and finished her third glass of seltzer.

Stryker was due home sometime on Friday. He'd be in time for the dance if it wasn't postponed. Although she didn't have anything to wear, she'd promised to go with him. There was always the thrift shop. Giselle got in new things weekly.

As her mind wandered, the television screen drew her eye. The weather report was on.

"And winds are whipping up. They're up to thirty miles an hour now but expected to rise to hurricane force by morning."

Her cell rang. It was Will.

"Leave early. I'm coming to get you."

"But my shift's not over."

"Have you looked outside, Jess?"

"No. Why?"

"It's pouring. Wind is blowing. Your old car doesn't stand a chance. I'm bringing the truck."

"All right. Let me get the okay from Homer."

Before she could look for him, he appeared. "Time to settle up and go home, folks."

"Aw, Homer," one man said.

"Wind is whipping up. Rain. It's a storm, Nate. I want everyone to get home safe. Come on. I'm closing up."

Jess texted Will. She could probably make it home safely in her car, but Will was right, the truck was sturdier. While she washed, dried, and put away glasses, she stared at the television. Would Stryker take a small plane to Oak Bend from New York City?

She chewed her lip. It might not be safe for a small plane. Her phone dinged. Another message from Will.

Dance postponed until next Saturday.

"Sullivan County residents, state troopers advise everyone to get home and stay there. High winds mean downed power lines. Safest place is your house," announced the weatherman.

She glanced out the window and spied Will.

"Skedaddle, Missy," Homer said, motioning with his hands. "I want you home safe."

"What about you?"

"I'm right behind you."

They were the last people to leave. Jess bowed her head against the driving rain as she ran to the truck.

"Thanks, Will," she said, shaking water droplets from her hair.

"Hey, don't get my truck wet."

"Sorry. Can't help it."

"You got smart. Leave that junk heap here. I'll bring you back tomorrow."

"Thanks. The dance is canceled?"

"Postponed. Next Saturday."

"Gives me a week to figure out how to get something decent to wear."

"Why don't you take some of the money you're making with the architect and buy something new?"

"Because we have a double electric bill coming in."

"Didn't pay last month?"

She shook her head.

"Okay," he said.

"I don't want them to shut it off."

"I get it. Wish I had money to give you. I'm plowing everything I'm making into tools. Charlie thinks I have everything I need to do the job. But I don't."

Jess put her hand on his arm. "That's a good investment. With your skill and the right tools, you'll have your business off the ground in no time."

"I hope. This is a big job."

"It's exciting that you're fixing up Minnie's house."

Will grinned. "After all your talk about the place, I'm kinda into it. I can see what you meant. We've sanded the cat pee smell out of the living room floor, foyer and front hall. It is a beautiful house. You were right about that."

"That's great! That was one of Stryker's reasons for taking it down."

"You stopped that."

"I did. Now I hope the old place can pay for itself."

"Me, too. West is laying out a ton of money."

"I figure he'll probably sell it."

Will took his eyes off the road for a moment to glance at his sister. "And?"

"And I'll deal with it when and if that happens."

"Maybe it won't. Maybe he'll decide to settle down in Pine Grove, marry the pretty blonde and run the joint himself."

She punched her brother in the arm.

"Ow! You're strong," he howled.

"Stop making fun. Stryker West isn't about to settle down in this rinky-dink town."

"You never know, Jess."

"And not with me."

"Why not with you?" Will raised his brows.

Exactly. Why not with me? Maybe because I'm not sophisticated, beautiful, or rich? All good reasons.

"Just drive, okay," she replied.

He steered the vehicle safely through growing puddles and into their driveway. Once inside, Jess turned on the television to watch the storm.

Chapter Fourteen

Stryker eased his seat back and closed his eyes. Taking the overnight flight on Friday meant he'd be in first thing Saturday. He didn't want to miss the dance. He promised Jess he'd be back in time, and though he had to postpone about five meetings, he was going to make it.

And he'd miss the storm. A pilot himself, Stryker had checked Friday weather conditions before making final plans to return to Pine Grove. The weatherman had predicted the squall would move out early Saturday morning, leaving clear skies for him to take his small plane to Oak Bend.

Chris would be at the airport to meet him. Everything was set. Picturing Jess in some sexy dress, smiling, happy to see him, he grinned. At first, the prospect of a dance made him laugh. Wasn't he a bit old for those things? The talk around town convinced him the dance would be one of the biggest events of the year.

He fell into an easy sleep while the plane winged its way across the ocean. Stryker had pushed thoughts about his plans to take his business to Europe out of his mind. No longer plotting out his life in advance, he now lived week-to-week.

An expert problem solver, Stryker Alexander West would overcome any obstacle that people, Fate, or the weather put in his path. He awoke refreshed and ready to enjoy the day.

As he made his way to the tarmac, he glanced up at the clouds. There were small breaks, allowing blue sky to peek through. He wondered what the conditions were in Pine Grove.

Jess had called him once or twice, but he let it go to voicemail because he had no time to talk if he'd wanted to wind up business and get back to her. She'd texted, too, and he'd ignored those, figuring she'd understand. The plane and the pilot were ready.

"Morning, Mr. West."

"Morning. Let's get started."

"Right away, sir."

Stryker boarded the plane, belted himself in, and gazed out the window. Now that he had a few minutes while the pilot got things going, he checked her texts. Ah! The dance for tonight had been postponed? So, what? He'd have time alone with her instead. He texted back that he was on his way and about to take off.

See you soon, honey.

Before long, the small aircraft taxied down the runway, then took off. Stryker never got tired of that sensation in his gut at liftoff. He peered out the window.

"We expect to touchdown in forty-five, Mr. West."

"Great. Thanks." *Just in time for breakfast at the Cozy Café.*

His thoughts were interrupted by the sound of something pelting the window. He peered out to see a curtain of rain surround the aircraft. The plane dipped and rocked.

"What's going on?"

"We just got word that there's a tail on that storm. Seems we're right in the middle of it now."

"Damn!" Stryker rose from his seat and slid into the seat next to the pilot.

"I checked the weather before we took off. There was no mention of this," the pilot said.

"Storms kick up out of nowhere in Pine Grove," Stryker said, remembering days he'd get soaked walking home from school when an unexpected storm hit.

The plane wobbled, the wings dipped and rose, as if the aircraft was a ship buffeted by giant waves. Queasiness hit his stomach, but he fought it back.

"We need to take her down," Stryker said.

"I'm looking for a place now. Control at Oak Bend is trying to find a location, too."

Sweat broke out under Stryker's arms and across his forehead. If the winds rose too high, the little airplane would be tossed around like a toothpick. He listened to the conversation between the pilot and the air traffic controller.

The pilot struggled to keep the plane level, with little success. Stryker stared at the ground.

"There's a big football field at the high school in Pine Grove," he said.

"Football field? Might be perfect."

He asked the controller for the coordinates. They waited in silence while the man pulled the figures together.

"Got it. Okay. Yeah. That looks good. You're about fifty miles away. Can you stay up that long?"

"We're sure gonna try," the pilot responded.

Stryker gripped the armrest until his knuckles turned white. Visibility had dropped. They'd be lucky to avoid trees while descending. Flying at about 120 miles per hour, they'd be at the field in twenty minutes. The bumpy ride alarmed the men, but they kept their cool.

"Do you know the foliage in that area?" the pilot asked him.

Stryker wracked his brain. "I think there's a parking lot that abuts the field. That might be as good a place to land."

"At least it's a side with no trees."

"Right."

"I see the clearing ahead," the pilot said, squinting.

"Good luck," came from the air traffic controller.

RELIEVED TO FINALLY hear from Stryker, Jess went to the Cozy Café to drop off pies. She breathed easy. Stryker was winging his way back.

"Do you have time for coffee?" Laura asked.

"Sure." Jess took her cup and sat at Stryker's favorite table. The radio was on. News interrupted the music.

"This just in. High winds and unexpected rain have taken down a small plane. The aircraft got caught in the sudden storm and went down. No information yet on survivors."

Jess froze. Could that be Stryker's plane? She picked up the phone and called. No answer. She sent a text. No reply. Panic rose her chest.

"No! No, no, no, no, no."

"What's the matter?" Laura asked.

Tears choked Jess.

"Honey? What's wrong?" the older woman approached the table.

"That was Stryker's plane. He said he was on his way here from Kennedy. That must be his plane. Oh my God!" she said, bursting into tears.

Laura hugged her. Sobs wracked her body as she couldn't deny the possible—Stryker's plane had gone down, and he'd died in the crash. Emotion rocketed through her body.

"We don't know if anyone died, Jess," Laura said.

Shaking, she let go of the older woman and sat back in the chair. "We don't."

"He could be fine."

"He could. But I doubt it. He was going to fly today to avoid the storm yesterday."

"Have faith. Let's listen to the radio."

"They don't have any news. I'm going to call Justin Barner," Jess said.

"The sheriff? Good idea."

Jess dialed.

"Howdy, Jess. What can I do for you?"

"The plane that went down. Was it Stryker's?"

"I'm not sure. I'm heading out there now. Where are you?"

"At the Cozy."

"I'll pick you up."

"Thanks." She put away her phone and stood outside. Siren blaring, Justin stopped in the lot. Jess jumped in the front seat and they took off. The police vehicle raced up the drive to the school. On the football field, tilted over on its side, the plane rested on one wing.

The ambulance siren followed. Jess threw open the door, and raced to the aircraft. With the emergency medical team right behind her, Jess put on speed she didn't know she had. Panting, gulping air, she moved faster.

Her heart rate doubled as she drew near the plane. *He's got to be alive.* As she rounded the corner, there were two men, sitting on the ground, sheltered from the rain by the wing, talking. As she approached, they looked up.

"Jess!" Stryker called, pushing slowly to his feet.

"You're hurt!" she said, rushing to his side.

"Nothing serious. A bruise or two. Twisted my ankle a little, deplaning. I'm okay."

Jess flung herself into his arms, sobbing.

"Hey, honey, it's okay. I'm all right. The pilot did a great job bringing us down."

"I thought. I thought," she said struggling for breath.

"You thought I was dead? Do I matter that much to you?" he asked, stroking her back.

She nodded. The realization struck her like a bolt of lightning. Damn, she loved Stryker West. Holy hell. This would be trouble. But her body made it completely clear that denial was fruitless.

"I'm so sorry. I didn't mean to scare you. But it's damn nice to know you care."

She raised her tear-stained face to gaze at him. "That's all you have to say?"

"Nope," he replied, pressing his lips to hers for a moment. "I care about you, too."

As the EMT's approached and Justin brought up the rear, their moment of privacy disappeared. Medics checked out Stryker and the pilot, who reported what had happened to Justin. Chris pulled up in the Bentley.

Jess stood around, waiting for her heartbeat to return to normal.

Stryker strolled over. "You still working? Can I give you a lift?"

"I left coffee at the Cozy Café."

"Perfect! I haven't had breakfast yet. Chris!"

In the car, Stryker snuggled her into his shoulder. She rested her palm and her cheek on his chest. The steady beat of his heart soothed her. Her nerves settled back to normal. His scent mixed with the smell of clean shirt and a dash of spicy aftershave.

"You smell good," she muttered.

He laughed. "Really? After that? I thought I'd sweated through this shirt twice."

"Nope."

"You're soaked. Should we get you dry clothes?"

"I'll be okay. It's warm at the Cozy."

He played with her damp hair as the car handled the twisty road with ease. When they arrived, Chris parked. While they waited for him, Stryker took Jess's face in his hands and planted a sweet kiss on her lips. When they got inside, there was a round of applause from the half-dozen patrons of the tiny shop.

"Thought you were a goner," Laura Dailey piped up.

"Nope. Not yet. I'm a pilot, too. Flew in the Air Force."

"Really?" Jess stared at him. "Who knew?"

"Who landed the plane?" Chris asked.

"The pilot. I'm not crazy," Stryker piped up.

"Yeah. What happened?" Jess asked.

"I'll heat up your coffee, Jess. Stryker, don't start without me. I gotta hear this."

Everyone in the place turned their attention to Stryker West. *Look at him. Loving having an audience.* She smiled to herself.

"Food for everyone. On me. Order whatever you like," he said.

A chorus of waffles, bacon and egg sandwich orders, and scones topped the list of popular food items. While the staff prepared the meals, Stryker launched into his tale.

"Everything was clear at Kennedy when we started out. Sure a few little clouds, but nothing to be concerned about," he began.

SINCE STRYKER WAS SUFFERING from jetlag, and a little sore from bruises and cuts, Jess returned home after breakfast. She loaded up her car and finished her deliveries. Working with the architects on the old house had eaten up any free time. The dance, scheduled for Saturday night, loomed large, and she had nothing to wear.

Jess tried to beg off, but Stryker wouldn't hear it.

"Not go? You not go to a Pine Grove event?"

"So many people don't talk to me, what's the point?"

"Bullshit. What's the real reason?"

She'd colored at his probing for the truth. No way could she admit her wardrobe didn't include a dance-worthy dress. She headed over to Pelletier and Grand for her afternoon appointment with Charlie.

"Let's talk about the study," he said.

"Oh, yes. Does the fireplace still work?" she asked.

They put their heads together for two hours, going over drawings and setting up a project for the next meeting. Charlie gave Jess a key to the place with instructions about what she was to check out before next week.

On her drive home, she passed the Thrift Shop. It was five, and Giselle Davenport, who owned the store, stood at the door, trying to place the key in the lock. Jess stopped short and backed up. She rolled down her window.

"Giselle! Got any dresses?"

"Yep. New ones yesterday."

"Can I take a look?"

"Sure."

Jess did a U-turn and parked on the street. Giselle had pocketed the key and gone inside. The bell tinkled as the door opened.

Giselle called out, "Jess?"

Forgetting her friend, who ran the place, was legally blind, Jess replied, "It's me."

"You picked the perfect day to stop by. We got new donations late yesterday. Great dresses. Some in your size, too. Come on."

Last thing Jess had money for was a new dress, even if it was second-hand.

"I'm just looking," Jess said, shuffling through the colorful garments. An ice-blue sleeveless number caught her eye.

"Try it on."

Jess shook her head. She never tried on anything she couldn't buy. Saved a lot of time that way. Unable to resist, she checked the price tag. Fifteen dollars. She figured the dress must have sold for two hundred bucks brand new. She only had three dollars in her purse. Jess sighed.

"Could we trade?" Giselle asked.

"Trade?"

"Yeah. Could you take me grocery shopping?"

"Sure. I'm picking up groceries for three ladies at The Meadow tomorrow. Can you go then?"

Giselle placed her hand on Jess's arm. "Only if you let me give you something in exchange."

"Don't be silly. I'm going anyway."

"Not doing it unless you take something."

"What did you have in mind?"

"That blue dress."

Jess's pulse jumped.

"Go. Try it on.

The garment fit like it was made for her. The bodice hugged her lus-cious curves and the full skirt, with a layer of gauzy fabric over taffeta swished provocatively when she twirled.

"Okay. It's a deal," Jess said. "Thank you." She hugged her friend. "I'll be by at ten. Does that work for you?"

"Perfect. I'll be ready," Giselle said, wrapping the dress in tissue and placing it in a bag. Jess hoped Stryker wouldn't guess the dress was sec-ond-hand. With a sigh she pushed through the door, making the bell sound. Then she broke into a grin. Nope, Stryker would only be inter-ested in how easy it would be to get the garment off her.

When she got home, she hung the dress in the closet and started on dinner. Tonight would be pasta with leftover chicken. After pulling out the ingredients, she opened a beer and turned on the radio. Humming along as she worked, Jess had the meal ready quickly.

At five thirty, Will banged through the door.

"What's for dinner?"

"Hungry?"

"I could eat an elephant," he replied.

"Ew, yuck. No elephant on the menu."

"Good. Was that Stryker's plane?"

"Yep."

"He okay?"

"Yep," Jess said, opening a beer and handing it to her brother.

"Good. Then I keep my job."

"Is that all you think about?"

"No, sometimes I think about Jennie."

"I'm glad to hear that. It was a close call."

"And if something happened to him, would you be heartbroken?"

Her eyes filled, and her chin quivered. "I'd be devastated."

"Aw, Jess," Will said, closing his fingers around her hand.

"I don't know what to do, Will," she said, her voice low. "I'm in love with him. And I know it's doomed. I mean, he's building an office in London. He has a life, a business. There's no place for me there. But I can't help myself."

Will pushed to his feet and hauled his sister into his arms for a hug. "Don't worry about it, Jess. We can't control our feelings. We love who we love. It'll be okay."

"Promise?"

"I promise. And if he hurts you, I'll punch his lights out."

SINCE STRYKER HAD A phone conference he had to attend, Jess had agreed to meet him at the dance. The event took place behind the town hall. The square had colored lights strung from a telephone pole to the building to another pole. Jory Walker, Mindy Winslow, and their spouses organized the refreshment tables while Mayor Mike and his band set up their instruments.

Jess eyed the baked goods. There were homemade chocolate chip cookies, pound cake, and more brownies and blondies than she could count. Another offered soft drinks, beer, and wine.

She'd volunteered to help and called Ida Billings, who had turned her down flat. "We don't need your kind around here," she'd said. Controlling her anger, Jess had simply hung up on her.

"Don't let that old witch bother you. She's jealous. You're young and pretty and she's an old hag with no husband and no kids." Jory had said.

The moist air clung to her skin as she made her way from the food to the drink table. A glass of merlot went well with the two brownies she snarfed down. People wandered in, crowding the tables as Mike and his buddies struck up a song. Will and Jennie arrived right behind Chip and his wife, Kathy. Jess nodded to Kathy who tossed off a stony glance.

Will and Jennie joined Jess.

"What's better, brownies or blondies?" he asked his sister.

"I'm a blondie's fan. But the brownies are great, too."

"Guess I'll have to have one of each," he replied.

"Hi, Jess, Jennie said, giving her a brief hug. The young woman had dark hair done up on the top of her head and a white eyelet dress.

"You look great, Jen. White is perfect on you."

"Thanks."

Jess had arrived early. She checked her watch wondering where Stryker was when she heard her name.

"Jess! Over here!"

There he stood, khakis, white button-down fitted shirt, navy sports jacket slung over his arm. The collar on his shirt stood open. As her gaze slid over the luscious man, her body heated. With a bright white smile and wide shoulders, he was the most handsome man at the dance. Stryker wended his way through the crowd to join her. With one arm, he swept her up against him and kissed her.

She melted. "I thought maybe you weren't coming."

"Stand you up? Never. You look beautiful." His gaze raked over her.

Jess took his hand and led him to the food. He wolfed down a brownie then popped open a bottle of beer. While the band played, he rested his palm on her shoulder and watched.

"Big crowd for this town," he commented.

"Yep. The dance draws all the cockroaches out."

"Cockroaches? There are some nice people in this town," he replied.

"And some not-so-nice, too."

"That's everywhere."

"True."

He put down his beer and took her hand, swinging her into his arms for a slow dance. She gripped his shoulders as his hands circled her waist. Leaning against his chest, she took a deep breath. He smelled awesome. Serious aftershave and his own unique scent.

"You smell good," he whispered in her ear. "New perfume?"

"Lily of the Valley."

"I like it."

In a loud voice came, "Well, well, well. Look at that. Jess Lennox is wearing my dress. Isn't that hysterical?" Anita Morrissey asked the woman next to her.

"Your dress?" her friend asked.

"Yep. I bought it ages ago. Just dropped it off at the Thrift Store a week ago. Sure didn't take her long to snap it. I'm surprised she could afford it," the woman continued.

Stryker tightened his grip. Tears of anger and humiliation stung the backs of Jess's eyes.

"Don't say anything. Ignore them," he whispered.

"I'm tryin,'" she replied,

"And she's got a rich boyfriend. He should be with you, Anita," her friend said.

That did it. Stryker dropped his hands. "You know, if you were guys, I'd take you out back and teach you some manners. Why don't you just shut up and go about your business? Jess and I are none of your concern."

"Some nerve," Anita mumbled as she beat a hasty retreat.

Jess fingered the skirt of her dress. Now, it looked shabby. She wanted to rip it off and toss it in the garbage. Gulping air, searching for control, Jess didn't hear someone clearing their voice. Giselle tapped her on the shoulder.

She spoke. "That's not her dress. She didn't donate it. She's lying."

Jess hugged her friend. "Thank you," she said, swiping at the tears that had leaked over onto her cheek.

"I don't care whose dress it was. It's yours now and you look great. Let's dance," he said, leading her to the middle of the floor.

Chapter Fifteen

They danced three more dances, but Jess's comfort level never returned.

"I think I should go home. I have stuff to do tomorrow."

"Don't go. I have a surprise. Come on." Stryker took her hand and led her to his car. He opened the door then eased behind the wheel. When he pulled into the driveway of the old house, Jess grinned. Somehow, they always ended up here.

He opened the trunk and pulled out a bottle of champagne, two flutes and a bag with other items. Then he led her to their spot beneath the tree near the pond and spread out a cotton blanket. She slipped off her sandals and plopped down. Stryker popped the cork and filled her glass. She took a healthy sip, then sat back, supported by one hand behind her and gazed up at the stars. The night was clear, and the air had cooled. It was a lovely evening.

"Thanks for speaking up for me. I'm not used to that."

"Jealous people are a pain in the ass."

She faced him. "Jealous? Of me? Really? Why? Who would be jealous of me?"

He laughed. "You're funny. You have so much going for you."

"Me?"

"Yes, you. You're beautiful. You're nice. You care about others. You're smart. Do I really have to do this?"

She smiled. "No, but it's nice to hear."

"You have a lot going for you. Oh, yeah. And you're an amazing baker."

She moved closer and cupped his cheek. "Thanks."

He turned his head and planted a kiss on her palm. Jess drew his mouth down to hers. His lips parted, and the tip of his tongue ran along her bottom lip. She opened and he plunged in. Stryker pulled her closer and closer until her breasts flattened against his pecs.

Desire awoke in her. She closed her hand over the back of his neck, her fingers crept up to touch his hair. The couple tumbled sideways, falling to the ground. He quickly repositioned her underneath him.

"I want you," he said, his voice husky.

Jess turned off her mind and let her senses rule. "Then take me," she whispered back.

While his mouth ravaged hers, his hand inched under her until his fingers reached the zipper. He eased it down, releasing the bodice. He kept going until it opened all the way. Stryker pulled up, his gaze seeking hers. She pushed both hands under the hem of his shirt and pulled it up. He unbuttoned it and shrugged it off his shoulders, tossing it aside., then ripped the undershirt over his head.

The moonlight cast his impressive chest in light and shadow, shading the muscles, making the smattering of dark hair appear darker. She ran her fingers through his soft fur, gently pressing her fingertips into his flesh. Touching him sent shivers of need down her spine.

"Cold?"

"Turned on," she replied softly.

He chuckled as he peeled her dress down to her waist. His gaze feasted on her breasts, his stare warming her skin and puckering her nipples. In response to a wave of shyness, she covered herself with her arms.

"Don't. You're beautiful. Please. Let me see," he said, easing her arms away.

Jess sucked in air and closed her eyes. His hands smoothed down her shoulders to her breasts. He bent down to kiss one, taking a hard bud into his mouth. Clutching his shoulders, she moaned at his caress.

He sucked and laved it with his tongue, sending shocks right to her groin. Heat spiraled up inside as his hands and mouth worked magic.

It had been so long, Jess had wondered if she'd ever experience love-making again. As if he knew, Stryker proceeded slowly, taking his time and being gentle. She arched her back, pushing her chest toward him, and raised one knee, her foot flat against the ground.

"Take it off," she said. "All."

"All?" he asked, raising his eyebrows.

"You heard me."

"Aye, aye, Captain," he said. Stryker pushed to his feet, unzipped his pants and dropped them and his boxers together. He shoved them to one side in a heap.

"All?" he asked, cocking an eyebrow.

"All."

He peeled off his socks. Her gaze traveled down his body. Damn, was he built. He had a faint outline of abs, slim hips, and an erection already starting. Staring at his dick, she exclaimed, "Damn. That's fine."

"Now, you," he replied, bending down and taking hold of her dress, sliding it down. She raised her hips and the blue dress disappeared, in a flash, to join his pants. She lay, squirming in white lace panties and nothing else.

"You're stunning. Now the panties."

As she rose to her knees, she grinned, taking her time easing them down. Stopping when they were at her knees, she leaned forward and took him into her mouth.

"Holy hell!"

She tried to stifle a laugh but couldn't. He grew rock solid within a few seconds. As quickly as she'd taken him, he stepped back.

"No, no. Don't. I'm only human," he said. "Now off with those panties."

Standing up, she dropped them, kicking them to the side. Stark naked, they faced each other. Her body burned for him.

"You're gorgeous," he muttered, his gaze traveling her length before stopping at the juncture of her thighs. She'd trimmed her pubic hair back to a neat landing strip. Stryker moved up against her, his hand squeezing between her thighs and up to her core. His fingers explored.

"You're wet."

"Yeah. I know."

He laughed.

"Okay. I'm easy. For the right guy."

"Nothing easy about you, babe. Not a damn thing."

"Oh, yeah?"

"Yeah. And I love that."

"You do?"

"Shh. Don't talk." His mouth captured hers again while his fingers stroked and circled. Need spiraled up inside her. She slid her palms up and down his chest, marveling at the delicious feel of his muscle and skin.

He slipped one finger, then another inside her, and she thought she'd lose her mind.

"Oh, God. Stryker. You're killing me!"

"Am I hurting you?" he asked, abruptly removing his hand.

"No, no! Don't stop, oh, please, don't stop," she said, grabbing his hand and urging it back where it was.

He bent down to kiss her neck. His tongue darted out to taste her skin. His fingers filled her, bringing her heat level to unbearable.

"Can a person die from sexual frustration?" she whispered.

He laughed. "Okay, okay. So impatient."

"I want you so bad."

He fished through his pants pockets, extracting his wallet. There he found a condom.

"But not without a taste first," he said, parting her legs and lowering his mouth to her hot flesh. As his tongue zipped along her slit, she thought she'd die. But she didn't stop him. The sensations flying through her body created an exquisite hunger, pulsating through down to her center.

"Stryker," she started.

"Okay, okay. I get the message," he said, unrolling the latex over his hard shaft.

He mounted her, manning his dick, rubbing it along her pussy before stopping at her entrance. With a quick thrust of his hips, he was inside her. She let out a small scream. Jesus, had it been that long? Could a hymen grow back?

"You're not a virgin, are you?" he asked, his voice filled with wonder.

Now it was her turn to laugh. "Hell no. It's just been a long time."

"I'd say. Man are you tight. It's amazing," he said, pulling out slightly and pushing in again.

"Oh, hell, that's good. Damn, good," she said as her eyes drifted shut.

Stryker's hips hit a steady beat, then slowly increased in speed. He repositioned her foot, hooking it over his shoulder and loomed over her. Reaching around his chest, she gripped his back, digging in slightly with her nails until she heard his groan.

She emitted a low chuckle.

"Like that?" she whispered.

"Hell yeah."

With her leg pulled up, Stryker buried himself balls deep. She moaned as he thrust into her. His lips made contact with hers. Then his tongue sought hers and they were connected on every level. Something about his closeness, the heat of their passion, swelled her heart. A sensation of peace, of protection, seeped into her. Every nerve in Jess's body jumped to life as he pumped into her. Passion hit a crescendo, as an orgasm burst into flame inside her. Her hips bucked then matched his rhythm. She called out his name as pleasure shot out to every part of her body—all the way to her fingers and toes.

"Oh my God," she moaned.

Cracking open her eyes, she spied his big grin. She chuckled to see how pleased he was that he made her come so fast. Keeping her gaze on him, she noticed a flush steal up his neck as his eyes became slits. *Looks like he'll be over the top soon, too.*

"God damn. You're so fuckin' sexy. I'm gonna blow," he said bending his forehead to hers.

"Do it."

As he moved faster and harder, tension built inside Jess. Unexpectedly, a second orgasm gathered speed. Faster and harder, faster and harder, he thrust until she thought she'd lose her mind. Suddenly, the orgasm reached the pinnacle and blew like a rocket at takeoff. Her hips went to automatic pilot as she worked him.

A loud groan from Stryker, then a hiss that sounded like her name indicated he'd found his release, too. He dropped his sweaty forehead to rest on her chest, kissed each breast, then her lips. Pushing up on his arms, he grinned. Jess ran her hand over his warm skin and through the perspiration glistening on his chest.

"Wow," he said, peering down at her.

"Yeah," she replied, raising her gaze to meet his.

The moon shone on half of his face. She searched for his reaction, emotion, but couldn't find any in the dim light. Was this just sex for him or something more?

"You're amazing," he muttered, once again placing his mouth on her chest.

"So are you. I'm like, I feel, so..." she started then stopped.

Stryker pulled out and sat back on his haunches. "Continue," he said.

"I can't. Words fail me."

He laughed. Stryker cupped her cheek and spoke softly. "You're even more beautiful when you've been loved."

"Am I?"

"Definitely."

Questions rose in her mind. She blurted out, "Why me? I mean, you could have any woman in the world. Why me? I'm not rich, or brilliant, or a model or movie star, or even beautiful. I'm just a small-town girl, scratching to get along."

"You're so many things. It's a shame, Jess, that you don't even know how wonderful you are. That's right, you're not the cookie-cutter girl, not central casting's version of the right girl for the rich guy. I love that about you. You're real. No phoniness, you're you—Jess being Jess. You speak your mind, don't pull any punches, and you're a survivor. Your life's been hard. I get that."

"Admiration is one thing, but, well, sex is another."

"Being a survivor makes you sexy as hell in my book. I'm a survivor, too. We have more in common than you know. I may not be as stubborn as you, but I come close."

She laughed. "I agree with that."

"You're a diamond in the rough. A four-leaf clover in a field of grass. And even more special because you don't know how special you are."

Love coursed through her, rising in her throat, making it to her mouth, but she tamped it down. No way was she going to confess to loving him first.

STRYKER STOPPED TALKING. Love circulated through him, knocking him for a loop. He couldn't be in love. There was no place for love in his life, but he'd never felt like this before. After making love to a woman, he'd often wished they'd stop talking and maybe even get dressed and leave. But not this time. He listened with rapt attention to Jess, weighing her every word.

As his arms tired, he rolled over and stretched out next to her. With one hand he raised her neck and slipped his arm around her shoulders, pulling her nakedness up against his skin. God, she felt good in his arms. All he could think about was how happy he was and when would he get another opportunity to make love to her? If it wasn't in the next five minutes, it wouldn't be soon enough.

He stroked her hair. "You came twice?"

"Uh huh. A first for me."

His chest puffed out a bit and a grin stretched his lips.

"Are you preening, like a proud rooster?" she asked.

"If the shoe fits…"

She laughed. "You're something else."

"I am when I'm with you," he said, his smile melting, his fingers combing through her locks.

Jess snuggled down, rested her cheek on his pecs, and snaked her arm around his waist. As he pushed unwelcome questions from his mind, a sense of peace washed over him. In a moment, Jess's breathing evened out. Glancing down, he saw her eyes closed. Asleep. Damn. He reached over to the spare blanket and pulled it around them. There'd be plenty of time to sort everything out in the morning.

Now, he had the opportunity of a lifetime, to sleep in the comfort of his lover's arms. He couldn't remember when that had happened last, if ever. He shut off his mind and listened to her breathing. In a cocoon of warmth, he let go, allowing sleep to overtake him.

Something sniffing at his hair woke up Stryker. He opened his eyes to stare straight into those of a fluffy, fat skunk. Clapping his hand over his mouth so not to holler and alert the animal, Stryker's eyes widened. The skunk waddled off before Jess stirred.

He lay back, wiping the sweat off his forehead. *A close call.* The air had grown nippy. Perhaps being outside in the middle of the night, naked, had something to do with his shivering. Or was it the sexy young woman tucked up close to his side?

Stryker turned his head, watching as the skunk went on his nightly forage for food. When the critter was at least two hundred feet away, Stryker nudged Jess's shoulder.

"Wake up, hon. Time to go."

"Huh? Wha?" she asked, yawning.

"Yeah. A skunk just checked us out. I think it's safer if we leave. Besides, it's cold." He eased out of the blanket, leaving her still cocooned, and dressed quickly.

"Oh, do we have to? I'm so comfortable," she sighed.

"Come on, babe. I'll help you," he said, offering his hand.

The minute she threw the blanket off, she protested. "Damn! Why's it so cold in summer?

He handed her the blue dress.

"Where are we going?"

"To my house. We can spend the rest of the night in a real bed."

She pulled on her panties and turned for him to zip her up. In the car, Stryker blasted the heat until they had to open the windows to cool down. They were the only car on the road.

"What time is it?" she asked.

He glanced at the clock on the dashboard. "It's three."

"I have to be up in two hours."

"But it's Sunday. Do you work on Sunday?"

"Sure do. Lots of people eat out on Sunday. They'll be expecting my pies."

"Maybe we should go to your house then?"

"Okay. Just don't expect anything fancy. It's clean but kinda run down."

"I don't care."

He parked in the driveway and entered quietly. Jess turned on the lights in the kitchen.

"Maybe I should put on coffee. No sense going to sleep just to get up in two hours, right?"

"Makes sense."

"How do you take yours?"

"My what?"

"Coffee?"

"Oh, yeah. Milk, no sugar," he said, grinning.

"I figured that."

Jess turned on the coffeemaker. "I have some pie left. Coconut cream or chocolate cream?"

"You made extras?"

"Sometimes a pie doesn't turn out right. Can't sell it, so we eat it."

"Can I have a piece of each?"

"You sure can."

After piling two generous pieces on a small plate, Jess poured his coffee and set it down in front of him.

"Doesn't look like anything's wrong with these.'

"Trust me. They got messed up. Sometimes I make a mistake and the pie crust isn't even or the filling is off kilter."

He took a bite and closed his eyes. "Fantastic."

WHILE STRYKER CHOWED down on pie and coffee, Jess got the ingredients for pie filling from the fridge. There were still fresh raspberries on the market, so she had enough to make a pie. The chocolate chiffon was always a winner, and two clients had requested coconut cream.

When Jess sensed his gaze following her, she smiled. She'd been doing this for so long, she could do it in her sleep. Gently mixing the berries with sugar, she lifted a spoonful to taste, then offered one to him.

"Perfect," he said.

"Agreed."

As she continued, he spoke up. "I have a meeting with Charlie Grand tomorrow. I guess that's today. He suggested I bring you. Can you come?"

"Do you want me there?"

"Of course, or I wouldn't have asked."

"What time?"

"Two."

"Perfect."

He pushed to his feet. Yawning, he stretched his arms above his head. Jess eased two pies into the oven, then stepped back. From behind, he wound his arms around her and bent his head to kiss her neck.

"Last night was awesome."

She leaned back against him and closed her eyes. "Uh huh."

"It's four. We should get some sleep."

"I might as well get my baking done now. I'll crash later."

"Will you come over and crash with me?"

"If you want."

"I do."

"I can be there at nine," she said.

"Good. Should I have coffee ready or will you want to go right to sleep?"

"Coffee would be nice."

"Done."

He released her. She faced him and raised her chin. Stryker kissed her slow and gentle.

"Don't want to get you too riled up since you have to work."

"I'm already running on adrenaline. Probably will 'til nine, when I'll crash."

"See you at nine?" he asked.

"Yep."

Jess walked with him to the door and stood on the front steps, watching him drive away. She waved, and he returned it. Leaning against the doorframe, she sighed. Cinderella had nothing on her. A timer chimed, drawing her back to reality. She returned to the kitchen and back to work. But her mind wasn't there. She relived every moment on the blanket with Stryker.

What an amazing lover. The cold, distant demeanor had melted away, revealing the tender, passionate man underneath. Everything he'd done had been for her pleasure. Well, almost everything. He'd treated her like a princess, or maybe a queen. As a lover, he'd set the bar so high, no other man could reach it.

Stryker Alexander West, mogul, billionaire, driven, ambitious businessman made love like the hero of a romance book. She laughed. Who would have thought that loving and considerate would be words she'd use to describe him in the sack?

Greed rose in her. She wanted more. All she had to do was hold it together until nine, then they'd have their reprise, round two, encore. Whatever it was called, it would be amazing. Her body tingled at the thought. Her fingertips were sensitized to the point where she had to use two potholders to keep from getting burned. Oh, yes, she'd run them up and down his body until he couldn't take anymore.

A feeling of warmth surrounded her, keeping a smile on her face as she toiled away, mixing fillings, baking pies, and rolling out dough to make and freeze shells for tomorrow. A lightness she'd never experienced before enabled her to bustle around expending little energy.

And the meeting. Stryker actually asked her to attend the meeting with Charlie Grand. She caught her breath. She couldn't believe he wanted to know what she was doing. Jess figured it was simply a ploy to give her some money, charity. Never in a million years would it occur to her that he or Charlie might listen to her ideas. But Charlie had. And now Stryker.

Will had argued with her that billionaires didn't hire people out of charity. That they were billionaires because they didn't waste money.

They spent it wisely. Or so her brother had said. Perhaps she'd have to agree with him. It all depended on how the meeting went.

Jess made the last delivery to Java the Hut. She turned the ignition on her ancient vehicle and headed for Stryker's house, praying the car wouldn't stall. When she knocked, a male voice called out, "Come in!"

She opened the door and entered a tidy living room. Though bigger than hers, she guessed it was probably much smaller than Stryker was used to.

"In the kitchen, Jess. And, if you're a burglar, I left my wallet on the coffee table. Take the money and leave. I'm expecting my girl."

She cracked up as she stopped to lounge against the kitchen door-frame.

"You're hilarious."

"Glad you appreciate that fact."

"I'm not serious."

He frowned. "I thought you liked my humor. Oh, well. Can't win 'em all." Striding over, he took her in his arms for a passionate kiss.

"Coffee or right upstairs?"

She yawned. "Guess I'm feeling kinda sleepy."

"Oh, I see. Yes. I am, too." He faked a yawn. "Why don't we go up-stairs?"

"Good idea," she said, grinning.

Following him to the stairs, goose flesh traveled up her arms as she watched his cute butt. Certain body parts tingled in anticipation. He turned, scooped her into his arms, and eased the door shut with his foot.

Chapter Sixteen

Rolling over, Jess cracked an eyelid. The clock read noon. Pleasure still flowed in her veins. Stryker had been a master lover, and she purred inside. Stretching her legs, she inched closer to his sleeping form. The warmth from him enveloped her. Snuggling closer, she disturbed him. He grunted.

"Time?" he asked.

"No."

"Hmm?" he muttered, pulling her closer.

Afraid to ask for what she wanted, Jess lay there, debating with herself.

"Hold me?" she asked, her voice barely a whisper.

"Hmm?"

"Please. Just hold me?"

He gave a lopsided grin and snaked his arms around her, drawing her head to his shoulder. She rested against him, her palm flattened on his chest. "My pleasure," he said, closing his eyes.

With his tight grip on her, Jess relaxed. Her muscles calmed, and her breathing evened out. Next to great sex, being held rang her chimes. In his arms, nothing bad could happen. He'd protect her, keep harm away, chase away bad people, and scary thoughts. Having been on her own for so long, with no support system, she hungered for safety. To let down her guard, give the reins to someone else, and be protected meant everything to Jess.

Taking a deep breath, she recognized his scent. Her fingertips lightly touched his chest. Heat transferred from his skin to hers. She pushed out the worry that this might not be forever and enjoyed it for now. Stryker Alexander West owned a huge business. He had responsibilities, money, meetings to take, employees to check on. He couldn't be spending his life following her around like a puppy. She accepted that his life would keep them apart, perhaps permanently. But for now, he wanted her, and she felt the same. Jess would enjoy time with him for as long as it lasted.

She rolled to her side. Stryker followed, spooning her, his knees up behind hers. He eased his arm over her middle and rested his hand on her breast. His breath ruffled her hair as he held her fast to his chest while his chin rested on the top of her head. Jess sighed. For the first time, she knew complete happiness.

The lovers arose by two and spent Sunday together. They grabbed a bite at Java the Hut, then strolled around the lake, hand-in-hand. They dined in Oak Bend at a romantic, new restaurant with candlelight and wine. The day ended with lovemaking and spending the night together.

Monday morning, Jess awoke at four. Stryker rose with her. He'd programmed the coffeemaker to start at 3:45a.m., so hot coffee awaited them. As he pulled down the covers, he shook his head.

"This is barbaric. And you do this every morning?"

"Yep. The first pie delivery is at seven."

"Doesn't give you much time."

"It's enough. If I'm a few minutes late, it's not a problem. I have the crusts ready in the freezer."

"And this pays the rent?"

"It does," she replied.

"You're amazing. This is a hard job."

"No harder than what you do. I bet you work 'til all hours at night, take long flights, and go right to work after you land. Stuff like that. That's harder, if you ask me."

"You have a point. But it starts at a civilized hour."

"That's your opinion. I love the morning. Watching the sun rise is wonderful."

"I've never risen with the sun before. I bet it's beautiful. Maybe I saw the sun after staying up all night a few times," he said, chuckling. "But those were drunken college days."

"It's awesome. Like nothing else. And I get to see it all the time. One of the benefits of the job." She poured out two mugs and handed one to Stryker.

"Thanks," he said, adding milk.

He took a sip and reached for Jess. His hand on her neck, he eased her into his embrace and kissed the top of her head. She clung to him, her breasts soft against his pecs. Hiding her face in his neck, Jess smiled. She could get used to this.

"You're amazing, you know that?" he said.

"I'm a survivor."

"Absolutely. And sexy as hell."

She laughed. "Really? Being a poor pie baker is sexy? Who would've thought?"

"We should get dressed. Or go back to bed?"

"I have to take care of the pies. Can I meet you at Charlie's?"

He nodded. "That's fine."

"Not that I wouldn't like an encore, but we had a few of those last night."

He laughed. "More curtain calls than a Tony-winning performance."

"You were amazing," she said, tightening her grip, kissing his chest, then letting go. The loss of the warmth of his body as she moved away reminded her that she had things to do. But, damn, all she wanted was to crawl back into bed with him. The sex had been awe-inspiring, completely over-the-top. He had dazzled her.

They finished their coffee, then she dressed while he watched.

"You going back to bed?" she asked.

"Yeah. But it won't be the same without you."

Jess laughed as she slipped on her shoes. After fishing her car keys from her purse, she headed for the door.

"Wait," he said, circling her waist. She stopped. He kissed her once more. Jess took a step back and cupped his cheek.

"Sometimes, you're just the sweetest man," she said, before disappearing through the door and down the steps.

JUST SOMETIMES? He grinned. That he could be the biggest son-of-a-bitch was well known. What billionaire wasn't a *my-way-or-the-highway* kind of guy? Nope, he didn't get where he was by being nice, or sweet, or whatever.

He fell back into bed and slept until seven. When he awoke, he remembered their parting. Stryker had wanted to tighten his grip, as if holding her would keep her there forever. But he didn't want forever, did he? He sighed. So much work lay ahead of him. The expansion of his private airplane service teetered before him. There was much to be done, and here he was, bemoaning leaving this young woman, spending his time in bed rather than on a plane back to London. What was happening to Stryker Alexander West?

He returned to his room to dress. By the time he got downstairs, Chris was in the kitchen finishing off the coffee.

"Have fun last night?" he asked, all innocent.

"As if you weren't listening with a glass to the wall," Stryker snickered.

Chris chuckled. "Hadn't thought of that. But it wouldn't have been necessary."

"Oh?" Stryker raised an eyebrow.

"When the house stopped shaking, I assumed you went to sleep."

Stryker burst out laughing. "Good guess."

"Way to go, boss."

"Thanks. Let's get breakfast at the Cozy before the meeting."

"Give me five to dress."

"Meet you at the car."

Stryker strolled outside. Turning to face the sun, he regretted that it was too late to see it rise. What would it be like to watch the sun rise every morning with Jess Lennox? Maybe tomorrow, he'd check it out. Oh, wait, no, not tomorrow. Tomorrow morning, he'd be on a plane to London, whether he wanted to or not.

He checked his phone. There were sixteen messages. He listened to his voicemail and returned texts while he waited for Chris. Falling for Jess would simply put a big roadblock on his schedule. He'd be mooning over and thinking about her instead of figuring the next strategy to opening another airport and placing orders for new planes.

The idea of sending a dozen roses, no two dozen—why not three?—to Jess crossed his mind. What was becoming of him? A softie, that's what. A lovesick schoolboy who didn't know one end from the other. In college, they had a much cruder term for what had happened to him. Forget it. So he cared for her, so what? Wasn't he entitled to a life, too? Was every waking moment taken up with how to make more money?

Aunt Minnie would say, "When is it enough, Stryker?" And she'd be right. He texted Chris to send the flowers. He promised himself, as soon as he wound up the European airports, he'd stop and take a breather. And maybe carve out a good life for himself, with a wonderful woman. But for now, there were decisions to make, plans to create, and permits to obtain.

"Ready," Chris said, tucking in his shirt as he moved toward the door.

They climbed in the car. Stryker thumbed through the papers in his briefcase, pulling out a few to review over breakfast.

"I have to get back to work, Chris."

"Everyone deserves a vacation."

"There's a vacation and there's stupidly letting my business slide because I'm, I'm—well, you know."

"I do. It's great. Nice to see you having fun for a change."

"Fun? A mind-blowing balance sheet is fun."

"There are other kinds, too, sir."

"I suppose. The right woman can make a difference."

"Yep," Chris said, as he turned into the parking lot at The Cozy Café.

"Of course, the jury is out. I mean, there are no decisions. Jess is great, but, well, we'll see."

"Don't rush into anything, sir. You might find happiness."

Stryker laughed.

JESS DONNED A NAVY-blue skirt and a white blouse. Looking professional for this meeting with the architect and Stryker mattered. Her nerves hit high alert. After serving Will breakfast, she paced. She'd have to hold her own with these knowledgeable men. Could she?

"Kick fuckin' butt, Jess," Will said, snarfing down a piece of coconut pie.

"It's not that kind of meeting."

"Then what is it?"

"It's to bring Stryker up-to-date on what Charlie's doing in the house."

"So? What's eating you?"

"Nothing. It's just that many of the ideas he's doing are mine. I hope Stryker agrees."

"Of course, he'll agree. He wants to sleep with you."

She snorted. "Will! This is business."

"And so is that. Between-the-sheets business. Don't think for a minute he's going to put you down and then try to make it with you."

"Sometimes you can be so crude."

"Only sometimes?" he asked, cocking an eyebrow. "I'm slipping."

"You don't understand," she said, putting her coffee mug in the sink.

Will closed his fingers around her elbow. "Listen, Jess. I damn well do understand. These assholes have got nothing on you. You're smart. You're a hard worker. And you know everything there is to know about that house."

"Not exactly."

"Enough. And how to use it. You've been in the food business for years. You're not some little kid. Don't let them intimidate you. Hold your ground. Stand up for yourself. They will benefit from what you have to say. Remember that."

"Thanks, Will," Jess said, planting a quick kiss on his cheek. "You're the best."

As she drove to Charlie's she pondered Will's words. He was right. She did have a lot to offer in this situation. Stryker wouldn't have hired her, right? If it was only charity, he would have given her a check and been done with it.

She parked and walked to the door. Stryker's car was there. He'd arrived early. Jess paused for a deep breath before pushing through the office door.

"Morning, Jess," Charlie called out. "Coffee?"

"No, thanks. I've had a ton."

"Hi," Stryker said, keeping his distance.

She caught herself in time, stopping before approaching him for a kiss. According to the expression on his face, Stryker Alexander West was all business. This was a business meeting—kissing was out.

"Take a seat at the conference table, I'll lay out the drawings," Charlie said.

Jess made a point of sitting across from Stryker. She didn't trust herself not to reach for his hand or his knee under the table.

"I've let Jess take the lead on how the house should be set up, Stryker. She seems to have a sixth sense about how people would move around and which rooms you need. We've got the living room, dining room, and kitchen. The extra room in the front has been earmarked as a library or den, with the fireplace uncovered and to be used for reading or writing. Will is constructing floor-to-ceiling bookcases."

Jess sat back and let Charlie do the talking. Stryker nodded from time to time or asked a question. Otherwise, it was Charlie's show.

"I'm afraid I have bad news," Charlie said, sitting forward.

"Oh?" Stryker raised his eyebrows.

"Yes. There's no way we can have the Inn up and running by Thanksgiving. Christmas will be a stretch, but we can do it. We tried every configuration, even hiring twice the men, but it wouldn't help. Some things have to be done in a certain order. I'm sorry." Charlie rolled up the plans.

"Wait! Wait." Jess stood up. She took a breath before continuing. "Maybe we can't open the Inn for guests to stay overnight. But we could have a Thanksgiving dinner there. Open just for that. Like a restaurant."

"Will the kitchen be ready?" Stryker asked.

"Oh, the kitchen will be finished by the end of next week. That was the easiest room. We did it first," Charlie said.

"Dining room?" Stryker asked.

"It will be okay. Not totally furnished maybe. We're looking for the right sideboard now."

"But the table and chairs are there," Jess put in.

"We have the light fixture. It can be connected in time," Charlie added.

"And the living room?"

"Again, we need more furniture, but we have enough now to accommodate a dozen people. And the fireplace has been cleaned, chimney, too. We'll test it first, but I think it'll be fine."

"If we can get the permits," Stryker said.

"If we don't serve liquor, we won't need a liquor license by then," Charlie said.

"We can try for one, and if it doesn't come through in time, take alcohol off the menu," Stryker said.

"Then why not? We could get some publicity from the local paper, maybe even take out a small ad. I bet we could get a dozen people there," Jess said.

"Do you have the equipment?" Stryker asked.

"Uh, no. But that's just a couple of shopping trips, right? I mean dishes, pots and pans, and silverware and stuff. Easy to find," Jess said.

"It has to be the right dishes, to go with the theme of the Inn," Stryker pointed out.

"Of course. Of course. With a historical flavor. Yep. I'm sure I can find everything we need."

"Then I see no reason not to go ahead. Charlie?"

"We'll put in for the permits this afternoon. Good idea, Jess," Charlie said.

"It's almost like a trial run. That gives us time to work out any bugs before Christmas. I expect the Inn to be filled to capacity at Christmas and New Year's, too. We'll need a plan for that," Stryker said.

"We're on it," Charlie replied.

"Oh, wait! The cook?" Stryker asked, staring at Jess.

Charlie turned his gaze on her, too.

"Me? You want little ole me to do the cooking?"

"Why not? You're already a baker. You'll have dessert covered," Stryker replied, a smile on his face.

"Come on, Jess. Who else could do this?" Charlie asked.

"Okay. Sure. Why not? I've got this." Her heart rated doubled.

"Good job. I like where this is going. It should be a real money maker once it's finished," Stryker said, pushing to his feet. He glanced at his watch. "I've got to run. I'm flying to London tomorrow morning."

"What?" Jess didn't believe her ears.

"I'm flying to London. There's much I need to do regarding my European expansion. I can't put it off any longer. Besides, you and Charlie are doing great. You don't need me."

Jess swallowed. "I didn't know."

"You didn't think I could stay here indefinitely, did you?"

"Well, I..." she started but her voice trailed off. That's exactly what she thought. A billionaire doesn't need to work. He can simply manage his money from his computer, can't he?

"Excuse me. I want to get my assistant working on those permits," Charlie said and left the room.

Stryker moved toward the door and Jess followed. Once they got outside, and away from the others, she spoke her mind.

"You're leaving? Why didn't you tell me you were leaving?"

"I thought you knew."

"How, by osmosis? she asked, hands on hips.

STRYKER DIDN'T LIKE the expression on Jess's face. While she appeared angry, her eyes gave her away. He saw hurt mixed with anger and betrayal as she glared at him.

"Look, Jess—" he began.

"Don't give me that 'look Jess' bullshit. You knew you were leaving, and you slept with me anyway. Just wanted to grab a little nookie before leaving?"

"It wasn't like that, and there was nothing little about that nookie."

"A fuck-and-run guy. My, my. Who would have thought? Not me. Stupid, naïve little me."

"It's not like that!" he hollered, grabbing her wrist as she turned away from him.

How could he say he was taking off while he still owned his heart? Where were the words to tell her how incredibly special she was, but he traveled alone? Sure, he was running away, and cowards never admit to cowardice, do they?

"Jess. You're an amazing woman. Incredible. But I have other obligations, responsibilities. Just because I have money doesn't mean I can sit around staring into space all day. There's so much riding on me—people's jobs, benefits. I can't just stop working. Even if I wanted to. Or should I say, when I want to."

"Blah, blah, blah. It's a lot of hot air. All I know is that you're leaving, and you probably won't be back. And I spread my legs for you for nothing."

"Don't say that. It wasn't like that. Not with you. It couldn't ever be like that with you." His voice softened, his heart thudded.

"You saying you're coming back?"

"Of course." Sure, he'd stay away forever if he could. That wasn't going to work. Leaving her would be the hardest thing he'd done in years. But he had to. He had responsibilities. And he needed to know if what they had was real.

"I'll believe it when I see it. Like I'll ever see you again—no." Her voice cracked, and her eyes filled suddenly, like a dam had burst.

"You will, you will. I promise." Pain shot through his heart. He'd wounded her, unintentionally.

"Sure, sure. Keep telling yourself that. And maybe, eventually, you'll believe it. Goodbye Daddy Warbucks." With that, she turned on her heel and ran to her car.

Stryker stood there, helpless. As the woman he loved left him, he searched for words that wouldn't come. What could he say? That he loved her, and he'd be back because he couldn't stay away? Stryker wasn't ready to reveal the truth. And maybe he never would.

As her car stalled, an idea struck him. He strode over and tapped on the window. She cranked up the engine again, but it died. He knocked again. But she ignored him and turn the key in the ignition.

"Jess! Open the window!"

She turned a tear-stained face to him and rolled down the window. "What?" Anger flash from her eyes.

"Thanksgiving. I'll try to make it back for Thanksgiving."

"That's two months away."

"If I can come back sooner, I will. But definitely for Thanksgiving. Save me a seat at the table, will you?"

"Okay. Two months," she said, shaking her head.

"Oh, and don't fall in love with anyone, okay?"

She raised her gaze to his. "Why not? What should I wait for?"

"Please. Jess. We have something amazing. Please give me time."

"Time," she snorted. "It's all I have to give."

"You have a heart to give."

"Yeah? Well, don't count on it being yours. Go do whatever. I'll be taking care of business here. There's a lot to do to get the house ready."

"And you're just the woman to handle it."

"Yeah. Right. I work cheap."

"There's nothing cheap about you, Jess Lennox."

She bowed her head and wiped her eyes. "Thanks," came out as a whisper.

He cupped her cheek and leaned in for a kiss. Words of love stuck in his throat.

"Promise me," he whispered.

She met his gaze. "No. If Prince Charming rides into Pine Grove, I'll be first in line."

"Let me be your Prince Charming."

"You're leaving for months. The prince would never do that."

"Promise me," he repeated.

"Promise me you'll be back," she replied, turning the key in the ignition. The engine hummed.

"I promise you I'll be back. Now you."

"Nope. I never make promises I can't keep. If someone else comes along, then that's life. Have a safe trip." With that, she threw the car in gear and roared out of the small parking lot.

Stryker sighed. His only hope was that Pine Grove was too small to attract men worthy of Jess. And maybe he'd have to wrap up business sooner than he'd planned. His heart squeezed. Had he made the biggest mistake of his life? Would he regret not staying? Would he lose Jess? A shiver stole through him as he walked to his car.

Sometimes the hardest decisions have nothing to do with dollars and cents.

Chapter Seventeen

Jess moped around the house for two days, until Will took over.

"What the hell are you doing?" her brother asked.

"What?"

"Your deliveries were late today. Two hours late."

"So? Nobody's going to die from pie withdrawal."

"Jess, you've been like a ragdoll. You can't let this guy get to you."

"Too late."

"Are you in love with him?"

"How can I be in love with a guy who takes off for two months?"

"Are you?" Will persisted.

She sank down on a kitchen chair. "Yeah. I am."

"I thought you hated him?"

"I thought so, too. He's really a nice man. He's had a tough time."

"You mean deciding where to spend his billions?"

"He has," she said, touching Will's arm. "Honest. And yet he's compassionate. Caring. Though he hides that well."

"You can say that again," he said, filling the coffee pot.

"You have to get back on track. Charlie's left two messages on your phone."

"You're checking my phone now?"

"Yeah. When it rings and rings and you don't pick up. He's gonna get on my case. Are you supposed to do something?"

"I'm supposed to buy all the kitchen stuff and plates and silverware, like from that era. You know when the house was built."

"Isn't that gonna take a lot of work?"

"Hey, it's only September. I have until Thanksgiving."

"Charlie told me about getting the house ready for the holiday. He said you're gonna cook."

"I stepped into that one, didn't I?"

"Why not?"

"Maybe because I've never cooked a turkey. Never made a traditional Thanksgiving dinner. I don't have a clue and don't know where to start."

"Then why did you agree to do it?"

"The two of them stared at me. What could I say?"

"How about *no*?"

"Don't be an ass. I didn't want to disappoint Stryker. And he's going to be there for the meal, too. He promised. I'm doomed."

"Call your friends." He shoved the last forkful of pie in his mouth.

"What friends?"

"Mindy, Jory, Giselle?"

"Oh, yeah. I could do that."

"Good. I've got to go. Bookcases aren't going to build themselves."

"Will the dining room and living room be ready by Thanksgiving?"

"Yeah. I think you need to order some furniture, too."

"Probably."

"Come by tomorrow. Charlie's going to be there, and we can figure out what to do next. Stop moping. Stryker'll be back. He wants you. And he's not the type of guy to let go of what he wants."

"I hope so."

Will ruffled her hair, then headed for his truck. Jess poured another cup of coffee. She needed help. Maybe if she immersed herself in getting the house ready, she'd forget about Stryker not being around. She sighed. At least she could try.

After adding milk and sugar, Jess picked up her phone.

"Giselle? I have a favor to ask."

At six, Jess packed up her pie and climbed behind the wheel of her rust bucket. Jess's friends sat around Giselle's kitchen table.

"I come bearing chocolate chiffon pie and asking for help."

"What do you need help with?" Jory asked, taking a forkful of the luscious dessert.

"I need to equip the kitchen at the Inn. And buy dishes and silverware."

"Cool! Who's paying?" Jory asked.

"Charlie gave me a credit card. I'm guessing Stryker is paying."

"I love shopping with someone else's credit card," Giselle said with a laugh.

"But I have to find things that go with the period the house was built. I think it goes back to 1850. Someone from the South built it. That explains the columns. Charlie did the research on the place. It's been in Stryker's family for a long time."

"I love historical stuff. We can search for that stuff on the computer. We'll get pictures of dishes, too."

"That would be good since I don't have a clue," Jess confessed, digging into her slice of pie.

When they finished, the women commandeered Giselle's computer with a large screen and searched through sites, showing plates and silver from the era.

"Lenox is showing up," Giselle said "Different spelling, but same name as you, Jess."

"That's weird, isn't it?" Jess asked.

Jory laughed. "Might be perfect. Lenox for Lennox."

"Says they didn't start selling china until 1889, though," Jess remarked.

"Maybe that's close enough?" Jory asked.

"Crap! Look. Two hundred bucks a place setting. That's out," Jess said.

"Federal platinum is only a hundred bucks per setting," Giselle said.

"Still too much. People break plates. And, if they're that expensive, they might steal them. We need to look for Lenox knockoffs."

The women searched until they found a much cheaper china design that resembled the early American ones. Then they zeroed in on flatware. Again, there were stainless steel versions similar to the ones from the 1850s.

"Next problem," Giselle said, hitting print.

"Do either of you know how to cook a Thanksgiving turkey?"

THE ROYAL SUITE, CLARIDGE'S, London, England

Stryker stood in the living room, at a bank of three windows, and looked out over London. John, his righthand man, paced.

"It's your fault, really," he began.

"My fault? How do you figure this mess is my fault?" Stryker asked, turning to face him.

"You're off screwing some piece of ass in that shitty little town when you should be here. Attending to things. Putting out fires."

"Watch the way you speak about Jess. And that's what I have you for. To put out fires."

"I suppose for handling the problems with construction—drunken workers, people stealing things, fine. But when the French minister wants a bribe to give you permission to fly—that requires you. And in Germany, they refuse to allow an American company to ferry passengers around Europe."

"How can I fix Germany?"

"I don't know. Maybe it has something to do with our government. Anyway, Germany's pissed. So you can cross them off your list of destinations."

"How can we have an air taxi service that doesn't land in Germany?" Stryker's voice rose.

"And you can pay off the Frenchman who thinks you have too much money and wants to share in the wealth."

"What does he want?"

"I'd say a million would do it," John said, stopping to plop down on the sofa.

"A million? Bullshit! I don't pay bribes."

"He's calling it a fee. But I'll wager the check would be made out to him, personally."

"He can stuff it. Is he the only one who can give us the permit?"

"I'm afraid so. I have Sofia looking into it, but she's had no luck finding anyone to go against him. Italy and Spain are pissed at the U.S., so permits there will be hard to come by."

"Shit! We're building this office in London, and I'm buying a town-house here and we have no business?"

"Seems like it."

"God damn, John! Why are you waiting to tell me this?"

"Because you've been too busy falling in stupid, insane, sex-crazed love to listen to me, or read my emails or my reports."

Stryker slumped down next to him. "I've looked at everything you've sent."

"With your brain, sir, not your dick."

"How can we repair relations with Germany, Italy, and Spain?"

"I don't know if it's worth it. If France won't give us permission to fly through their airspace, you can forget Spain."

"Is there any good news?"

"Switzerland gave us the go ahead. I have the permit right here," he said, fiddling with a file folder.

Stryker put his hand on John's arm. "It's okay. I believe you. Wonderful. We can fly from London to Geneva. Big fucking deal."

"You could start a New York to London shuttle."

"I'd need bigger planes for that. How many planes are on order?"

"Only two. I stopped ordering after talking to France."

"Good move. Can we cancel those?"

"No, but we can probably resell them."

"At a loss. We can use them in the States."

"They're too small to fly Chicago to Dallas," John said.

"We're screwed. How much do you think we'll lose on a resale?" Stryker asked.

"Hard to say. The Bombadier is thirty-two million."

"I'm guessing we can get seventy-five percent of that back. Twenty-four, twenty-five mill," Stryker said.

"At a loss of seven million each."

"Damn. Fourteen million down the toilet. How about the London office?"

"You can always sublet that. In fact, you can probably make money on it," John replied.

"Yeah, but it will have to be finished and renovated again to suit the needs of tenants."

John looked at his watch. "The contractor is due in half an hour. Lunch will be brought up in fifteen. It'll be set up in the conference room."

Stryker pushed to his feet and followed John. He loved the dining room, which doubled as his conference room, in the Royal Suite. The dark wood table, Prussian Blue walls with white trim took elegance to a new level. Anger and confusion bubbled up inside him. How had this happened? He'd lost his grip and now the plans for his European expansion crumbled before his eyes.

"Cancel the offer on the townhouse, John."

"Don't know if I can."

"Call right now. Get us out of it. I'm losing enough money on this." Stryker pushed aside a chair and stood at the window. His brow furrowed, his lips pressed together. Stryker Alexander West doesn't have failures. He'd struck the word "failure" from his vocabulary.

It wasn't that he couldn't afford to lose the money. In fact, the loss would morph into a nice deduction at tax time. But his plans had been scuttled, the rug pulled out from under him. Politics had entered his boardroom, and he didn't like it.

And what was the cause? He smiled ruefully to himself. All because he couldn't give in on that stupid, fucking house. He couldn't back away from that fight, but stayed, hoping to prevail. He'd lost anyway, and now his dream of luxury air travel in Europe had ground to a halt. Maybe he'd met the love of his life, but at what price?

As the Claridge staff set up a sumptuous luncheon, he remained at the window. He'd risked everything and lost. And he hadn't even secured Jess. No commitment from her, no European business, and time down the fucking drain. Could he clean up this mess, get the office construction on the right track to be turned into a money-making sublet in time to return to Pine Grove for Thanksgiving?

He rubbed the back of his neck. He had no answer.

JESS SPENT HER AFTERNOONS in the library. She researched cookware, where to buy china and flatware, and Thanksgiving recipes. There were so many magazines with articles about food for Thanksgiving, her head spun. Seemed like plain, simple food no longer existed on the holiday tables of Americans anymore.

Every specialized dish required more ingredients, and a ton of time to prepare. How could she get it all done? She'd need a helper. Janet, the librarian, brought a tissue to a weeping Jess.

"What's wrong?" she asked, sitting down next to the young woman.

"Do you know the expression, 'bit off more than you can chew'?"

Janet laughed. "Some days I think I invented it. What's the problem? How can I help?"

Jess explained her predicament.

"You need a helper. Find out how much you can pay, and let's put up a sign here in the library. Lots of high school girls are looking for part-time jobs during the holidays."

"Great idea."

"Why don't you take these magazines home?"

"But you don't allow them to be checked out," Jess replied.

"This is an emergency. I trust you to return them. When you select your dishes, we'll make copies of the recipes."

"Thank you. I'll try them out on my brother," Jess said.

Though it was only the end of September, Jess hummed a Christmas tune as she drove home. Saturday, she and Will planned a shopping trip to Home Depot to stock the kitchen with pots, pans, and cooking utensils.

Stacking the magazines on the kitchen counter, happiness filled her heart. Jess Lennox would be preparing and serving Thanksgiving dinner in the house she adored. Could it be that her dream had come true? Her phone rang. It was Charlie.

"Just in case you're thinking of backing out of that Thanksgiving dinner, I'm calling to tell you we have already signed up six people. We took their money, so it's too late."

"Really? Six? Already?"

"Yep."

"Save a seat for Stryker," she said.

"Stryker?"

"He said he'd be home for Thanksgiving."

"Home? Is Pine Grove his home?" Charlie asked.

Jess sensed heat in her cheeks. "He owns a house here. So that makes it his home."

"How are things coming?"

"Great. I've got recipes. Will and I are stocking the kitchen this week and I've found a pattern that's cheap enough and close enough to the times to be perfect. We've ordered the dishes. They should arrive in two weeks."

"Excellent. This is actually coming together. When Stryker hired us, I thought there was no way this could be done."

"I'm excited."

Charlie laughed. "Just be prepared for anything, Jess. We'll be lucky to be ready on time."

"We'll be ready. I can feel it."

When she hung up, Jess opened *Southern Living* to the Thanksgiving menus page and pulled out a notebook. She flipped through the pages until she reached the section on side dishes.

"Hmm. Brussel sprouts almondine. Interesting," she muttered to herself. The call of the chickadee drew her eye.

"Sorry, little guy. I've got work to do. I'll refill the feeder in a bit."

Charlie had approved her spending money at the grocery store to experiment on dishes to serve at the Inn. Will entered, opened the fridge and grabbed a beer.

"What the hell is all this?"

"Experimenting to find the right dishes for Thanksgiving."

"And what the hell is that?"

"A turkey. Gotta learn how to cook it."

He smiled. "I get to eat this stuff?"

She whipped around, grinning. "Yep."

"This is our first turkey," Will said, his voice filled with wonder.

"Yeah. Kinda weird. I mean everyone else eats turkey all the time."

"Can't wait. I've been in a few houses, doing repairs, when they were cooking the turkey for Thanksgiving. It smelled fantastic."

She patted her notebook. "You're my guinea pig, Will."

"Don't much like the sound of that."

"Don't worry. I promise not to kill you."

"That's cold comfort," he said, pushing to his feet and grabbing silverware.

STRYKER PICKED UP HIS gin and tonic, took a mouthful, and swallowed. "What's the schedule for tomorrow?"

"Let's see," John said, leafing through his notebook. "Hmm. We're meeting with the contractor. He's declaring bankruptcy. Seems his partner was snorting the company profits up his nose. He can't finish the office."

"What the hell?" Stryker pulled himself upright on the luxurious sofa at Claridge's.

"We have to agree to a settlement. His lawyer will be here."

"Great. I'm not paying him shit if he doesn't finish."

"Let's wait and see what the lawyer says." Shuffling through a few pages, John stopped and pointed. "Aha! There it is."

"What?"

"Your flight info to Germany tomorrow. You're meeting with the man in charge of Munich airport. Maybe he can rent us some space and help with the permit."

"Does he speak English?"

"Oops. Forgot. We need a translator. Be right back."

Stryker turned his attention away from the drone of John's voice on the phone and let Jess Lennox drift into his mind. He went to the window and returned to pacing.

How were things going at the Inn? Geez, they didn't even have a name for the place yet. He cringed to think things there were falling apart like in Europe. Uneasy, he picked up his phone.

"Stryker?" came a feminine voice.

"Hey, Jess. How are you?" he asked, scratching a scruffy cheek.

"Good. You?"

"Things here are kind of a mess. I was wondering, how's the house coming? Will you make the Thanksgiving deadline?"

"Oh, yes. We have to. We actually have people signed up for the dinner."

"You do?" he asked, unable to conceal his surprise.

"Of course. Didn't you think we would?"

"With the way things are going—well...the ad is working?"

"It is. We have six signed up."

"And the construction?"

"Will's finished the bookcases. He'll finish the floor in there this week, the light fixture in the dining room has been connected. The place is coming together."

He sighed. "That's great."

"And I've picked out dishes. We ordered them and the flatware. They should be here by mid-October."

"Fantastic."

"I've been researching recipes, too. Will is eating like a king."

Stryker laughed.

"Yep. I'm closing in on the perfect menu."

"Sounds like you and Charlie have everything under control."

"We do. Barring catastrophes, floods, blizzards—we should be okay. I'm saving your seat."

"Great news. I'll be there. Looking forward to it."

"Me, too."

"I, uh, miss you," he said, fumbling for words. Why didn't he tell her how he felt? Because he didn't know, not for sure, did he?

"Me, too."

"Okay. I'll check back with you in a week or two."

"Fine. Good luck with stuff over there."

He clicked the phone off. Thank God something in his life was going right. He chuckled to think that Jess played a key role in launching the Inn. Men with ten times more experience in business that she had couldn't pull things together here. But Jess took the reins in Pine Grove. He grinned. Jess Lennox was a woman like no other.

"Gunter said the airport guy speaks fluent English. We don't need a translator," John said, bursting to the living room.

Stryker nodded and retreated to his room. As he filled a small suitcase with his belongings, he couldn't help wishing the trip ahead was to Pine Grove instead of Germany.

The next morning, Stryker arose grumpy. He peered outside. Dark rain clouds roiled around the hostile sky. Anger gripped him. When the ride got bumpy, he clutched the armrests in the small aircraft. Fortunately, they landed safely.

Once in the office of the director of the airport, they discovered that he did not speak fluent English and they needed a translator. The German looked annoyed.

Stryker yelled at John and stomped away. Wiping his face with his hand, his stomach squeezed, making him nauseous. There had been no time for lunch. While John scrambled, calling everyone he knew, searching for a translator, Stryker returned to the airport, seeking food.

Not speaking the language, he had to point to what he wanted and toss money on the counter. Fury raced through his veins. Why was he in Germany? What was he doing, trying to fix a business that had been broken beyond repair?

After downing a sausage and bread, he came to a decision. He picked up his phone.

"Forget the translator, John. Book us on a flight back to London immediately."

"What about our deal here?" John asked.

"Let it go. I've made a decision. We're shutting down this business. Starting today."

Chapter Eighteen

*P**ine Grove, NY*

Jess awoke at five and tripped down to the kitchen. First thing she did, which she did every day, was cross the day off on the calendar taped to the refrigerator. She'd sketched a heart in the space for Thanksgiving Day. Another day closer to seeing Stryker again.

Yesterday, staring at the calendar, Will had asked, "Aw, a heart. Got a thing for West, huh?"

"That's about the big meal. The opening of the Inn," she'd lied.

"Bullshit. Can't fool me. You're gaga for that guy."

Jess had turned away, hiding the heat in her face. "And what if I am?"

"Don't hold your breath waiting for Mr. Mega Bucks to pop the question."

"One minute you tell me I'm God's gift to the world, and now you don't think I'm Stryker's equal?"

"You are—In some ways. And in others, uh, no."

"Don't you have someplace you gotta be?" She had snatched the dish from under Will's nose as soon as he took the last bite of egg and shooed him out the door.

Jess opened the fridge. Switching on the radio, she sang along while she prepared pie filling. Although her new job helping to prepare the Inn paid her more than the pies sales, she needed to continue that business. She'd worked hard to build her reputation and had a satisfied clientele. Besides, this business would go away after the holidays.

A larger for-sale sign graced the front lawn. Eager real estate agents visited weekly. Jess prayed no one would buy it but admitted to herself it was simply a matter of time until the Inn found a new owner.

In the meantime, she'd be living her dream. Although the dream extended only until the new year, she hadn't made any plans beyond that. She'd always have her pie business and had put away some savings from the new income.

Forcing herself not to hope for a life with Stryker didn't work. At night, in bed, too tired to control her thoughts, she'd go to sleep picturing a small wedding in the mansion and a reception for her friends.

At daybreak, reality crept in. The billionaire had a growing business in Europe and would never settle for Pine Grove when he could live in London, Paris, or Rome. She'd sigh and push negative thoughts from her mind. Each week she distracted herself by trying two new recipes. On October fifteenth, she hung around at the Inn, waiting for delivery of the kitchen appliances.

She wandered through the old mansion. The first floor was almost done. She checked on the den. The fireplace, bricked up at one time, was now open. It needed TLC and to be tested and cleaned.

Then she stopped in the dining room. The dark wood floor and table gave a warm, old-fashioned feeling to the room. The blue walls with crisp white trim added style. Charlie had located the perfect sideboard at a garage sale. It was old, but Will had refinished it and the piece glowed with a new pride. She hadn't planned on decorations but saw that the room needed artwork on the walls, candlesticks, and some crystal bowls with fruit or gourds on the sideboard. She pulled a small pad from her back pocket and made notes.

A trip upstairs brought her up-to-date on the progress of the guest rooms. The first two appeared to be ready for furniture. The others, not yet. The faint odor of cat or wild animal pee haunted the hallway. Will had assured her the smell would disappear after all the rooms and the hallway were done. She opened several windows. Fresh air couldn't hurt.

When she heard the crunch of tires on the gravel drive, Jess took off, flying down the winding staircase to the first floor. She opened the door and signaled the men to pull around back. Loping down the long hallway to the back door, she let them in. With big eyes, she watched them work, pretending that every spanking new item belonged to her.

By the third week in October, the kitchen was ready. She wiped down the new cabinets and cleaned the professional refrigerator and stove. Her eyes widened when she examined them. How different her pie business would be if she had equipment like this.

Right after they finished the kitchen, the new dishes and flatware arrived. She loaded everything into the dishwasher, then she arranged the sparkling new plates, cups, and saucers in the sideboard in the dining room.

Next, Jess unloaded the bags with linens. As she worked, she created a list of necessities yet to be purchased: soap, scouring pads, cleanser, and more.

Taking a break, she texted Stryker.

Kitchen is ready. A few more basics and it will be good to go.

He replied.

Thanks for the good news.

She wrote back.

I hope your business is going well, too.

When there was no reply from him, she frowned. With a shrug, she figured he'd been too busy to take time to fill her in on anything. Hell, what did she know about the airline business anyway?

Climbing into her rust bucket, headed for the store, she frowned. It wasn't like Stryker to not respond. Even if it was only to beg off because he was busy. A nagging feeling that something wasn't right settled between her shoulder blades.

ROYAL SUITE, CLARIDGE'S, London, England

Stryker stood at the window, eyeing the overcast sky and drinking coffee.

"Now what?" John asked.

"I'm thinking."

"That's good. We're extended beyond belief on this."

"But we can't continue. I'm not going to pay off the French, and I refuse to toady to the rest to make up for our government's policies. This whole idea has become politicized. Damn it! That's the last thing I wanted."

John moved next to Stryker. "And I repeat. What are we going to do about it?"

Stryker paced. It was already November and he had problems the size of the Empire State Building. The clock was ticking as Thanksgiving drew near.

"You're not still planning to go back to that God forsaken shit hole, Pine Grove at Thanksgiving, are you?"

"I made a promise."

"But business is business."

Stryker rubbed the back of his neck. "I know. It's beginning to look like either I run out on you and the men trying to finish the job on the office or I run out on the best girl I've ever known."

"Might consider that a lose/lose proposition."

"Ya think?" Stryker cocked an eyebrow as he faced John.

"More coffee?"

"Yeah, and can you add a little cyanide?" Stryker replied.

John gave a laugh as he left the room. Stryker paced. The planes would be ready by December first. That was the original launch date for the European service. He had to find some way to make money with those planes. Sell them for fifty cents on the dollar and lose thirty-two million? No way. Taking a hit like that had never been acceptable to Stryker. He could always think his way out of a tight spot.

As he stared out the window, watching the rain, a plan formed in his brain. John returned with refilled mugs for both. He handed one to Stryker.

"Okay, John. I have it. First, I want you to research all our current sites. I want a spreadsheet showing me which ones are most successful. Which make the most money? Which are booked up consistently? And I want it this afternoon."

"This afternoon?" John's eyebrows rose.

"Yep. When will Dallas be up and running?"

"January one."

"How many planes?"

"Two. We always start with two."

"And they're due to arrive, when?"

"Right after Christmas."

"Fine. Get me those figures. I'll be damned if I'm eating thirty mill on those planes. Next, I want a plan for rental of our office space right up until our lease expires."

"Okay. Got it. You want the sublease plan by when?"

"As soon as possible. Hire help. We need to get this fixed. The sooner the better."

"I'll need a couple of days for the spreadsheet. I have to contact every airport separately. Geez, we have L.A., New York, Boston, Washington, Atlanta, Toronto, and Chicago, now. Remember, there are time differences, too."

Stryker frowned. "Do the best you can."

"I'd sure hate to interfere with your love life," John remarked.

"Yeah, sure you would. Jealous and horny, John?"

His right-hand man laughed. "Maybe."

"Get on it. We're going to keep those planes. I'm not selling anything at that kind of loss."

"Got it. I'm on it," he said and left the room.

Stryker opened his laptop and pulled up a map of the United States. "Hmm, if I can't go to Europe, where else can I go in the U.S.?"

Three hours later, he called a meeting. John and his secretary joined Stryker in the dining room. Room service delivered lunch. Stryker spoke.

"This is what we're going to do. We're going to open up a Dallas/Houston shuttle and a Los Angeles/San Francisco shuttle. If we can't go to Europe, we'll go West."

"And the new planes?"

"Once you get me the data on usage by market, we'll put the new planes in the markets that are sold out consistently. We'll expand there first. After plans are set for the new markets, we'll buy new planes. Unless the ones we're shifting to our busiest markets aren't needed. If that happens, we'll send those out west."

"Great plan!"

"How'd you like to live in Dallas or San Francisco, John?"

"Really?"

"Yep. You can keep your eye on the sublet by coming to London two or three times a year."

"I'd love to be back in the states."

"Good. Then let's go. Call our best people and have them fly out to check out those markets. I want a report in two weeks."

"Done," John said, smiling.

"I thought you loved it here," Stryker said, sitting back.

"I do. But I miss my kids. I'm gonna have my first grandchild, and I'd sure as hell like to be home for the birth."

"Marnie?"

"I'm happy here."

"Good. You can be our anchor in London. Work with John on a way to keep track of the sublet and troubleshoot any problems."

"Great. A promotion?"

"Yes," Stryker said.

As figures came in from the various airports and preliminary studies of the new markets, Stryker lost himself in his work. Work days stretched endlessly, with only short breaks for food. At night, he fell into bed, exhausted, and rose again at six to begin his day. Deadlines drew near faster than expected. Thanksgiving became simply a number on the calendar.

PINE GROVE, THREE DAYS before Thanksgiving

"Why do you need to practice? Millions of people cook turkeys every year. How hard can it be?" Will moaned, slumping into the kitchen of the Mansion.

In the dining room, three workers took a break from the renovation to eat the dinner Jess had promised.

"It's only a small turkey. We still have to wrestle with a big one."

"I don't understand what you need me for?" Will complained.

"I need you to help me turn the turkey."

"Turn the turkey?"

"Yep. Laura said she always cooks hers upside down. Then the juices run into the breast not out. She said Barney turns the turkey right side up for her."

"So call Barney."

"You're standing in for him. Come on, Will. We need this to be a success."

"Besides, if you want to eat it, you have to turn it first."

"You got me there."

He groaned and approached the oven. Jess pulled out the roasting pan and tossed a pair of oven mitts at him.

"Here you go. Turn this sucker," she said, resting her hand on hips.

He put on the mitts and placed his hands on the wings. He yanked, but the bird was stuck.

"Oh, wait. It's stuck to the metal thingy." Jess reached for a knife and slid it along the edge. "There, now try it."

He did. But he couldn't get it unstuck.

"Try top and bottom," Jess suggested.

He snorted and shot her a hostile glare before placing one hand on the neck and the other on the tail. "Like this?"

"Yeah," she said, nodding.

He gave a huge heave and the bird became unstuck at the same time as it became air born. It flew from his hands, up in the air and landed with a splat on the floor.

"Oh, shit!" Will and Jess said together.

"Pick it up," she commanded.

As he bent down, he responded, "you're not going to serve this to the guys, are you?"

"Five-second rule. Get it off the floor!" she shouted, then lowered her voice, her gaze stealing to the door to the dining room.

Will bent down and picked up the bird.

"Good. Now turn it. Put it right side up."

"Jess," he said, shaking his head.

"I just washed the floor. It's fine. I'll wipe off the turkey."

"I'm not eatin' that thing."

"Oh, yes you are!" she said, facing him, her brows drawn together.

"You tryin' to kill me?" he asked.

Jess grabbed two paper towels and wiped away at the turkey.

"You're taking off the skin, Jess."

"Isn't that what you want? It's totally clean underneath."

"You'd better clean up that stuffing on the floor before somebody slips, breaks their ass, and sues your beloved Mr. West."

Jess stuck out her tongue at Will. "You're mean."

"Just honest."

"You're eating this turkey. And no telling the guys it fell on the floor."

Will raised his palms. "Okay, okay."

"Go get the cranberries and bring them to the table. I still have to carve this sucker and mash the potatoes."

"I'll mash the potatoes," he said, picking up the cranberry dish. On his way to the door, he didn't see a piece of stuffing. He stepped square on it and went flying. The dish with the cranberries flew up in the air and landed with a crash. The glass dish broke into a million pieces, scattering cranberries all over the floor.

Jess shrieked, Will yelled, and the three men at the table rushed in. She sank down cross-legged on the floor and burst into tears.

"I guess there's more to making Thanksgiving dinner than I thought," one of the workers said.

The men helped Jess get the food that was left on the table. The mashed potatoes and the sweet potatoes were a big hit. So was the turkey—what the guys didn't know, wouldn't hurt them.

Thursday morning, Jess delivered two pumpkin pies to the Inn. She wore jeans and a long-sleeved T-shirt. She'd made several dishes the day before and felt ready to tackle the turkey and other fixings she'd left for Thanksgiving Day.

Will made a fire in the fireplace in the living room, and one in the den, as well. He popped in to check on Jess.

"Den fireplace seems to be working, but I'd keep my eye on it, if I were you."

"Can you do that? I have enough on my plate."

Once she started cooking, time flew. Will came to help. He opened the wine, brushed the dusting of snow off the front steps and stood by his sister. Jane, the high school girl they'd hired to help donned an apron and followed Jess's instructions.

"Are we turning the damn turkey again?" Will growled.

"We are. This time, I've made sure it's not going to stick."

"Damn well better."

She smiled. Bustling from one end of the kitchen to the other, supervising Will and Jane, Jess lost track of time. She took a sip of hot, mulled cider as she thought about her next move. The doorbell rang. Will ushered in the eleven people who had paid to eat this sumptuous meal. Jess peeked out to watch the guests take off their coats. Her nerves kicked up.

She donned a fancy apron and strolled to the living room.

"Dinner is served. Please, take a place in the dining room."

The sideboard groaned under the weight of the carved turkey, stuffing, mashed potatoes, sweet potato casserole, green bean casserole, two types of cranberries, a caesar salad, and a Brussel sprouts casserole.

The guests exclaimed as they sat down. All the seats were filled, except the one for Stryker. The doorbell rang again.

"Leave it to Stryker to be late," she said to Will.

Her heart flip-flopped as she ran to answer. But it wasn't Stryker. A delivery man with a giant bouquet of red roses stood on the steps. Jess took the flowers and retreated to the kitchen. With trembling fingers, she opened the card.

Sorry, babe, please forgive me. Too many fires to put out. See you at Christmas.

Love,

Stryker

Tears pricked at the backs of her eyes. Will popped his head in and interrupted her thoughts.

"Where's the gravy? Hey, who sent those?"

"Stryker."

He shrugged.

"Gravy's coming." She put down the flowers and poured the gravy into a small pitcher.

GRATEFUL TO HAVE JANE helping, Jess put the girl to work washing and drying pots and pans. Will helped put away the dishes and silverware. Before her energy ran out, Jess paid Jane, sent her home, and poured a glass of wine. Will popped a beer and joined her at the kitchen table.

"Wow. That was amazing. I can't believe you pulled it off."

"Me, neither."

"Everybody raved about the meal. The turkey was perfect."

"Thanks to you for turning that huge bird." Jess stared out the window. Hunger finally hit her belly. She hadn't eaten much dinner and had saved her plate. Picking up her fork, she picked at the meat and took a dab of sweet potato.

"What was your favorite dish?" she asked, turning her attention to her brother.

"Hmm. My favorite dish. Let's see. The turkey. No. The stuffing? No. Mashed potatoes—hey, what did you put in those? They weren't like what we have at home."

"Heavy cream. We can't afford heavy cream."

"Sure made a difference. I don't really have a favorite dish, Jess. Everything was my favorite," he said grinning. "And the way they all blended together was awesome. People eat like that every year?"

"So I'm told."

"Are you okay?" he asked, squeezing her hand.

"Sure. Fine. Just tired."

"It's that West guy, isn't it?"

"Don't start with the 'I told you so', okay? Just leave it."

"I wasn't going to. Just, just—I'm sorry," he said, his voice soft.

Will's sympathy broke her control, or was it exhaustion? She lowered her head, covering her eyes with her hand.

"Aw, come on. I'm sure he had a good reason."

"Doesn't matter. He promised, and he broke it."

"Hey, guys with his money, shit happens, you know?"

"I'm sick of hearing about his money. Maybe I'd be better off with a poor man."

"You're just tired, Jess," he said, rubbing her back. "You've been working like a dog. Here at the Inn, then the pies, getting up at daylight, working until late at night. You need rest."

"No time for rest. We have to have those rooms ready for people before Christmas, which is only four weeks away." She dried her eyes with her apron.

"We'll be ready. We got a lot of stuff done this week. You'll see."

"I'm tired. Everything went okay?" she asked.

"More than okay. They're already planning to come back next year."

"Really? You're not making that up?"

"Nope. That's what they said. Oh, I forgot. Here," he said, reaching into his back pocket and pulled out some bills. "Fifty bucks. Their tip for the cook."

He thrust the money into her hand. She plucked out a twenty and tucked it into his shirt pocket.

"That's for helping. Damn if you hadn't done anything except flip the turkey it would be worth twenty. Thank you." Jess pushed to her feet and he followed. He drew her into his arms for a hug. Jess rested her head on his shoulder.

"Those Lennox kids. They're a team," he said, before releasing her.

"Time to rest."

"Finish that plate first, young lady," Will said, pointing.

She managed a smile and gave in to her hunger pains. "You seeing Jennie tonight?"

"Yeah."

"You going over there?"

"I don't feel comfortable at her parent's house. So I'm picking her up, and I thought we'd eat leftover pie and watch TV at our place."

"Sounds like a plan. Have fun."

Will kissed Jess's cheek, then headed out. Slowly she lifted forkfuls of food to her mouth. Damn. This was good. Her first Thanksgiving dinner. Not bad. She grinned, pride flowing through her. Her phone rang. It was Charlie.

"Happy Thanksgiving, Jess. Thanks for making this first event such a success."

"Same to you, Charlie. It was nothing."

"It was a helluva lot of work. You did a great job. Will told me what the guests had to say. I've received some email, asking to reserve places for next year. Way to go!"

"Thanks."

"Can you stop by tomorrow? I'd like to discuss Christmas, and I have a bonus for you."

"A bonus?"

"Stryker's orders. And I agree. When can you come?"

"Three okay?"

"Fine. See you then."

She washed and dried her dish and added water to the roses before leaving the Inn and locking up. On the way to the car, she got a text from Stryker:

Heard Thanksgiving was a success. Not surprised. Congratulations.

Jess turned off her phone, put it in her purse, and turned the key in the ignition.

Chapter Nineteen

Jess opened the door to Pelletier and Grand. Perched on a chair by his big desk, Charlie waved her in. She eased down on a loveseat across from him.

"We're getting inquiries from the Christmas ad. I've got a photographer to take pictures of the finished rooms. I need you to get bedroom furniture in at least two rooms as fast as possible, so we can get pictures up on the website."

"Website?"

"Yeah. Stryker came up with a name. Didn't he tell you?"

She shook her head. Her heart pounded. Why wasn't she in the loop.

"Yeah, he called two days ago. His lawyers are filing papers now. It will be the Pine Mountain Inn. How fast can you have those rooms furnished? Remember, it's just for photography. I mean, you don't need to have sheets on the beds or anything. Just bedspreads. Dressers, lamps, nightstands, the usual stuff. Oh, and a couple of pictures for the walls."

"I'm on it. I'll get back to you with a date by tomorrow afternoon."

"Great. That works. This is gonna happen, Jess. Ruth, the real estate agent is getting lots of interest in the place. The folks from Thanksgiving left some nice reviews on Yelp, too."

Jess wore a half-smile. Should she be happy or sad? What would happen if someone wanted to buy the place? She swallowed before speaking. "I'd better get going."

"Right. Talk to you tomorrow."

As she drove home, fear sprang up in her heart. Surely Stryker wouldn't sell the place that meant so much to her? Every day, working at the Inn became more real. Will kept reminding her that it wasn't hers and she shouldn't get too attached, but it was too late. She loved the place, adoring every moment she spent there.

The smell of fresh paint, wood furniture polish, and pine boughs she'd brought in to decorate the staircase set her mood. She looked forward to snowy afternoons when she could curl up with a book in front of the fire in the library.

The next morning, after pie delivery, Jory joined Jess for breakfast at The Cozy. After eggs, Jess drove them to Oak Bend. They bought what they needed at a fine, local furniture store, which scheduled delivery for the next day. Jess cringed at the prices, but Stryker wanted the best.

At two, Jory rushed off to her job at the newspaper and Jess returned home. She called Charlie.

"We're all set. The furniture is coming tomorrow. I'll pick up linens today. You should be able to take pictures by Friday."

"Excellent! That's amazing."

"I don't mess around when there's a job to do."

"You're great, Jess. Oh, by the way. You forgot to get your bonus check. Why don't you stop by on your way to the store?"

"Will do."

She pulled into the Pelletier and Grand parking lot. An envelope awaited her on the front hall table. She took it and opened it in the car. Her eyes popped—a thousand dollars! She couldn't believe it. She never expected anything like that. She'd hoped for a hundred bucks, but this...wow!

She stopped at the bank then continued to the nicest store within thirty miles. They had a good selection of linens. She bought sheets, towels, comforters, pillows, towels, and blankets in coordinating colors.

After hauling everything into the Inn, she made a cup of tea and put her feet up. The creaking of the front door alerted her. She sat up and jumped to her feet.

"Jess!" came a voice from the foyer.

"Coming!"

She rounded the corner in time to see Ruth, the real estate agent, with two other people.

"Hi, Jess. This is Martine and Albert. They're here to look at the Inn."

"Oh."

Jess bit her lip. The middle-aged woman and man were babbling in French as they walked into the living room. They smiled as they perused the space.

"I'm sorry. Do you mind if I show them the kitchen?"

"No, please. Go ahead," Jess said, standing back, out of the way.

Did she mind? Damn right she minded. Strangers in her kitchen, opening her cabinets, peeking into her drawers—it was a violation. But she held her tongue, took her tea and her jacket, and went outside on the back deck. A twinge shot through her. No way could she watch people trudge through the Inn, checking it out, looking it over, with an eye to buying it. The men were still working upstairs, and the racket from the third floor indicated it was under construction, too.

Maybe these people wouldn't like the Inn? Maybe they wouldn't buy something that wasn't finished? Maybe the price was too high? She could hope, couldn't she? Unable to stand the invasion, she drove home, picked up a book and stretched out on the sofa. Within minutes, she fell into a restless sleep.

THE ROYAL SUITE, THE Claridge, London, England

Stryker rubbed his neck and sat up straight. He'd been poring over documents since the wee hours of the morning.

"New contractors. Coming by this morning. They'll be here in an hour. Have you eaten anything?" John asked.

Stryker shook his head. "I need a shower."

"I'll get breakfast up right away. Go. This is a big firm. You need to be your best."

Stryker trotted off to the bathroom. He stripped off his clothes and stood under the warm water. Damn, it felt good— but not nearly as good as it would feel if Jess Lennox had been there with him. The feel of her skin, her beneath him, never left. It haunted him every night when he turned out the light.

If he could have just one kiss, it would give him the determination to carry on. With a rueful smile, he admitted to himself that he'd never stop at one kiss with Jess. No, he'd have to have her completely. He soaped up his body, wishing the hands on him were her hands. But there was no time for that, even taking care of business in the shower. People were coming, a million decisions had to be made. And he had to protect his empire from the catastrophes that had befallen his business in the past two months.

Thank God, the U.S. business grew steadily. In moments of quiet, he wondered how the Inn was coming. He didn't want to press Jess to send him pictures because she worked two jobs. At moments of high stress, when John yelled, or France refused to speak to him, he pictured the living room of the Inn. In his mind's eye, he saw a huge, comfortable sectional sofa, a roaring fire, and Jess pouring a bottle of Merlot, his favorite wine.

While he lived in outrageous luxury at Claridge's, he yearned for the comfy warmth of the mansion and the company of his girl. Back to his roots? What roots? He'd not returned to Pine Grove because there was nothing there for him except a broken-down old house that had become a money pit and a batty old aunt who gave away his money without a thought.

The images he conjured tugged at his heart. He wanted to go home. Yes, home, that's what it would be now, wouldn't it? But business snarls, tangles, problems, and decisions held him in their grip. He had to fix things in Europe before he could flee and find respite.

He turned off the water, dried himself quickly, and slipped into a charcoal gray suit. With a light blue shirt and a black and gold rep tie, he faced the day.

Breakfast awaited him on the coffee table in the living room. He checked his watch. John strode in.

"You have exactly fifteen minutes to eat."

"Got it." Stryker took the silver top off the dish presenting Burford brown eggs, scrambled, sweet cured bacon, and a raisin scone. Of course, a silver pot of coffee proudly took its place on the large tray. The aroma awoke his appetite and he chowed down.

As he added milk to his beverage, he heard the murmuring of voices in the vestibule. He figured John would show them into the dining room, which doubled as his conference room. Stryker finished the last two bites of his meal, wiped his mouth with a napkin and pushed to his feet.

It was time to get control of the office renovation. He checked his watch again. Damn. December twentieth. He only had four days to wind this up before heading back to Pine Grove. No, he would not stand up Jess again. Business be damned, he had to be there. Sometimes his heart had the right to come first.

He shook hands with the three men from the new firm and took his seat at the head of the table.

"Gentlemen. Thank you for coming. Let's get this project back on track. I must sign off on your plans no later than December twenty-third."

"That's pushing it," one man said.

"I know. And I apologize. We've been thrown a few unexpected curve balls. The project stalled and until we could come to an agreement with the old company, we could not proceed. I'm willing to agree that a ten percent rush fee be added to your original estimate."

"Of course if you need Stryker to meet with you over Christmas—" John began.

Stryker smacked the flat of his palm down on the table. The loud noise silenced the room.

"That's not going to happen."

PINE GROVE, DECEMBER 22

The two weeks before Christmas flew. The two rooms had been booked, as well as a big Christmas Eve buffet, a caroling event, and a Christmas Day dinner. Everything was sold out. Jane was hired for Christmas Eve but refused for Christmas Day. Jess sat at the kitchen table at the Inn making lists. A slight noise startled her, she looked up. The French couple stood in the doorway.

"You have done a marvelous job here, Miss Lennox," the man said.

"Ah, yes. So true. But once the Inn becomes ours, we will be in charge. Of course, we'll need some help in the kitchen and cleaning up. Especially a maid to clean the rooms. In case you're interested," Martine said.

Anger rose in Jess's chest. "No, thanks," she spit out, fire flashing from her eyes.

The man approached and put his hand on her forearm. Jess yanked away as if his touch burned.

"We understand. It must be very difficult for you to have done all this and to lose it."

Words froze in her throat. She couldn't speak.

"We understand. But if you change your mind, come by right after New Year's. I'm sure we can find work for you," Martine said, a cold smile on her lips.

"New Year's?" Jess choked out.

"Yes. We hope to have the contract signed by then and be handling the New Year's Eve party ourselves."

"I take my orders from Stryker West, not you. I doubt you can have things done by then. So until then, I will plan the New Year's Eve party," she replied, her voice dripping ice.

"Suit yourself. It's wasted work," the husband muttered, before turning to leave.

"Wait, Albert! We have some questions about the Inn," Martine continued.

"You can direct them to Ruth. I'm very busy. Now if you don't mind showing yourselves out." Jess turned her gaze back on her notebook.

"Well! Don't bother to come around. We prefer to hire people who are amenable, who will take direction," Martine said, turning away.

"Suit yourself," Jess muttered.

When she heard the door close, she let out a breath. Rising from her seat, she stood at the window, looking at the chickadees at the feeder. What if they were right? Neither Charlie nor Stryker had said a word about the couple buying the Inn. She didn't know who to believe, so she called Charlie.

"A couple buying the Inn? That's news to me. But Stryker doesn't tell me everything. You should ask him."

She couldn't stand the suspense, so she texted him. He was probably right in the middle of a meeting. Tough. This question needed to be answered.

Some French couple says they're buying the Inn. Is this true?

She hit send. Returning to the table, she continued making her list. Damn, there was so much to buy and do before Christmas. She needed more help, but she'd have to make do with Will.

A pop alerted her to a text.

That's news to me. I'll check with Ruth and get back to you.

Tears of relief filled her eyes. So, it wasn't true. Excellent. With renewed energy, she completed her list, then parceled out the tasks by day. There was plenty to do today. And she had extra pie orders for the holiday. Well, who needed sleep anyway?

As she drove to the store, she had an idea. It would be perfect, and she'd add that to her list. Humming along with Christmas music on the radio, Jess grinned. Stryker would be back for the holiday, in time to see her do her big event.

Returning to the Inn two hours later, she hit the stairs to make up the beds in the two guest rooms. Might as well get those out of the way. She found holiday music on her phone and sang along as she fluffed pillows and tucked in sheets. Calico print duvet covers complimented the color schemes of the rooms.

When she finished, she leaned against the doorjamb and surveyed her work.

"Wow! These are great. Like out of a storybook," Will said, appearing behind her.

"Or out of my dreams. This is just as I pictured it."

"I know I gave you shit about your stupid dream and the house and stuff. I was wrong. The place is lookin' pretty damn good. You were right, Jess," Will said, patting his sister on the shoulder.

"Thanks. I'm not sure I'll survive. But at least I'll die happy," she said, grinning.

Could life get any better?

"WHAT DO YOU MEAN EVERY flight back to New York is sold out?" Stryker's voice rose in volume.

"I thought for sure you'd have to stay here until after Christmas," John said, his face reddening.

"You idiot! I told you I need to be in Pine Grove on Christmas Eve."

"You always say stuff like that and it never happens. Work has always come first with you. I thought this would be more of the same."

"You thought wrong. Damn. *Damn*! Get me on a flight, any flight out of here tomorrow."

"Christmas Eve?"

"Yes, Christmas Eve. I want to leave in the morning."

"I'll try."

"If you have to charter a plane, then do it."

"Okay, okay. Keep your shirt on."

"And send this FedEx to Will Lennox, in Pine Grove. Okay?"

"Got it."

"I'm going to pack," Stryker said, shoving an envelope in John's hand then leaving the room.

Two hours later, John had tried to charter a plane, but they were all booked. One pilot took pity on him. John read the email to Stryker.

"Can he co-pilot? Mine wants to stay home with his family. If this guy can fly, I'll take him."

Stryker jumped up in the air and let out a whoop. "Tell him, yes. Where do I go?"

It took hours to get Stryker and his luggage to the airfield. The weather had turned foul, and snow clogged the streets.

When they arrived, the pilot grabbed him by the arm.

"Where the hell have you been? I've got a full flight and if we don't take off in fifteen minutes, it'll be too late. The airport's gonna close. Come on!"

Stryker climbed in while John loaded his luggage. The plane taxied down the runway and lifted into the skies as the storm intensified.

Once they got out over the ocean, the storm let up. But the news from the States wasn't good.

"All major airports on the North East coast are closed. Here, find us a place to land."

Bad weather on Christmas Eve should not have been news to Stryker. With everyone wishing for a white Christmas, it was no wonder there were snowstorms in Boston, New York, Philadelphia, Baltimore, and Washington. Stryker perused the map. There had to be someplace they could land.

"Atlanta?" he asked the pilot.

"Works for me. Beats crash landing. Folks will have to find other ways to get north. Maybe train? Drive?" the pilot asked.

"It's a damn long drive from Atlanta to New York."

"So, look for a closer airport. How about Charlotte?" the pilot asked.

"Okay. Charlotte. It's a long drive but possible," Stryker replied.

The pilot radioed Charlotte and received permission to land.

"How the hell are you going to get to New York?"

"I don't know. I need to get to upstate. No train going there," Stryker said.

"Must be a girl," the pilot replied.

"Yes. An awesome one."

"Ah, love and Christmas. It'll work out. She'll be there, waiting for you."

"I don't know about that," Stryker replied, his brow creased.

John was in London. Stryker was on his own.

When the plane landed, he made his way to the nearest car rental kiosk. But they were sold out. So was every other car rental place. There were a few taxis waiting. Out of options and almost out of hope, he checked his watch. December 24, eleven o'clock. He approached one driver.

"I'll give you a thousand bucks to drive to New York tonight."

"Tonight? No way. But maybe tomorrow."

Exhausted and out of options, Stryker attempted to find a room. But the hotels were booked. He texted Jess.

Stuck in Charlotte.

He didn't get any response. One glance at his phone and he realized he was out of juice. Where was that phone cord? He tore apart his luggage, but the cord wasn't there. He'd been so distracted, he'd neglected to grab it.

People bustled around the airport, hurrying to their destinations or hanging at the bar, drinking to pass the time until the northern storms passed. He asked a few people if he could borrow their cords, but they refused, politely. Seems as if everyone had a place to go and people to see.

Out of options, Stryker found a chair and tried to get comfortable. It would be a long night. He hoped something would break in the morning. How mad would Jess be if he missed Christmas? He cringed at the thought. It hadn't been his fault, had it? Maybe it was, waiting until the last minute to leave. He closed his eyes. Of course, it had been his fault. Lack of planning.

Jess would be there but maybe mad. Could he pick up something to smooth things over? She wasn't a diamond bracelet kind of girl. Stores would be closed tomorrow. He'd simply have to beg her forgiveness, humble himself. Ah, yes! It came to him. There was something he could do.

Settling his nerves with a possible solution, he drifted off to sleep.

THE SIDEBOARD WAS LADEN with serving dishes. A ham, an escalloped potato casserole, a Caesar salad, Brussel sprouts, butternut squash soup, twice-baked potatoes, and a cheesy broccoli casserole filled the air with tempting aromas.

The table was set with fine china. An evergreen centerpiece, created by Will, added the scent of piney freshness to the air.

Guests drank mulled wine, hot cider, and beer in the living room. Jess checked her watch. It was seven. The carolers had just left, and it was time to call people in to dinner. Where was Stryker?

"Come on, Jess. You can't wait any longer. I'm sure Stryker's coming. There's a shit ton of snow out there. He's probably delayed," Will said.

"Okay, okay. Yes, I'll call the people to the table."

She went out and sounded the dinner bell. The seven-foot tree and the fire created a festive atmosphere. After people took their seats, Jess plopped down on the sofa and stared at the flames. She sighed. Where was Stryker? She gathered, from their brief phone conversations, things had not gone well in Europe. She didn't know exactly what that meant.

But he said he was coming, and she'd believed him. Where was he? She stared at the wrapped gifts under the tree. They were for the guests staying in the Inn, not her. Charlie had handed her another bonus. Two thousand this time.

As she searched her soul for holiday spirit, Ruth Bledell came through the front door.

"Hi, Jess."

"Ruth," Jess said, nodding.

"Look, I don't want this to surprise you. Here it is. The contract I'm going to present to Stryker when he arrives. Martine and Albert are offering a million dollars for the Inn, as is. In other words, they would finish the renovation themselves. I don't see how Stryker can turn it down, do you?"

Jess simply stared at the woman.

"I just didn't want you to be blindsided."

"Thanks, Ruth. I have no idea if he'd turn it down or not."

"It's way over market value for the property. Can you match it?"

Jess chuckled. "Nope."

"Maybe you can work for them?"

"Nope."

"Okay. Well. I'm sorry. But I have to present this to him."

"I understand. It's fine."

Ruth nodded and left.

Jess went through the scenario. She'd known that the house could never be hers. Someday someone would want to buy it, and how could Stryker turn down that kind of money? Besides, he never wanted the place anyway. This solves two of his problems at once. He'll recoup his money and unload the albatross around his neck.

She sighed. Did she have a Plan B? Not a well-formed one, but she had an idea of what to do. Listening to the clink of knives and forks made her hungry. Will appeared.

"Well? Come on. I'm not eating alone," he said.

She joined him in the kitchen. There she had set an elegant table for them. She'd put aside some of the same dishes the guests were having. As she sat down, hunger gripped her belly.

"I'm starving!" she admitted.

"Good. You need to put on a few pounds. You've been working too hard, doing too much. This looks great. Let's eat."

They joined hands, said grace, then dug in. She'd made a delectable meal. When they finished, he cleared their dishes. Jane bustled in, carrying empty plates and used flatware.

"They're ready for dessert," she said.

Jess rose and handed one platter of cookies to Jane and took another one herself.

"Will, you grab the cake."

Jess had made a holiday-themed chocolate sheet cake. As soon as she entered the dining room, people clustered around her, pelting her with questions.

"What kind of sauce did you make for the ham?"

"What was in the baked potato? It was delicious."

"I love the Caesar dressing. Did you make it yourself?"

She answered as many as she could. By ten, she could barely drag herself outside. The people at the Inn were still up. Will had agreed to put out the fire and lock up the place so she could rest. There had been no sign of Stryker, no gift under the tree from him, either. She left the box with vintage cufflinks she found for him there, drove home and collapsed.

Tomorrow was Christmas. Her texts had gone unanswered. Was Stryker in trouble? Did he need help? Was he buried under an avalanche of snow? Was he with another woman? Did he stay in London to do work and not have the heart to tell her? These questions filled her head until it ached. She popped two ibuprofen and crawled into bed. The sound of a tweet woke her. She read it, nodded, sighed and pulled up the covers. Tomorrow was another day.

Chapter Twenty

Christmas Day proved to be as busy as the day before. At least Jess didn't have to deliver pies as the places that sold them were closed. But she hustled her butt over to the Inn to make breakfast. After that, she prepared a platter of ham sandwiches and cold salads for lunch.

Then there'd be an early dinner of turkey with all the fixings. She barely had time to think about Stryker. Will arrived at eleven, just in time to help set up dinner. The two worked until the last dish was washed, dried, and put away. When the grandfather clock in the hallway chimed nine times, Will spoke.

"Time to go home, Jess. Have our own Christmas."

"But the fire?"

"I'll come back at midnight and make sure it's out."

She nodded. Before heading to the parking lot, they stopped to take one last look.

Fresh pine boughs, with pine cones and red berries nestled between branches, draped gracefully around archways and down the banister. The huge Christmas tree in the living room glowed with colored lights and silver and gold balls. A hand-crafted wreath decorated with tiny ornaments hung over the fireplace in the den.

"Christmas decorations look nice," Will said.

"Thanks."

The beauty of the Inn shone with a patina of elegance crafted by age and love. Her gaze darted from wall to wall, from sofa to desk, from clock to mantle. Pleased with the progress the old mansion had made, she smiled, then went out the door.

Her chest filled with pride at a job well done. Will got behind the wheel of his truck. Jess turned the key in her vehicle and steered for home.

Jennie joined them. Jess doled out mugs of hot, mulled wine. Will put Christmas music on before he went to their spindly tree and pulled a package out from underneath.

"Jess. This is for you. You deserve something great this year, but this was all I could afford." He handed her a long, rectangular package.

She opened it to find a high-quality immersion blender. "Wow, Will! How did you know I wanted one of these?"

"Maybe 'cause you kept sayin' so?" he joked, raising his eyebrows.

Jess teared up as she handed him a heavy present. "This is something you should have."

He opened it to reveal a heavy-duty, portable jigsaw.

"Wow. This is great," he said, rolling the box around in his hands.

"And it has a laser light to help get cuts straight. It's corded so you don't have to worry about batteries. That makes it lighter, too. You should have had one before, instead of renting one. Now there's no stopping you."

"I can make furniture, too. This is awesome. Thank you, Jess." He leaned over and kissed his sister on the cheek.

It was time to do something she should have done long ago. She put her hand on his arm.

"I'm getting an early start tomorrow."

"So? You usually get an early start."

"I'm leaving, Will."

"You're what?" His eyebrows shot up.

"I'm leaving. My work is done here. I've taken a room in Willow Falls. Guy at the bakery there said if I ever wanted a job to look him up."

"Why, Jess? Just when everything is going good?"

"With the jigsaw, you'll have enough work to afford a real house. Maybe for you and Jennie," she said, glancing at the young woman by her brother's side. "There's nothing left here for me. Stryker didn't come. He didn't text. Ruth said that French couple is ready to offer a million bucks for the mansion. How can he turn that down?"

"Aw, come on. Jess. This is your home."

"It's not much of one, is it?"

"It's been okay for the past fifteen years."

"We've made do because we had no choice. I need more. It's time to move on. I can't keep working at the Inn, even if the couple doesn't buy it. It's too painful to be there all day and come home to this." She gestured at their meager surroundings. "And the Inn'll never be mine."

"I know how you feel, but what about Stryker? Maybe something happened?"

"Maybe it did. He's just a pipe dream, too. I've always done best relying on myself. Stryker can't fix my life. Only I can do that. I realize what I can do now, and it's time to save up to have my dream. Maybe not in a mansion, but in a house of my own."

"But you have friends here," he said.

"And enemies, too. Time for a fresh start."

Will teared up. He swallowed but uttered no words. Her eyes filled. "I know. There's not much to say. No one could have a better little brother than you. I never could have made it without you."

"I'll miss you," he said in a small voice.

"Me, too."

And then she was in his arms, sobbing. He stroked her hair and held her close.

"It's okay, Jess. I understand," he whispered into her hair.

She parted from him and headed for her room. Packing was easy. When you have no money, you don't acquire things. She was up until midnight. Finally, she slid between the sheets. Was Stryker coming? If he was, why didn't he say something? And if he wasn't, why?

STRYKER ROLLED INTO Pine Grove at one in the morning. Chagrined he'd missed Christmas by a couple of hours, he had to shower and sleep before he saw Jess. He thanked the man who drove him and handed him a check for $1000. Fortunately, he'd taken a year's lease on the house in Pine Grove, so it was still his.

With no phone, he couldn't call or text Chris or Jess. He showered and eased under the covers. His body warmed the cold sheets and his thoughts turned to Jess. Warmth surrounded his heart. It wouldn't be long before she'd be in his arms, and he could spring the surprise on her. He sighed and was out like a light within minutes.

The next morning, he got up, pulled on his warmest clothes and hitched a ride into town. Able to recharge his phone at the Cozy Café, he ordered breakfast, then called Chris. When he finished, he got a ride to the Inn. People were packing up and leaving. They stopped him.

"You own this place? It's a gold mine. We had the best Christmas we've had in years," one man said.

"I just loved the food," said a woman.

"And the fireplace and mulled wine. It was wonderful," said another woman.

Compliment after compliment flowed. Stryker beamed. "I hope you'll come back next year."

"Where's Jess? We wanted to leave her a little something," the man said, offering an envelope.

"I'll make sure she gets it. Thank you," Stryker said.

It was an hour before everyone cleared out. Stryker looked in the kitchen, but Jess wasn't there. She probably went home to sleep and recover. He checked the tree. There it was, hanging there. The envelope, sporting a red bow, still hung on the tree. It was on the side, though.

Obviously, Jess hadn't seen it. Her name was written on it in blue ink. He frowned.

Damn. Part of his surprise had gone unseen. He climbed the stairs, peeking in the two guest rooms. They were a shambles with bedclothes all over the place and towels on the floor. Looks like he'd have to hire a chambermaid. He shook his head. Nope, that would be Jess's responsibility.

As he left the second bedroom, he glanced down the hall. There was his old room. Curiosity drove him to twist the knob and open the door. His mouth hung open. Freshly painted walls, a new spread gracing the bed—one with an airplane motif—met his eyes. His old books, now dust free, filled the two small bookcases. *The Hardy Boys, Call of the Wild* hard-bound editions had survived.

It had to be Jess who restored his room. Even the windows had been cleaned and the view to the bird feeders in the backyard was clear as a bell. Stryker teared up. He'd suffered a terrible loss as a young child, but his aunt had created a haven for him in this room—his room. Jess had dusted it off and polished it up good as new.

The crunch of gravel under tires indicated Chris had arrived. Stryker climbed in the front seat.

"To Jess's house."

"Yes, sir. And welcome back."

Stryker knocked, but no one answered. He didn't see her car, but Will's truck was there. Stryker repeated the action several more times. If Jess wasn't home, he wasn't leaving until he knew where she was. A sleepy Will answered the door.

"Mr. West?"

"Hi, Will. Where's Jess?"

"She's gone," the young man said, rubbing his eyes and yawning.

"Gone?" He raised his eyebrows. "What do you mean gone?"

"She left town. Moved away. Left early this morning. At least that was her plan."

"Why?"

"She figured you'd be selling the Inn. I mean, with an offer of a million dollars, who could blame you?"

"What offer? I told Ruth to stop showing it. I told her I wouldn't sell at any price."

"That's not what she told Jess. She said she had a couple who'd pay a million for the place. Who could turn that down?"

"I could. That's who. I'm not selling. Where's Jess? I need to straighten this out."

"Where've you been? She waited but didn't hear. Thought you weren't coming." Will narrowed his eyes.

"My phone lost its charge. I couldn't get a flight. Then I couldn't get a car. I drove for eleven hours with a cabby through the snow yesterday. I got here at one last night. I'm sorry I'm late, but it couldn't be helped."

"Damn!"

"Yeah. So, where is she?"

"All I know is she rented a room in Willow Falls."

"Okay. Thanks." Stryker got back in the car. "We're going to Willow Falls, Chris."

"Okay. What street?"

"I don't know. We'll just drive around until we see her car."

"You're the boss," he said, putting the Bentley in gear.

An hour later, they rolled into the small town. After driving around for forty-five minutes, Chris spotted her car first.

"There it is," he said, pointing.

Stryker smiled. For the first time, he was glad she drove such an old and disreputable vehicle.

"Pull up to the curb. We'll just wait," Stryker said.

THE ROOM WAS SMALL but tidy. It had two windows and a faded red bedspread. Jess slung her suitcase on the bed. She'd only been there an hour and already felt homesick. The room was clean enough, but whoever decorated it must have been color blind. The loud colors clashed. She slumped down on the bed and sighed. Maybe leaving Pine Grove wasn't such a good idea?

Was she running away? Shame filled her. Of all the things she'd ever been, she'd never been a quitter. Maybe she could get her money back. She smoothed out the bedclothes and picked up her suitcase. Jess texted the landlord, she asked if she could terminate her lease and get her deposit back. She was going home.

As she headed for her car, she kept texting, trying to convince him she hadn't damaged anything and to refund her money. With head down, staring at her phone in one hand and lugging her suitcase with the other, she didn't see anyone in her path. Boom! She bumped right into Stryker West. She looked up, and her mouth fell open.

"What are you doing here?" she asked.

"Looking for you. And getting mowed down."

"Oh, sorry about that. Why are you looking for me?"

"Come on, Jess. Come home. We have some things to straighten out."

"Like what? You're selling the place, so we don't have the Inn anymore."

"Nope. I'm not selling. I told Ruth to take it off the market weeks ago. She's just trying to finagle a fat fee."

"You took it off the market?"

"I did. Besides. I can't sell it because it doesn't belong to me."

Her eyebrows knitted. "What do you mean?"

"You owe me a dollar. Do you have one?"

"Silly man. You don't even have a dollar on you? Of course, I do."

"Good. Give it to me."

"Okay." She dug the bill out of her purse and handed it to him.

"Perfect. Here," he said, handing her an envelope and stuffing the single in his pocket.

She opened it. Inside was the deed to the mansion, made out in her name.

"What's this? A joke?"

"I just sold the Inn to you for a buck. Now we need to find a notary and get your signature on the deed and it'll belong to you."

Jess shook her head. "No, wait. This can't be. I'm dreaming. Wake me up."

"You're not dreaming. I've known for a long time that you should have the Inn. You love it. You'll take good care of it."

"I will. But. Hey. This is crazy!"

"It's not crazy. It makes perfect sense."

Jess threw herself in his arms. He laughed and held her close.

"This was on the tree. It was to be your Christmas present."

"I never saw it," she said, pulling herself together. "I thought you'd forgotten to give me something for Christmas."

"Never. I got your airplane cufflinks. Very appropriate. Thank you. Jess Lennox, I love you. Can't stop thinking about you. Life without you sucks. Please marry me." He dropped down to one knee.

In shock, she stared at him, her mouth open. He fished around in his pocket and brought out a black velvet box. Jess covered her mouth with her hands. "No!"

"Oh, yes. Here you go," he said, flipping the box open to display a gorgeous round cut diamond nestled in a cluster of smaller ones. "Please, sweetheart. Say yes."

"Yes! Oh, yes, yes, yes, I do. Oh, yes." She clapped her hands and gave a little hop.

Stryker took her trembling hand and slid the ring on.

"Now it's official. Can we go home?"

"Yes," she said, heading for her car. He put his hand on hers.

"Oh, no. Not in that thing. We'll have it towed to the junkyard and get you a real car."

Stryker took her suitcase and placed it in the trunk of his luxury vehicle. He held the door to the backseat open and joined her there.

"Chris, please keep your eyes on the road. Next stop, Pine Grove," Stryker said, taking Jess in his arms. His lips found hers as the car moved toward their new life.

Epilogue

At sunrise, Jess stretched her arms up and her legs down, then snuggled under the down comforter and against the warm, naked body next to her. The bedroom was chilly. She pulled the blanket up so that just her eyes showed.

Stryker groaned and rolled over, slinging a careless arm over her middle. Though only early April, trees were budding outside the third story window. Stryker had renovated the third floor of the Inn into a master suite, including a small kitchen and his-and-hers bathrooms.

Thrilled she could look out from the bed into the trees and watch birds on the wing, Jess struggled to leave her perch every morning. But today, was her wedding day, and she simply couldn't lie still.

Unconsciously twisting her engagement ring on her finger, she grinned so wide her cheeks hurt. Having assumed she'd never get married, Jess had no plans for a wedding. Her friends Jory and Mindy had taken control, borrowing Stryker's limo for a trip to New York City and an appointment at Kleinfeld Bridal for the perfect gown.

Unused to sleeping this late, Jess calmed down. She lay still, listening to the bird songs floating in the open window, along with the cool breeze. With her closet door ajar, she spied a bit of the most gorgeous white dress she'd ever seen peeping out. It was hers. Was this a dream? Soon, there would be the sounds of Laura Dailey and her crew, setting up downstairs for the wedding brunch. That's right, for once, she wasn't cooking and serving. Hey, she could get used to this.

Jess and Stryker would be married on the glassed-in porch, facing an old maple tree, decorated with three bird feeders. Will had insisted on giving her away. She hadn't told her mother because she didn't trust her not to write to Stryker, asking him for money, or a lawyer for a new trial.

They'd invited only a handful of people. Jess slipped out of bed and tiptoed across the cold wood floor to her dresser. Quickly, she donned a tank top and matching pj bottoms. As her gaze rested on Stryker's sleeping body, she smiled. Recalling their passion from the night before, she sighed. The man had amazing staying power. He'd worn her out.

Jess padded through the archway to the kitchen. Having their own suite made it easy for her to run the Inn and still have private space with Stryker. She turned on the coffeemaker.

The view from the third floor took her breath away. On the side with no trees, the vista was broad, reaching to the Catskills. On the side with trees, she had the same view as a bird in a nest.

"Good morning," came a deep voice.

She turned. With the covers up to his waist, Stryker pushed up on one elbow. He ran fingers through his unruly dark hair and stared at her. His sexy, wry smile brought goosebumps to her skin. His gaze traveled her length.

"Dressed?"

"Cold."

He nodded. "It is chilly in here. I have an excellent, foolproof method of warming up my future wife." He sat up and threw down the covers.

His future wife. A zing of desire shot through her at his words. They had been engaged since the holidays. She wondered when she'd be used to the idea. Probably never. She strolled over to him.

"While you're taking your time, the sheets are growing cold," he said.

"But you're my very own sheet warmer. So, I'm not worried." His stare, as she pulled the tank top over her head and shed the pj's, warmed her. Stryker patted the mattress.

"Get in, I'm freezing."

She climbed on the bed, and he enveloped her in his embrace. Giggling, she fell back, with Stryker on top. Immediately the heat from his body chased the cold from her bones. She opened her legs and he slid to his knees.

"Hmm, I could slide right in," he remarked.

"Uh, yeah."

His dark eyes danced with merriment. "But what fun would that be?"

She laughed.

He kissed her, then trailed tiny ones down her neck. "We don't want any body parts neglected," he said, capturing her nipple with his lips.

With a sharp intake of breath, she arched her back, giving him open access to her chest.

"Love these," he murmured as he devoured her. His lips, his tongue stoked her fire. Desire sparked. Stryker pushed up, then eased down lower. He buried his face in her belly, swiping his tongue down until it came in contact with her sex.

"Oh, God. You're not going to?"

"Oh, yes I am," he replied, cutting her off.

Her body stiffened.

"Let go, Jess," he said, softly.

Hah, easier said than done. Holding tight control on her life and her brother's had kept them alive, housed, fed, and clothed.

"I love you. Believe it. We're getting married. Jess..."

"I will. I am. I'm trying."

She took a deep breath and glanced down. His gaze connected with hers. Warmth, love, and lust mixed in his eyes.

"Let me love you."

He kissed her belly, then traveled down, his tongue exploring her folds, then wiggling in deeper. Lust flew through her. Need so intense it pulled her toward him took over her body. He flattened his tongue against her hot flesh and rotated. She gripped his shoulders, sinking her fingertips into his muscles.

Heat ratcheted up and up, spiraling toward oblivion. Her hips bucked, then every muscle in her body squeezed tight and let go. Burning pleasure rippled through her as he continued.

"Oh, God. Stryker!" broke from her throat as she closed her eyes. She threw her arms around his neck and hugged him.

He kissed her neck. "My turn," he said, slipping his hands under her behind and lifting her hips up. She reached down and grabbed him, closing her fingers around his erection.

"Jesus. That's hard," she remarked.

"You do that to me."

She attempted to sit up, but with the flat of his hand, he coaxed her back down.

"Not now. It's too late."

"Really?"

"Oh, yeah. I want to come inside you."

She nodded.

Stryker removed her hand, gently, and substituted his own. He directed his dick to her entrance, rubbing it up and down her slit a couple of times.

"Oh, God, when you do that..." she said, leaving the sentence unfinished.

Before she could gather her wits, he was buried deep in her. He repositioned her to his liking, one heel over his shoulder, the other leg raised slightly so he could curl his fingers around the underside of her thigh. He pulled her to him and spread his legs slightly, to get his balance before he pumped.

Passion grew slowly in Jess. She ran her hands down his back, thrilling to the feel of muscle. There was something about him being on top of her, protecting her, shielding her from life, that turned her on.

"I love you so much," she whispered in his ear. Her eyes drifted shut, leaving touch as her dominant sense. Every inch of her came alive, nerve endings primed to their most sensitive threw tiny sparks inside her.

He increased his pace and pushed harder. Jess picked up his rhythm and they rocked together, almost moving the big bed. He hid his face in her neck, groaning against her damp skin. An orgasm swirled within her, growing.

"Damn, Jess. Oh, God," he muttered, sweat coating his back and chest.

Just before he came, she did, her hips moving on their own, her body tingling. Then he groaned her name, thrust one more time and stopped.

She held him to her, closing her mouth over the soft part where his shoulder met his neck. Damn, she loved her man and the way he made her feel. He brushed her hair off her forehead, then combed his fingers through it.

"You're beautiful in the morning."

"Just the morning?" she teased.

"Every minute of the day."

As the call of the chickadee drifted to her ears, she began the most perfect day of her life.

JORY AND MINDY FUSSED over Jess.

"What's going on up there?" came a masculine voice on the stairs.

"Don't come up here, Stryker! You can't see her," Jory called.

"Okay, okay. People have arrived. Can I send Will up?"

Jess nodded.

"Okay. Send him up," Mindy called.

Dressed in a tuxedo and looking completely uncomfortable, Will stood in the doorway.

Mindy and Jory hugged Jess. "Good luck," Jory said.

"You'll be great," Mindy added, giving a final adjustment to the garland of flowers Jess wore.

The women left. Will spoke.

"Damn, Jess. You look awesome!" he said, approaching his sister.

"So do you. And, yes, as soon as the brunch is over, you can take that off."

"Thank God!" he said, tugging on his shirt collar.

She walked to the window. "I never thought this would happen."

"Marriage to Stryker?" he asked, following her.

"Marriage to anyone. No one wants the child of a criminal."

"Stryker's not just anyone," Will replied.

"You're telling me!" She laughed.

"This is the right decision. He really loves you."

"I know. I'll miss you, Will," she said, turning full eyes to her brother.

He dropped his gaze to the floor. "Me, too."

"We've been a team for a long time. You've been my biggest support."

"We're still a team. Lennox's to the end."

She reached over to brush his hair out of his face. "I love you, Will."

"You've been the most incredible sister. You always put me first. No one's ever done that before," he said, his voice low.

"'Cause you're the best brother that ever was."

"If Stryker doesn't treat you right, you come to me. I'll straighten him out," Will said, pounding a fist into his palm.

She laughed. "Thanks."

"I'll always have your back."

"And I yours. But I think Jennie will be there for you, too."

"Kinda looks like that."

"I'm glad. I want you to be happy. To have your own family," Jess said.

"You'll always be my family," he replied, handing his handkerchief to his sister.

She blotted her eyes. "Won't do to be crying before the ceremony even begins."

"Let's do this," Will said, offering his arm.

She took it and together they descended the winding staircase, through the hall and out to the porch. As they approached, the guests rose from their chairs, and Nancy Collins, from the vet's office, played the Wedding March on a keyboard set up in the corner.

Jess's gaze met Stryker's. All fear evaporated as she stared at him. Love shone through his dark, warm eyes. When she reached the groom, Will gave her hand to him.

"Who gives this woman?" the judge asked.

"I do," said Will, his voice cracking as he brushed a tear from his eye.

The End

If you enjoyed this book, please so kind as to leave a review. Thank you.

You might also like the first two, stand-alone books in this series:

Books by Jean C. Joachim

<u>ECHOES OF THE HEART</u>
HEATHER & MIKE: THE ONE THAT GOT AWAY
SANDY & RAFE: SECOND PLACE HEART
LIZ & NICK: NO REGRETS
PAIGE & BILL: ONE FINE DAY
ANTHOLOGY
<u>HOCKEY</u>
THE FINAL SLAPSHOT
<u>BOTTOM OF THE NINTH</u>
DAN ALEXANDER, PITCHER
MATT JACKSON, CATCHER
JAKE LAWRENCE, THIRD BASEMAN
NAT OWEN, FIRST BASE
BOBBY HERNANDEZ, SECOND BASE
SKIP QUINCY, SHORT STOP
EXTRA INNINGS
<u>FIRST & TEN SERIES</u>
GRIFF MONTGOMERY, QUARTERBACK
BUDDY CARRUTHERS, WIDE RECEIVER
PETE SEBASTIAN, COACH
DEVON DRAKE, CORNERBACK
SLY "BULLHORN" BRODSKY, OFFENSIVE LINE
AL "TRUNK" MAHONEY, DEFENSIVE LINE

HARLEY BRENNAN, RUNNING BACK
OVERTIME, THE FINAL TOUCHDOWN
A KING'S CHRISTMAS
<u>THE MANHATTAN DINNER CLUB</u>
RESCUE MY HEART
SEDUCING HIS HEART
SHINE YOUR LOVE ON ME
TO LOVE OR NOT TO LOVE
<u>HOLLYWOOD HEARTS SERIES</u>
IF I LOVED YOU
RED CARPET ROMANCE
MEMORIES OF LOVE
MOVIE LOVERS
LOVE'S LAST CHANCE
LOVERS & LIARS
His Leading Lady (Series Starter)
<u>NOW AND FOREVER SERIES</u>
NOW AND FOREVER 1, A LOVE STORY
NOW AND FOREVER 2, THE BOOK OF DANNY
NOW AND FOREVER 3, BLIND LOVE
NOW AND FOREVER 4, THE RENOVATED HEART
NOW AND FOREVER 5, LOVE'S JOURNEY
NOW AND FOREVER, CALLIE'S STORY (prequel)
<u>MOONLIGHT SERIES</u>
SUNNY DAYS, MOONLIT NIGHTS
APRIL'S KISS IN THE MOONLIGHT
UNDER THE MIDNIGHT MOON
MOONLIGHT & ROSES (prequel)
<u>LOST & FOUND SERIES</u>
LOVE, LOST AND FOUND
DANGEROUS LOVE, LOST AND FOUND
<u>NEW YORK NIGHTS NOVELS</u>

THE MARRIAGE LIST
THE LOVE LIST
THE DATING LIST
<u>PINE GROVE SERIES</u>
UNPREDICTABLE LOVE
BREAK MY HEART
RENOVATING THE BILLIONAIRE
<u>SHORT STORIES</u>
SWEET LOVE REMEMBERED
TUFFER'S CHRISTMAS WISH
THE HOUSE-SITTER'S CHRISTMAS

About the Author

Jean Joachim is a USA Today best-selling, award-winning, international romance fiction author, with books hitting the Amazon Top 100 list since 2012. She writes contemporary romance, which includes sports romance and romantic suspense.

Liz & Nick: One Fine Day won second place in the erotic romance category of the Oklahoma Romance Writers of America's International Digital Awards.

Dangerous Love Lost & Found, First Place winner in the 2015 Oklahoma Romance Writers of America, International Digital Award contest. *The Renovated Heart* won Best Novel of the Year from Love Romances Café. *Lovers & Liars* was a RomCon finalist in 2013. And *The Marriage List* tied for third place as Best Contemporary Romance from the Gulf Coast RWA.

To Love or Not to Love tied for second place in the 2014 New England Chapter of Romance Writers of America Reader's Choice contest.

She was chosen Author of the Year in 2012 by the New York City chapter of RWA.

Married and the mother of two sons, Jean lives in New York City. Early in the morning, you'll find her at her computer, writing, with a cup of tea, and a secret stash of black licorice.

Jean has 48 books, novellas and short stories published. Find it here: http://www.jeanjoachimbooks.com. Chat with Jean in her Facebook group, JJ's Book Buddies. Join here: https://www.facebook.com/groups/489790604419710/